GHOSTLAND

SHAUN WHITTINGTON

SEVERED PRESS
HOBART TASMANIA

GHOSTLAND

Copyright © 2018 Shaun Whittington
Copyright © 2018 by Severed Press

WWW.SEVEREDPRESS.COM

ISBN: 978-1-925840-03-2

Ghostland is a work of fiction, and many of the events in the book occur in real places. However, in these areas I have taken the liberty of exaggerating certain things that suited the book. Other places that are mentioned may not be real at all, so if you are from the area that I have written about, try not to be too upset that I have twisted a few things.

This is a book about after the apocalypse, so it does contain tension, gore, and scenes that could upset individuals, especially scenes involving children. It needs to be as real as possible, and in reality nobody would be exempt from such an unforgiving world.

Thanks,

Shaun.

The Canavars are coming, so you better hide and pray.
If you don't believe me then you're going to die today.
They'll eat your flesh, they'll eat your brains, and they'll eat your heart and more.
The Canavars are everywhere; you better lock your door.

Tyler Washington
Aged 10

CHAPTER ONE

He released a long moan and put his head back, staring into the darkness. His daughter had finally fallen asleep, and as soon as Simon Washington could hear the eight-year-old girl snoring gently as she laid her head on his lap, he leaned over and blew the candle out. He had no idea what time it was. Ten? Eleven?

She wasn't a big fan of the dark. She was not exactly terrified of it, which was a near-miracle considering what they had been through, but if the candlelight helped her go to sleep then her father was happy to use up some of the wax.

He ran his fingers from his right hand through his bushy beard whilst stroking his daughter's head with his left, and closed his eyes. He was sleepy, his eyes were stinging, but the adrenaline coursing through his veins was making sleep a hard task to achieve.

He was getting that feeling again.

He hadn't experienced it in days, but it was happening. He sat up, straightened his back, and tried to ride it out. He stopped stroking his daughter's head and put the two fingers of his left hand on his neck, feeling for the carotid artery.

His pulse felt normal, kind of, so where was the surge of adrenaline coming from? And why was he finding it difficult to breathe? Was it all in his mind?

He tried a few breathing exercises, like he normally did in this situation. He took in a deep breath and held it for eight seconds, then slowly released for another eight. He continued to do this, and after a few minutes the episode had come to a close, like it normally did. He had no idea why this was happening. Yes, he and his daughter, Imelda, were in a dire situation, but these panic attacks had only started a couple of months ago.

Why didn't it start straight away? Why didn't it start a year ago when the country, and possibly the world, went into chaos? He didn't know what it really was. Was it really a panic attack? Did he have high blood pressure? Something else?

When it first happened he thought he was having a heart attack. Just the thought of dying frightened him, so his panic grew and it seemed to make the situation worse. The fear of leaving his daughter alone was petrifying for Simon. Leaving his daughter to fend for herself was what frightened him the most. He had taught her things. He had shown her how to catch game by setting traps, how to skin rabbits, filtering water, but being eight years old with no parents, walking these barren lands alone, was something that broke his heart just thinking about it.

He closed his eyes and felt tiredness creep up on him. He nodded off for no longer than ten seconds and suddenly gasped, getting a fright, the hairs on the back of his neck standing to attention. Was there something outside?

He unzipped his blue fleece jacket, careful not to wake his daughter, and left the jacket opened; it wasn't so cold. He was sure that it was around springtime; maybe April or May, he wasn't exactly sure.

The winter seemed like a lifetime ago now, and he and his daughter had been on the road for a few months; he guessed three. They had stayed in their house for nearly nine months before they had to leave. When they were at their house and had run out of food, they had to spend their time raiding neighbours' houses. Most of the houses were empty, because in the beginning, when the Canavars were in their droves and most people fled to a different place, going elsewhere seemed a better option for most folk. Since the bombs had fallen, people, as well as the Canavars, had been depleted. Simon hadn't seen one in months, and his daughter hadn't seen any since *that* day. The day she lost her mummy and her brother; the day Simon lost his wife and his son.

He had no idea where to go next once morning had arrived, and knew that staying in the wooden hut for another night was not an option.

For months the pair of them roamed from one house to the next, picking up scraps here and there, and he knew that this couldn't go on forever. Food was going to dry up eventually. Water was fine, for the time being. He knew how to filter water, although the process wasn't entirely perfect. They had a few jars with them that also had lids, and a couple of old soda bottles that Simon kept in his rucksack. The soda bottles were cut in half, and had, at the top of the bottle, small pebbles. Underneath the pebbles was sand. A cloth was below the sand, tied with an elastic band.

Once the water had been filtered Simon would filter it again, boil it for a minute, and then let it cool down. The water had to be filtered to remove waterborne cysts that could harbour and protect bacteria from chemical treatment or even boiling, but he was aware that the cysts were capable of withstanding high temperatures.

The filtering process would remove some cysts along with pesticides, herbicides, sediment, insects and other debris. It was a lengthy process, and was quite frustrating that it took up a lot of their time.

In the beginning, the Canavars were the problem, but after the bombs fell, other humans were now a danger. He knew that not *every* individual was a danger to him and his daughter, but he had to be wary of any stranger, male or female. Times were different, and people were resorting to any methods in order to survive. He had seen it with his own eyes.

He felt a throbbing in the back of his mouth and placed his fingers in and touched one of his back teeth. He winced when his fingers made contact and knew it had to come out eventually.

He had no tools to deal with the situation, but was sure he could wait a while. He had only felt the discomfort a few weeks ago, and although it was painful, he was certain he could hold on for another few days or so. It wasn't exactly keeping him awake at night. Not yet.

He stroked his daughter's head once more, leaned over and kissed her. Her hair needed washing. The last time she had washed her hair was a couple of weeks ago when they came across an abandoned house that had no food available, but had bottles of lemonade and bars of soap.

The days of old seemed like a lifetime ago now. His daughter went to gymnastics on a Friday evening, and back then all she worried about was her technique for her one handed cartwheel and what the new move was going to be. Now, she worried about other things. She worried about where the next meal was going to come from and if they were going to run into any trouble.

They had been very careful.

They had remained in the countryside since they had escaped from their house, after her brother and mother were attacked, but Simon had told her that they needed to head to somewhere more residential—a place that was reasonably populated in the old world. He was hoping to come across more houses, shops, maybe even a friendly community that had been created by some locals, but he was aware that a place with numbers could also mean danger for him and his daughter.

Most of the houses that they had checked recently had nothing left. The food had either been taken when the owners had packed up and left, when the Canavars had exploded on the scene, or other people had raided the house during that period, maybe even after.

The arrival of the Canavars was bad enough and had depleted the nation severely, but when the country was attacked from the skies, mainly the cities, there didn't seem to be anyone around. That, of course, wasn't the case, but that's what it felt like for Simon Washington and his eight-year-old daughter.

Simon and Imelda felt like they were the last people left on this earth.

How wrong they were.

CHAPTER TWO

NEXT DAY

He woke up with a start, and at first was unsure where he was. He was still sitting up and his eyes scanned around the dusky area and immediately placed his hand on his daughter's head. He smiled. She was still there, still with her head on his lap. He tried to sit up without disturbing his daughter. He had no idea how long they had both slept. Maybe they had had plenty of hours or maybe not enough, he wasn't sure.

He could see that it was light outside because there was light shining through the tiny cracks of the shed that they were in.

He and his daughter had weeks of monotony, walking from one place to the next. To relieve the boredom they talked about how their lives were when things were normal. He openly talked about his wife and son, his daughter's mother and brother, as he thought it was healthy to do this, rather than forgetting they ever existed.

He had no idea how long it had been since their passing. A couple of months? Longer? It felt like years. He was sure they had died in January.

Sometimes it felt like it had always been just him and his little girl, and the flashbacks that consisted of his wife and son were just his imagination. It sounded silly, but that's how Simon felt sometimes. He had no photographs of his family, no video footage to remind him what life used to be like ... nothing! Everything he could remember about his past was in his head. He couldn't remember it all, but a lot of the memories would come flooding back if his daughter would say or do something. Sometimes, however, the memories would sneak up on him like an assassin, without warning, and twang his heartstrings, forcing his throat to harden.

His daughter began to moan and stir and this made him smile. He waited a minute and allowed his little girl to sit up in her own time. Eight-year-old Imelda Washington sat up and stretched her arms. Still sitting, she released a yawn and then looked at the outline of her dad who was sitting next to her.

"Morning, babe," said Simon in a soft voice.

She never responded verbally and looked around, almost as if she was unsure where she was.

"Sleep well?" He looked at the little scar that was on the right side of her forehead, just below her hairline.

"Uh-huh." She nodded and gazed around once more before adding, "Had a weird dream."

"Oh yeah?" Simon smirked and could hardly see his beautiful girl. The dusky shed hid her blonde hair, blue eyes and perfect skin. "What was it about?"

"Erm..."

She seemed reluctant to tell him and Simon decided not to push her. The dream could have been too silly to describe, or it could have been one about her mum and older brother.

"You know what?" Simon gently touched Imelda's cheek and said, "Why don't you tell me once we're on the road."

She nodded and groaned, "So we're moving again?"

Simon smiled and nodded. "We need to go where the food is."

"Nowhere then."

Simon decided to ignore her moaning, stood to his feet and stretched his arms. He then put his arms out straight in front of him and stretched his back. He smiled as he remembered that this was the type of stretch, as well as others, he used when he went to the gym.

The gym, he thought. That seemed like a lifetime ago now.

'You hungry, babe?" he asked her.

"Not really."

Simon cupped his right hand, brought it up to his mouth and breathed into it, immediately sniffing his breath. He twisted his nose. He needed to brush his teeth. He hadn't brushed them in days and his teeth were beginning to hurt. They had two worn toothbrushes in the bag that he had, but had little toothpaste. They had managed to acquire some toothpaste from the last house they were in, and it had also been days since Imelda had brushed her teeth.

They had no plan. They simply wandered from one place to the next, from one town to the other. He just wanted the pair of them to survive. That was what his wife would have wanted. If he had lost his whole family on that terrible day he would have killed himself, but he had Imelda. She was the only thing that was keeping him going, keeping him sane. He had responsibilities, and the thought of him dying and leaving his little girl, alone, upset him. He saw what it did to her when she lost her mum and Tyler, her older brother.

"Ready to go?" he asked her.

She stood and straightened her back and nodded in the dim shed. He picked up the rucksack and went over to the door and pushed the door open. The pair of them squinted as the sun flooded the inside of the wooden hut, stinging their eyes. Both raised their hands to shield their eyes, and slowly stepped outside to a beautiful day, with Simon leading the way. He hadn't eaten for a day and decided to rummage through his bag.

Because of his daughter, he didn't want to use the supplies, but he was no good to her dead. He looked around at the garden they were in and could see the long grass. The houses that stretched along were in ruins. Some were unrecognisable as houses anymore, and yet, bizarrely, the shed that they had stayed in stood untouched. Maybe the houses in front had shielded it from the bombs that had been dropped months ago. He wanted to keep away from the ruins, the areas that had been affected, but last night they had no choice.

Noises from the previous night, coming from males, had forced father and daughter to flee, and the shed was the first thing they saw whilst their bodies were engulfed in panic.

Simon put the bag on the floor, unzipped the rucksack and began to rummage through. Inside the bag he had:

Two steak knives.
One claw hammer.
3 tins of beans.
A tin of sardines.
A packet of Frosties (out of date).
3 bars of soap.
3 carrier bags.
Two jars and soda bottles to purify water.
One empty plastic bottle.
A hairbrush.
An assortment of candles.
A shaving mirror.
Peter Benchley's Jaws paperback (This book was in the bottom of his bag. It was his favourite film, and had read the book when he was a child).
One pair of spare trainers for his daughter.
Two pairs of knickers.
An *OMG* black T-shirt. OMG was in pink lettering.
One black V-neck T-shirt.
Two worn yellow toothbrushes.
Green disposable lighter.
An adult blue T-shirt.

He pulled out a tin of beans and shook it in front of Imelda. "You sure you're not hungry?"

"I'm sure." She nodded, and scanned around where they were with fear scrawled on her face.

"Okay. Maybe I'll have a tin later." Simon could see the concern on her face and pointed up ahead. "Let's go this way."

Simon put the tin in his pocket, threw the bag over his shoulder and moved away from the ruins that was once a street full of life. He took a quick scan around the broken street and imagined brand new cars parked on the drives, children playing, and people out walking their dogs. He had hardly seen any animals since he had been on the road. He didn't know why. There must have been a lot of domestic pets, mainly cats and dogs that had lost their owners and had to fend for themselves.

He placed his arm around his daughter's shoulder and his mind went back to that day—not when they announced the first crisis, but weeks after, when the bombs fell.

Before the bombs had fallen, Simon and his family had been hiding in their attic, away from those things, living off scraps, and occasionally going out and taking supplies from abandoned houses that had been left when the country was in stage one of this crisis.

He hated going out. It frightened the life out of him when going out for the first time, but he couldn't let his family starve. Thankfully, the neighbours to his left had decided to chance their luck elsewhere and had fled, but hadn't taken all the food with them. He didn't know why. His elderly neighbours to the right had decided to commit suicide. When he broke into the house, he found them on their bed, on their backs and holding hands. They had taken an overdose of painkillers. The positives from this was that they had left a house with cupboards full of food, and this told Simon that they must have killed themselves in the first week.

Stage One was what Simon and Imelda called it. Stage One was when the dead began to attack. Stage Two was when the bombs fell.

When Stage Two began, Simon had a feeling what was happening and relocated his family to the basement, to lower ground, to be safer. Getting to higher ground was better for Stage One, when the dead were out in their numbers, but going to lower ground was more beneficial when Stage Two began to happen, getting his family away from potential falling debris and shattered glass from the windows.

When the bombs had stopped and he was brave enough to get to the roof of his house, a couple of weeks after, he could see that the area he was in looked unscathed. There was the usual smashed up cars from the Stage One era, as well as bodies and blood, but after the explosions had stopped, he could see that the streets near him looked untouched. He could see from afar that certain buildings like high-rise flats and churches, as well as a shopping centre, weren't there anymore, but his area was fine. Whoever dropped the bombs, it appeared that there were specific targets, but his street, as well as dozens around him, hadn't been damaged.

"Dad!"

Imelda had brought Simon out of his daydreaming of yesteryear, and he turned to his daughter to see what she wanted. They were walking side by side and it looked like they were heading towards a small cluster of trees.

"What is it, babe?" he finally spoke up.

"How come those trees look okay?"

"What do you mean?"

"Remember the last time we tried to go to the woods and all the trees were bare and burnt?"

"I think they were affected by Stage Two," Simon said. "And anyway, that's not exactly the woods, is it?" He pointed over to the trees. "We need to walk through and see what's on the other side. We're running out of water, so we need to fill up our jars once we find a pond or a stream … or something."

"Oh, okay."

"Hold onto my hand." He held out his hand and his daughter took it.

"We haven't seen people for days," Imelda sighed and moaned further, "And when we do, we run or hide from them."

Simon never responded and it only took them a minute to get out of the trees. He looked down at his worn boots and Imelda's dirty white trainers. Thankfully there was another pair for her in his rucksack.

In front of them were miles of fields, nothing else apart from a farmhouse in the distance.

"Now what, daddy?" she asked with a little attitude in her tone.

Simon pointed ahead of him and said, "We're going to that farmhouse, but first..." He sat down, placed the bag on the floor and pulled out the tin from his pocket. "I'm gonna have something to eat."

CHAPTER THREE

After finishing his beans, Simon and Imelda Washington trudged with weary feet through the long grass. He held his daughter's hand for a few minutes, but once their palms became sticky they both agreed to release their grip. There were fields all around, but a small group of trees were in front of them and they went round them to reach a picket fence. He climbed the fence first and then helped his daughter over. The pair of them were now standing on a grassy bank, and a country road stretched by them. They needed to cross the road to reach a small iron gate. They crossed the road and Simon opened the noiseless gate. The pair of them stepped carefully down the garden path and headed for the front door of the farmhouse. Imelda tried to speak, but Simon shushed her and tried to see if there was a way of opening the door without breaking it down.

Simon looked at the concerned face of his daughter. "Let's try round the back."

They both went to the right hand side of the house where a drive stretched from the front and passed the house, stopping at the back of the place. It took just over ten minutes to check out the outside area of the farm.

"Now what, daddy?" Imelda asked once the back door gave way.

"I don't know." Simon gently waggled his head.

"Does that mean there're people inside?"

"I don't know."

They stepped inside to be greeted with a basic kitchen and cupboards that looked like they had been around since the eighties. He closed the back door, once they were both inside, and could also see that the now defunct oven was archaic, something that Simon's granny used to use. Maybe old people used to stay here, he thought.

He told Imelda to stand in the corner of the kitchen, by the sink, and not to move. He placed his rucksack by her feet, told her to be brave, and then took a quick look around the house.

He stepped into the empty living room and went over to open the curtains slightly, letting some light spill in. He then opened a door and was now at the front door that they couldn't get in. He had his back to the front door and was looking at the stairs in front of him.

He went to the first floor and checked the bedrooms. Each door was closed; so opening each one was a scary task. The final room to check was the bathroom, and once that was achieved, Simon smiled and was pleased that the house was clear.

He descended back to the ground floor and could see the main/front door. He noticed that the door had a bolt, like the back door in the kitchen, so at least it could be locked from the inside.

Simon wasn't surprised that there were no supplies, but at least it was safe and clear inside the farmhouse itself. It had a barn but was empty, and no farm vehicle was present, no tractor, combine harvester … nothing. What *did* surprise him was that the back door that they went in was unlocked, which delighted *and* concerned him.

He had always wanted to try a farm, but was scared that the owner would shoot him or his daughter once they were spotted. He didn't live in a country where they were blessed with guns, but you could guarantee that a farmer would have a shotgun stored somewhere.

He entered the living room and told Imelda to come in and join him. He sat down in the living room area in a dusty chair, and was going to check out the place more thoroughly once he found the energy to get back on his feet. Imelda came in from the kitchen, placed the rucksack by her daddy's feet and sat on the couch, opposite her dad, and leaned her head back. Both were hungry, tired, despite the day being so young.

"Is the place safe?" she asked him.

Simon nodded timidly. "Appears so."

His eyes looked around and couldn't understand why others hadn't snapped up such a place. And why did the owners leave?

"I'm tired, daddy," she moaned.

Simon smiled. "Tired or just dehydrated?"

"Tired and … both." She rubbed her throat. "Could I have the rest of that water?"

"I thought you said it tasted horrible," he gently teased with a thin smile. She never responded and he could see she wasn't in the mood.

He reached into his bag and pulled out the rest of the filtered water in the jar and passed it to her. There wasn't much left, maybe four or five gulps, but he urged her to hold her nose and finish it. She did as she was told, twisted her face in revulsion, and then passed the jar back to her father.

She lay down and curled up on the sofa.

It was still the morning, but sometimes the pair of them did this. They would sometimes have a couple of short naps a day. It was rare that they ever got seven to nine hours a sleep a night, so they just slept whenever their body told them that they needed to, providing it was safe.

He gazed over at his little girl and then stood to his feet. He quite fancied a nap himself, but he needed to open a window to let some air circulate and wanted to close the dusty curtains of the living room window, despite only opening them a few minutes ago.

He shut the curtains and looked over at the silhouette of Imelda once more and strained to see her face in the dusky room. It didn't seem that long ago she was born. Like her old man, she had beautiful thick red lips and blue eyes. The eyes were from her mother's side of the family. Simon had dark brown eyes and they were narrow, like Clint Eastwood's in his spaghetti western movies, and his eyebrows were dark and quite thick, like his beard. Imelda's eyebrows were quite thick for her age, and Simon knew that as she got older she wasn't going to thank him for giving her the thick eyebrow gene.

Maybe that didn't matter now.

He was certain that when she reached puberty, boys would be the last thing on her mind; especially the way things were now.

Simon was dreading that day. The day she would become a young woman. Not only would he be looking for food, water and medical supplies, but he'd also be looking for sanitary towels, maybe even bras for the young girl. They hadn't had 'the talk' yet, but he was sure she was aware that the time of young womanhood would come.

He could hear Imelda lightly snoring and although a little tired, he didn't feel the need to sleep. He closed his stinging eyes and decided to relax and lose himself for a while.

His thoughts didn't go back to the days when his world turned to shit; his thoughts went further back. He thought about their last holiday together as a family. They decided to stay in Britain and went to a place called Flamingoland. It was a great holiday and they were blessed with good weather for the week. Tyler had made some friends and claimed that a 'fat boy' had been picking on him. That was the only negative part of the holiday.

The routine of the caravan holiday was the same every day. The whole family would get up between seven and eight. Whilst Diana would be rushing around, making the kids their breakfast and getting them dressed, Simon would escape from the madness for an hour and take the five-minute walk to the complex's gym. He would use the treadmill for an hour then return to the caravan, shower, get dressed and head to the amusement park and zoo that was right next to their caravan with the rest of the family. They would spend all day in there, and the only ride that Simon didn't like the look of was the high swings.

Tyler and Diana freaked about every ride apart from the pirate ship and the water rides. Imelda had no fear of any of them, despite being the youngest, and she especially liked the Mumbo Jumbo, a roller coaster that wasn't for the faint-hearted. Then they would go back to the caravan, eat, and then get dressed for the nighttime.

The club on the complex wasn't the best entertainment, so Simon and Diana would sometimes let the kids play in the park that was opposite the caravan, whilst the parents sat on the decking of the caravan, talking, and drinking red wine.

Simon sat with a smile on his face.

The memories of Flamingoland were so vivid that it felt like there was a projector showing the highlights of the holiday in his mind.

He gazed back over to his daughter and lost his smile.

He knew that his holidays with his family had happened, but it didn't feel real now. He felt like it had happened to someone else.

There were many things that he was concerned about, apart from overall survival. He began to worry about dying and leaving Imelda all alone, like he did every day. Even though he had taught her everything he knew about survival skills, which wasn't a great deal, he wasn't sure she would cope. She was only eight years old.

The other thing that scared him was killing another man. He had only killed two Canavars so far, but there were very few of them left now, or so he thought. Whenever he or Imelda had heard the sounds of footsteps or vehicles, they would always hide. They had managed to avoid humans, but their luck was going to run out one day.

Could he kill another man if his daughter was in danger? Of course he could. He didn't want to, but his only goal was to get his daughter through this. It was the only reason why he was still alive. Could he kill another man for his supplies, if it meant those supplies would keep him and his daughter alive for a few more day or weeks?

He wasn't sure.

His daughter began to toss and turn, and Simon stood up, fearing that she would fall off the sofa and hurt herself. Her movement was reducing, but now she was beginning to mumble.

"The ... coming ... hide and pray. If you don't believe me you're ... today."

She suddenly stopped talking. To a stranger, her words would have been confusing and nonsensical, but Simon knew exactly what she was talking about. It was a poem—well, *kind* of a poem. It was more of a song that Tyler had made up many months ago.

When Stage One was in its infancy, ten-year-old Tyler used to taunt his little sister, as big brothers do, and used to frighten her to death about what was happening in the outside world. He had made up a poem and used to mumble it to Imelda to scare her. He never used to do it in front of his parents, although he had been caught a couple of times and had been told off.

Obviously, in this early stage, Tyler, as well as Imelda, had no idea how bad things were, and were going to be. They did nothing but moan about the lack of food and not being able to see their friends. Then when the power went, things became worse.

Seeing that his daughter was beginning to settle again, Simon sat back down and leaned his head back. This time he thought about the two weeks they had in Benalmadena from two years ago.

He closed his eyes, smiling from ear to ear, and began to daydream about the best holiday he ever had.

CHAPTER FOUR

A noise made Simon jump up out of his chair. He stood up, confused, and had a quick look around. His daughter was still sleeping and he realised that he must have dosed off as well.

He remained still, too scared to move, still standing, and trying to listen out for any further sounds. Over a minute had passed and the sound of scratching could be heard. It was coming from the back of the house, from the back door.

Unsure whether to wake his daughter or not, Simon was smothered in confusion; he remained standing and had no idea what was the right thing to do. He made slow steps in the dim quarters and stopped once he was in the kitchen, where the back door was. The scratching grew louder and he had realised that it was coming from behind the door that was situated in the kitchen.

He took two steps closer and then went onto his knees. He made the rest of the small journey to the back door by crawling, and once he reached the door he placed his ear against it. Simon had just realised that he hadn't checked if this door was unlocked or not. He looked to see the door was bolted. He supposed that it didn't matter in this situation anyway, as he was sure that whatever was behind the door was an animal of some kind and was unable to open doors.

He kept his ear against the door, held his breath, and seconds later the clawing had stopped. Now snarling came from the animal that Simon was now certain was a wild dog.

Weren't most surviving dogs *wild* these days?

The dog could smell him, he was sure of it. And now the scratching began once more, but this time more frantic. The dog must have been starving. It was so hungry that it was prepared to claw its way through a wooden door to get to its next potential meal.

He was unsure what to do next. Should he kill the dog, or let it continue to scratch its way through and hope it became tired, gave up, and went elsewhere?

He stood up and left the kitchen on his tiptoes, like a drunk coming home late and hoping not to wake his wife. He went over to his daughter, bent down and put his hands under Imelda's back. She moaned a little as he picked her up, and he made the arduous walk up the stairs. He then reached the landing and picked a bedroom to put his daughter in. He placed her on top of the bed and shut the door behind him as he left. He knew if she woke up she'd freak, but he was hoping that that wasn't going to happen.

He went downstairs, returned to the kitchen and unbolted the door. He then entered the living room and reached into his bag. He took out a steak knife and a claw hammer from his bag, and headed for the front door. He put the hammer and knife in a pocket each, and then took off his blue fleece and wrapped it tightly around his left arm. He kept the hammer into his deep pocket and took out the steak knife as he slid the bolt back.

He took in a deep breath as he stepped out and closed the door. He had a look around the desolate fields that stretched around him and checked if the blue fleece was tight enough around his left arm, then headed for the back of the farmhouse, where the scratching had been coming from. He was certain that the dog wouldn't give up and felt he had no choice. He didn't want to kill a dog. He didn't want to kill *anything*. But the safety of Imelda was his main goal.

The other concern he had was that he had no idea what type of dog waited for him. Alsatian? Rottweiler? Pit Bull? He hoped that it was only a Schitzu or a Pug, but it didn't sound like a small dog.

He held his breath as he reached the corner of the farmhouse that was at the back, and peered his head around to see a black and white Collie scratching at the door. He puffed out a breath of relief and wondered if he had anything in his bag the dog could devour.

Simon smiled and bent down. He clicked his fingers to get the dog's attention and said, "Hello there. And what do you think you're doing?"

The dog glared at Simon, cocked its head to one side and began to whimper.

Bless it. Poor thing's probably starving.

"Come on." He continued to click his fingers, trying to beckon the dog. "Come here."

The dog took a step forward and then began to growl, showing its teeth.

Simon was saddened by this and hoped that maybe he and Imelda had gained a companion. In hindsight, he should have gone through his bag and taken some food round with him, but there was no going back now.

He stood up, knowing that walking or running away would make the dog run for him, and raised his knife. He stayed motionless as the canine stepped closer towards him. It looked hesitant, but at the same time it didn't want the 'meal' to get away.

Simon took one step backwards and the dog galloped towards him.

With his heart in his mouth, Simon raised his arm, waiting for the dog to pounce, and gripped the knife handle tight. The black and white Collie jumped at Simon once it was just a metre away, and predictably sank its teeth into the blue fleece wrapped around his arm. It growled and shook its head from side to side, trying to rip the man apart, almost pulling Simon's shoulder out of its socket. He waited a few more seconds, heart beating out of his chest, and then drove the knife into the side of the dog's neck, quickly pulling the blade out. It released a short yelp and let go of his arm immediately.

It took a step backwards, its legs wobbled, and Simon watched as the blood poured out of the mutt's neck. He looked down at his knife and could see the blood running off the steel, then turned his attention back to the dog that had now fallen and lay on its side. He watched as the animal's middle went up and down as it breathed, but then it stopped.

Simon released a breath out and was about to pick the dog up, but then paused. He was paranoid about his little girl waking up, alone, in a strange room. He made a decision to run upstairs and move Imelda back to the sofa before moving the dog.

And so he did.

*

After gathering some branches and making a spit for the fire he had just lit at the back of the farm, Simon filtered some water, ready to boil once the dog was cooked. They sat waiting patiently, both salivating. They had eaten cats before, a fox, squirrels … but never a dog. Simon had gutted and skinned the animal before placing it over the fire. Making a fire was dangerous, especially on a night, but they needed to eat.

"Your beard's going grey, daddy," Imelda remarked with a smile, trying to kill time. Both sat next to one another and gazed at the dead canine, willing it to hurry up and cook.

"I know, babe." Simon smiled. "It's only grey at the sides of my chin. Anyway, I'm not getting any younger."

She looked at her father strangely. "Neither am I."

"It's just a saying," Simon snickered. "It's just something adults say. You don't have to take it literally."

"Adults are strange."

Simon smiled thinly and wondered about the future of his daughter. He thought about her going into womanhood once more, and wondered what to do when she needed to wear a bra or when she started her menstrual cycle. He had years to play with before this scenario occurred, but if they were going to survive, it *was* going to happen.

"Once this thing's cooked," Simon nodded to the animal on the spit, "then we'll get back inside. Maybe go for a cheeky nap."

"What about the rest of it?" Imelda asked her father. "We'll never eat it all."

"I can carve the rest up and put the meat on a plate for later."

"Can we eat the meat cold?"

"I think so." Simon hunched his shoulders. "You can eat chicken cold, so why not? Remember that time we ate a cat for the first time?"

Imelda nodded. "I wouldn't touch it."

"That's right. You hadn't eaten for two days and I was getting mad."

"I did in the end," Imelda said with a smile "Only because you told me it tasted like chicken. It looked and tasted nothing like chicken."

"I know, but at least you ate some of it."

She nodded and looked up and seemed lost in thought. Before her father could ask her what was wrong, she said, "I keep on thinking about that song that Tyler used to tease me with."

"Song?" Simon ran the nail of his thumb across his left eyebrow, trying to understand what Imelda meant.

"Yeah. *The* song."

"Oh yes. Funny you should say that," said Simon. "You were mumbling it in your sleep when you were lying on the couch."

"Was I?"

Simon nodded.

He gazed at Imelda and could see her beautiful features, and began to lose himself. She was sitting next to the fire as the flames licked the air.

"What's wrong, daddy? You're staring."

Simon shook his head, shaking himself out of his hypnotic state and apologised to his daughter. "There's nothing wrong."

"Are you sure?"

Simon nodded. "It's just that…" Simon gulped and allowed his sentence to trail.

"What?" Imelda queried her daddy further.

"Sometimes…" Simon began, but paused. "Sometimes I look at you and feel like bursting into tears."

Imelda's forehead tightened and she said, "I don't understand."

"It doesn't matter," he laughed timidly. "You're not a parent, so it's hard to explain."

"Okay." She glared at the cooking canine and salivated as the smell tormented her senses. "Do you think it'll be ready soon?"

"Shouldn't be long." He reached to the side of him and picked up two plates he had taken from the kitchen. He leaned over and gave his daughter one and then took a fork from his pocket and passed it to her.

"After we've finished, we'll go straight back inside, okay?" he asked her.

She nodded.

"Okay. A couple more minutes and we'll carve this baby up."

CHAPTER FIVE

Since killing the dog, the rest of the day had passed by with little excitement. The rest of the animal was carved up and placed on a plate from the kitchen cupboard, although there wasn't much. Simon and Imelda had stuffed their faces and gave themselves a protein overdose.

Simon had put the plate on the side of the sofa and he and Imelda spoke about their old life, in the afternoon, whilst picking at the meat.

The evening was maturing and Simon had made sure both doors of the house were locked before heading upstairs with his daughter, bag in hand. Simon picked the room that had the double bed, dumped the rucksack, and both of them kicked off their footwear before lying on the bed, on top of the black and white duvet.

Both of them were fully clothed when they lay on the bed, their heads resting on the soft pillows that were dressed in black covers, and Imelda laid her head on her father's chest. He stroked her hair and then kissed her forehead.

"I want to dream about mum and Tyler tonight," she groaned.

"Do you, babe?"

"Uh-huh. Do you?"

Simon thought for a few seconds and pulled a face. "Well ... I don't need to dream about them. They're in my head."

"But dreaming is different."

"Is it?" He continued to stroke her hair.

"Yeah. In your dreams you can touch them, smell them. You do things that we never did when they were alive."

"Your dreams must be a lot more vivid than mine." Simon smirked and continued to stroke her head.

"What does vivid mean?"

"Clear." Simon cleared his throat and added, "Anyway, I don't like to dream about mum and Tyler, because when I wake up I then realise that they're not here anymore."

"Oh."

"Do you like dreaming of mummy and Tyler because you miss them and want to be with them, or because your dreams take you back to how the world was before...?"

Simon never finished his sentence. He didn't need to. If he had finished his sentence, how would it have ended? Before... Before... their world turned to shit? Before... mummy and Tyler were killed in front of their eyes? Before ... the Canavars came and started ripping people to pieces. Before ... what?

"I just like dreaming about them," Imelda said, her sentence was in a tone to suggest she was a little bit angry with her dad. "That's all."

"Try and get some sleep."

"I'll try, but that nap before might keep me awake."

"I know. In that case, we'll just lie here and see what happens. It's still quite early, isn't it?"

"Okay, daddy."

A silence enveloped the pair of them and Simon closed his eyes, but Imelda disturbed his short-lived peace. He could hear her sighing, fidgeting and groaning. He bit his bottom lip and tried to remind himself that she was staying in a room for the first time and that she was only eight years old.

She said, "Daddy?"

Simon sighed, "Yes, what is it?"

"Remember our guinea pigs?"

"Of course I do." Simon released a short chortle. "They were a bloody pain, weren't they?"

"I miss them." Imelda released a long sigh.

"I know you do, but we couldn't take them with us. We had to let them go in the garden when me, you, mummy and Tyler left the house."

"Do you think they're still alive?"

"Probably not." Simon didn't think there was any point lying to her. They probably didn't get as far as half a mile before a cat or a fox took them into their mouths and carried them away.

The guinea pigs that Imelda was referring to had been bought months before things had turned for the worse. He remembered the day Diana had bought the guinea pigs very well.

The guinea pigs were bought whilst Diana was out shopping with Imelda. She had texted Simon and asked if they could get a hamster. He said yes, but she had returned with two thirteen-week-old guinea pigs instead. Imelda and Tyler had one each. Imelda called hers Alvin and Tyler called his guinea pig Ham Sandwich. It was either Ham Sandwich or Nibbles. He was going to call it Nibbles because it had bitten Diana when she first held it, but Tyler stuck with Ham Sandwich. Amusingly, Tyler had said to his dad, "I don't know where I got the name from, dad. It just came to me."

When the family had to leave their home, Alvin and Ham Sandwich couldn't go with them and were let out in the wild. Simon knew that they wouldn't last a week, but after Stage One and Two, his only concern was for his wife and two kids.

They also had an old cat called Beckham, which Diana and Simon had bought when they moved into their house, years before the kids came along.

When the kids were under the age of four they bought a black Labrador puppy. They called it Buddy, but it died after just five days. It had some kind of bladder problem and had to be put down. A year later they bought another black Labrador, and called this one Buddy as well. 'Buddy Mark Two' was a nightmare from the beginning. It was totally disobedient, hyperactive and did its own thing. They both thought that it was to do with it being young. Simon took it to six weeks of puppy training, but it never did any good. After the sixth week of training, Diana and Simon were watching the TV and Simon looked over to see Buddy chewing one of his slippers. "Well, that was money well spent," he remarked. Then a week later they gave the dog to a friend.

After the two Buddys, Diana wanted another cat. They bought one and called it Azrael. It was eventually given to the neighbours as it managed to get fleas and had passed it on to Tyler's room. Tyler had to sleep in his parent's room for a week until the problem was removed. His back had been bitten on a number of occasions, and a mixture of Rentokil and fumigating the room themselves and a lot of hoovering finally removed the pests.

To Simon's dismay, this incident hadn't put Diana off getting another cat. She bought another black one, just like Beckham, but after a year it had disappeared and was never seen again. So the reluctance from Simon about getting more pets was justified. Their history with animals wasn't great. Their two goldfish, Bruce and Nemo, had lasted longer than most of their domestic pets.

Simon looked over at the bedroom door and realised he hadn't put anything against it. Both doors were bolted downstairs and he was a light sleeper; even in the old world he never slept great, so he wasn't too worried. He decided to move the chest of drawers against the door anyway.

"Babe, I'm just going to get up and block the door."

There was no response from Imelda.

"Imelda?"

He smiled as he could hear her lightly snoring. He decided to leave the door.

He stroked her face with his forefinger and planted a gentle peck on her plump cheek. "Love you."

CHAPTER SIX

NEXT DAY

The bedroom was slowly filled with daylight. Simon was the first to wake up and could see that he had forgotten to pull the curtains together before they went to bed.

He yawned and could see that Imelda was stirring to the side of him. The pair of them had slept most of the night on their sides with their backs to each other. He was facing the window, where the light was spilling in, whereas Imelda had her back to it, which explained why she was still asleep.

He turned onto his other side and kissed his daughter on her hot cheek. He stroked her hair and leaned in for another kiss, but he released a gasp instead. A noise from underneath them could be heard, and all Simon could do was stay still in shock.

Who was it? How the fuck did they get in?

He began to gently shake his daughter awake. She moaned and wriggled and once her eyes opened, her dad had something to tell her.

"Babe. I think there's someone inside the house."

"What?" she yawned, then suddenly sat up and gasped. "What, daddy?"

Simon shushed her and told her to stay where she was whilst he went over to the door. The only reason an individual would be inside would be for supplies. He looked over to his bag that sat at the side of the bed and went over to get a knife. He was unsure what to do.

Should he attack or scare off the intruder? After all, it only sounded like it was the one. Or, should he and Imelda hide?

Does he allow the man to see for himself that there's not much here and wait for him to leave? But if they hid, there could be a chance they'd be found.

And then what? A fight? Someone getting hurt? Killed?

Imelda had left the bed now and tied her hair in a ponytail as she went over to her old man.

"Are we going to hide, daddy?"

He shook his head. "No, but *you* are."

"What?" she gasped and widened her eyes. "I … I…"

"Get under the bed."

Imelda began to panic and said with tears in her eyes, "But what are *you* going to do?"

22

"I don't know yet." Simon puffed out an anxious breath. "I'm staying here, but if he comes in, *if* it's a he … I'll … I'll talk to him. Well, I'll *try* and talk to him."

"Talk? He might hurt you, daddy."

"Just..." He could feel his nerves making his body judder. He felt tense and Simon was trying to keep it together. He didn't want to snap at his little girl. She was scared. "Just ... get under the bed, please. It'll be okay."

"Okay," she whimpered. "If you say so."

Simon gazed over and felt for the petrified Imelda as she went under the bed and lay there on her belly. He reminded her to be quiet and took an intake of breath as the person in the house began making their way upstairs.

"Oh shit," Simon mumbled.

"Daddy, what is it?"

Simon shushed his little girl.

He could hear the footsteps growing louder as the individual progressed to the landing, to the first floor. Simon had tears in his eyes. *Please don't hurt us. Please don't fucking hurt us.*

He clasped onto the handle of the knife tightly as the footsteps continued. Simon placed his ear by the door and heard the man—he assumed it was a man—going through the bedroom next door to them. The bedroom door closed, as the individual exited, and opened the door of the smallest bedroom.

Simon turned and faced the window. Still clasping his knife, he placed his left hand on the door handle, waiting for the intruder to try it. He knew he was going to.

Then the moment came.

Simon heard three slow footsteps coming towards him, towards the door. He held the door handle tight and pushed it up so that it wouldn't move once it was tried.

There was silence, hesitation from the person behind the door. And then Simon felt it. The handle was being tried and Simon managed to keep control of it. It moved maybe about half a centimetre, but Simon made sure that it never went down further.

An awful, terrifying silence engulfed the bedroom and Simon placed his ear to the door and couldn't hear a thing, not even breathing. Had both men held their breaths?

"Is there anybody in there?" a male voice spoke up from behind the door.

The query made Simon's heart giddy-up even more. Simon breathed in, gulped hard and replied, "Yes, there is."

23

That was it.

No more words were exchanged between the two males, and the stranger in the house walked away from the room where Simon and Imelda were staying, and then Simon could hear fading footsteps which suggested that the man was making his way downstairs. But was he leaving the house altogether?

Silence was present in the room for a matter of minutes, both Simon and Imelda too scared to speak out.

Simon still had his hand on the handle and finally released it, but kept a hold of the knife in the other.

"Daddy?" Imelda finally shattered the silence from under the bed, and added further in a soft voice, "Has the man gone away?"

"I don't know, babe. I'm gonna check. Stay where you are."

There was no protest from Imelda as her dad prepared to leave the room, to leave her alone. There was no response at all.

Simon finally built up the courage to open the door and stepped out onto the landing. He gently closed the door behind him and could see that the intruder had left all doors of the other rooms open, both bedrooms and the bathrooms. Simon was certain that the man was downstairs and that the fading steps wasn't some kind of trick, but he gave the rooms a quick check anyway, and then sauntered to the top of the stairs.

He looked down and remained gazing for seconds, unsure whether going down was the correct thing to do. The right hand that was clasping the knife was clammy and shaking, so he swapped hands and wiped his right palm on his black combat trousers before putting the knife back in his grip.

He made the descent very slowly, pausing with each step he made. In order to survive in the long term, he knew that eventually killing another man was something that needed to be done to protect himself and his daughter. He just didn't want that day to be today.

He finally reached the bottom of the stairs and then hesitantly peered into the living room, like someone would peer over their cushion during a horror movie, and could see that the room was empty. The kitchen was the last room in the house to check.

He made nine steps across the living room and reached the kitchen with his knife now raised. The door was still shut, but he could see that the intruder had forced open the window of the kitchen and that's how he had managed to get in. Simon went over to the window and pushed it back down, wondering what the stranger had used to prise the window open. The weak lock had been busted. He was so obsessed with the two doors that he never thought about the downstairs windows of the house as another way that intruders could get in.

Although he was still shaken from the arrival of the intruder, Simon was relieved that the house was clear and that the individual, their brief uninvited guest, had decided to flee.

He decided to go back upstairs and tell his daughter the good news.

He made slow steps to the bottom of the stairs and scratched his head. He put his knife back into his pocket and wiped his sweaty hands on his trousers once more. He looked up to the landing and gasped as he could see a man standing at the top of them.

Simon gulped and said, "But … how? The other two bedrooms are empty."

The man was of similar appearance to Simon, but this guy's hair was longer and so was his beard. The stranger said with a smile, "You forgot to check the bedroom wardrobes."

CHAPTER SEVEN

"What do you want?"

Simon remained calm on the outside, but panic ran through his veins as he knew that the intruder was just yards away from the room where he and his daughter slept, away from where Imelda was right now.

Please don't get out from under that bed. Stay where you are, babe.

The man at the top of the stairs remained gazing at Simon. He was dressed all in black. He was a skinny fellow, had dark features with a thick dark beard and had a hairdo that was reminiscent of Liam Gallagher in his 90s Oasis days.

"I'm not here to harm anyone," the man spoke and held up his hands as if he had a gun pointing at him. As soon as the man at the top of the stairs had said those words, Simon began to relax. He believed him straightaway. The man was calm and had no malice laced in his words.

"So ... what are you after, mate?" Simon asked him. He hadn't called an individual 'mate' for a while. It was probably because he only addressed males as mate, and he hadn't talked to another man in a good while.

"I thought this place was empty," the man began. "I came to seek for food and shelter, but ... you're here."

"I am." Simon nodded.

"Is it just you here?" The man gazed around and added, "The place looks big enough to share."

"Yes, I'm here on my own." Simon stroked his beard and gazed at the man menacingly, trying to scare the man away by using false bravado. "And I don't do sharing."

"Why so hostile, friend? I'm just a normal guy, like you, just doing my best to survive."

Simon gave no answer, and he dismissed the question. He thought for a few seconds and asked the man to come downstairs so they could have a chat, face-to-face.

The man smiled and made the descent. Once he was five steps away from the ground floor, Simon put his hand into his pocket, feeling for the knife in case it was needed. They both headed for the living room and Simon told the man to follow him. The skinny individual stepped into the living room and Simon asked him to sit down in the armchair. The fear that Simon had before was now gone. Going by the behaviour of the intruder, it appeared that *he* was the one that seemed a little nervous, and also a little paranoid.

"I'm sorry I broke in, sorry about your window," said the man. "I'm just desperate."

"It wasn't really my place until a couple of days ago."

"Still…"

"Give me a minute, mate," said Simon, and headed for the stairs and left the living room.

"Wh-where are you going?"

"I need to do something. Won't be long."

Simon ran up the stairs and went into the bedroom where he and Imelda had slept.

"It's okay, babe," he announced in a whisper and looked under the bed. "It's me."

"What's happening, daddy?" Imelda gasped and her eyes were large with fear.

"There's a man here," Simon tried to explain.

"A man?" she cried.

"It's okay. I think he might be alright," he tried to calm his frightened little girl. "I just need you to stay here while I get to know him, to make sure he really is a good guy."

"Do I have to stay here, under the bed?"

"You can sit on the bed, if you want, but if you hear any noises downstairs or footsteps making their way up here, get back under the bed and stay hidden."

Imelda looked confused and began to crawl from underneath the bed. "Why would I hear noises from downstairs?"

In case we're fighting, Simon thought. Fighting to the death.

He decided not to speak his mind, and told her to be quiet and not to leave the room until he came back.

Simon went over and kissed the confused child on the forehead, then left the room and galloped downstairs to the ground floor.

He tapped his right pocket to make sure his knife was still there before returning to the living room.

The intruder was still sitting in the armchair. He greeted Simon with a smile and then began to gaze around the room. Simon sat on the couch, opposite his intruder, and sat back, giving off a relaxed impression. Now both men were glaring at one another and Simon was the first to speak after a thirty-second silence.

"Why here?" Simon asked the man.

The man opposite smiled and said, "No introductions first?"

"Okay," sighed Simon. "I'm Simon. And that's all you need to know ... for now. And you?"

The intruder nodded the once and announced, "People call or called me Dicko. Or D, if you prefer. It's up to you."

"Dicko?" Simon snickered.

The man who called himself Dicko looked at Simon coldly. "The last people that I were with used to call me that. It's quite a recent nickname, if that's what you want to call it."

"No. What's your real name? I was good enough to give you mine."

"Look, Simon," the man began and revealed a skinny smile. "Dicko was a nickname I was given months ago and it sort of stuck. I don't go by my real name anymore. My real name reminds me of the past. And in the past I have lost people. Understand?"

"Not really. I've *also* lost family members, but I'm still Simon."

"We all have different ways of dealing with this."

Simon didn't understand the way of the stranger's thinking, and said, "You can change your name all you want, but does it stop you thinking about friends and family before you go to sleep?"

"Let's change the subject," Dicko said with a smile. "I won't pry about your past, if you do the same for me. Okay?"

The conversation had dried up temporarily, even though Simon had many questions to ask the stranger, and queried him once more. "You never answered my question. Why here?"

"Why do you think?" Dicko ran his fingers through his scruffy beard and added, "'I've been walking miles, even went into the city."

"The city?"

"Yeah. The place has been bombed to shit." Dicko stroked his hairy chin and added, "I'm from the countryside originally, so being on the road and seeing cities and large towns that had been bombed was a new thing for me to witness. I suppose it was the government's way of reducing the problem."

"Have you come across any ... unsavoury characters on your travels?"

"You could say that," Dicko laughed.

"Tell me."

"You're not from around these parts, are you?" Dicko asked, quickly changing the subject.

"Originally I'm from down south."

The intruder nodded. "I thought so."

"These characters you mentioned. How bad were they?"

"From the old past or the recent past?"

"Recent."

Dicko shook his head and snickered, "You've lived a sheltered life, haven't you?"

Simon nodded. "I've tried to avoid conflict. Nothing wrong with that, mate, is there?"

Dicko never answered and changed the subject. He said, "I was recently with a gang. I was with them for just a couple of days, but they wanted me to join them on a permanent basis…"

"But…?"

"Their … methods, shall we say, were too brutal for me, so I did a runner during the night."

"Brutal?" Simon looked puzzled. "What do you mean? How brutal?"

Dicko snickered, "Let's just say that people just aren't the same anymore."

"How?"

The man that called himself Dicko leaned his head back and released a puff of breath out. He stroked his beard, gazed over at Simon, and then leaned forwards with his hands clasped together.

"Just remember this," he began. "Friends don't exist anymore. A lot of good people don't exist anymore."

"So I should be wary of *you*," Simon snarled and leaned forward. "So I should throw you out of here right now. Maybe I'll kill you."

Dicko said with a thin smile, "I'm one of the rare good guys."

The stranger didn't seem flustered at all with Simon's so called aggressiveness, which diluted Simon Washington's confidence a little.

"How many men have you actually killed?" Dicko asked with a grin, knowing the answer anyway.

Simon didn't think there was any point lying to the man. He gulped hard and flushed a little. "None ... yet."

"Jeez." Dicko began to snicker. "Have you been living in the shadows or something? How are you still alive?"

Simon gulped and asked, "How many have *you* killed?"

"A few."

"A few?"

Dicko nodded and said, "I've had to. It was either them or me. It's nothing that has ever given me pleasure, I can tell you. Also…"

"Yes?"

Dicko lowered his head and mumbled, "It doesn't matter."

"I know I'll have to do it eventually," Simon said. "I know that we've been lucky so far."

Dicko smiled and said, "What you need is another housemate. Someone that has a bit more experience, because—"

"That's not going to happen." Simon spoke up with a snarl in his tone, hoping that his face wouldn't quiver with fright like it did when his boss gave him a present and a presentation for his 21st birthday in front of the whole workforce.

"Is it not?" Dicko looked solemn, showing no emotion.

Simon shook his head.

"So no sharing. Finders keepers. Is that the way we're playing this?"

"I'm not playing."

Dicko slowly stood to his feet and looked like he was ready to leave. "You mentioned earlier that *we've been lucky so far.* You're not alone in here, are you?" Dicko smiled and looked up at the ceiling. "Somebody up there?"

Simon now stood up and placed his hand in his pocket, feeling for the steak knife. "Leave ... please."

"Is that what you really want?"

Simon nodded and now seemed unsure. Dicko could see the uncertainty in Simon's face and gave off a thin smile.

"Yes," Simon finally answered Dicko's query. "It's what I really want."

"Okay, friend." Dicko nodded. "I'm going."

Dicko walked into the kitchen, unbolted the door, opened it and stepped outside. Simon went to the door and watched as Dicko descended down the grassy bank and headed for the cluster of trees at the bottom. Once Simon saw Dicko disappear and swallowed up by the greenery, he relaxed a little.

Dicko seemed like a reasonable fellow, Simon thought. If he wanted to hurt him, then he would have. Dicko even left when he was asked to. Simon hoped that asking him to leave was something he wasn't going to regret in the future.

CHAPTER EIGHT

An hour had passed after Dicko's leaving, and Simon had told his daughter that the man that had broken in had now gone for good. He was going to tell her that it was a stray animal that had managed to get in, just so she wasn't scared, but she already asked him who was down there as she heard voices.

Simon had found a yellow plastic bucket in a cupboard, underneath the sink, and wanted to go out and find running water. They could fill the bucket, take it back to the house and filter it in their jars. Imelda didn't want to go out with her dad, but he wasn't leaving her alone, especially since the visit from Dicko.

He took the yellow bucket, a knife in his right pocket, and went outside, taking a reluctant Imelda with him. He was wary because of the visitor from earlier, and also the fact that they had to leave the house unlocked whenever they left the premises.

"How long is this going to take?" Imelda was moaning already, and they had only walked twenty yards. Simon had decided to walk the same way Dicko had gone when he left. The stranger must have headed that way for a reason. He must know the place better than *he* did, Simon thought.

Simon had been concerned for Imelda. She never drank enough.

Even before the incidents happened, when things were normal, Imelda never drank enough fluids and was always constipated. Simon and Diana used to moan at her all the time. She would take a full bottle of water to school and would return six hours later with the bottle still full. There had never been a problem with Tyler keeping hydrated. But he had his own problems. He was the fussy eater out of the two. He would eat meatballs but never touch normal mince. He would eat a roast potato but claimed to hate mash. And would eat pizza from Pizza Hut but wouldn't eat a square one because it was the wrong shape.

Imelda would try any food once, but keeping her hydrated had always been a problem. The problem was even worse now, as the water, after being filtered, didn't taste great. Luckily, Simon had found some blackcurrant cordial juice in the kitchen, and was going to add that to the water to make her drink more.

"We'll be out for no more than an hour," he told her, holding her hand with his left and clasping the bucket with his right.

"What if we don't find any water, daddy?"

Simon shrugged his shoulders. "We will. Don't worry."

They continued with their walk and he could now feel his daughter staring at him.

"You okay, babe?" he asked her.

She hunched her shoulders and said, "Not bad. I'm a little sad today, daddy, that's all."

"I know, babe."

She gazed at her daddy, gulped, and said, "I was thinking about mummy."

"Oh?"

She looked at her dad with wet eyes and said with a quiver, "I was thinking about when she used to take me to gymnastics."

Simon raised a smile and remembered the Friday evenings well.

Diana used to take Imelda and her friend Sophie every Friday. Sophie was more advanced than Imelda. His daughter was a new starter and began with practising forward rolls, then went onto handstands, and then the crab. Months later she had progressed to cartwheels and one-handed cartwheels. Imelda always used to be high as a kite whenever she came back. She used to have one new move a week, and would drive Diana mad when practising her moves in the bedroom or the living room where there was a hard floor. Diana was concerned that Imelda could end up hurting herself, but she did them anyway, whenever her mother wasn't around. Sometimes Simon would catch her doing a cartwheel in her room, but he never told Diana. Imelda had found something that she loved and he didn't want to discourage her, although he could see Diana's point.

"I miss mummy," Imelda said with a sad sigh. "I miss Sophie as well."

"Of course you miss Sophie," said Simon. "She was ... *is* your best friend."

"Do you think I'll ever see her again?"

Simon scratched his eyes and had a face that looked puzzled. "Who? Mummy?"

"No, silly. Mummy and Tyler are dead." She squeezed her father's hand tighter than normal and added, "I mean Sophie."

"I don't know. I don't think so." Simon decided to be brutally honest with his daughter. There was no point lying to her. "When the Canavars came, and then the bombs fell, we hid for months. A lot of people died during Stage One, and others fled to go to the countryside or to be with relatives. Sophie and her family had relatives up north, so I'm guessing her family probably left to go there."

"Maybe the bombs killed her."

"I don't think so," said her father. "Sophie lives just a couple of streets away. If just a couple of bombs had hit near her house, we wouldn't be here either."

"Why did they bomb us, daddy?"

"We've been through this before. I'm not entirely sure, but..."

They both started walking again, still holding hands, and Simon was trying to think how he could word his explanation to Imelda. They reached a group of trees that were all huddled together and passed the trees that were to their right.

"Look, daddy," Imelda shrieked and pointed over at the trees. "A fox."

He narrowed his eyes to try and focus and shook his head. "I don't think it's a fox, babe. Looks like a red squirrel. Very rare. Even more so now."

"Daddy?"

"Yes?"

"Why didn't we go somewhere safe when the monsters came?"

"We just hid," Simon said. "Me, you, mummy and Tyler only left the house once we realised it wasn't safe anymore."

A while after Stage Two, a few unsavoury, or maybe just desperate, survivors broke into their home. Luckily they were all in the basement so no one got hurt. It sounded like three or four men that had broken in, and Simon came to the decision right away that their home was no longer safe anymore. Their home had been good for Stage One and Stage Two, but desperate survivors had killed his confidence. Not only that, but the scumbags had ransacked the place and had broken the door whilst trying to get in. But at least they didn't take the car—not that it was much use in the long term anyway.

In the first week, Simon siphoned his vehicle and took the wheels off just in case it was stolen. The trouble with doing this meant that it could highlight to looters that people may be inside. When the men came and broke down his door, they were clearly in for food, and not for the car or looking for other people.

Simon sighed, "I miss home, our street."

"I miss nana. I wish we could have driven to her house when we had the car."

"We've already been through this before, babe, many times. I think nana, papa, grandma and granddad, your uncles ... are all ... gone."

"How do you know that grandma and granddad are dead? They live four hundred miles away."

"I just know, okay?"

Simon thought it was easier, mentally, to assume that everybody he knew had died. He didn't want to have false hope, to be travelling to places where relatives once lived, only to be hit with disappointment.

Assuming that everyone was gone allowed Simon to solely concentrate on looking after his little girl.

"Daddy, look," she shrieked.

Simon had been walking with his head in the clouds, thinking about yesteryear, and had a fright when Imelda squealed.

He looked in the direction she was pointing, and a wide smile emerged on his features. Three hundred yards in front of them was a pond, behind the pond looked like the start of a forest.

"Thank the Lord," Simon said with a smile. "Water."

CHAPTER NINE

"How long is this going to take?" Imelda moaned once they reached the pond. "My legs are tired."

"It's just a simple matter of dipping the bucket into the pond and walking back to the house," Simon huffed. "I'll probably spill some on the way back. Water can be quite heavy, you know. Especially when you've got half a mile or so to walk."

Imelda turned to face away from her father whilst he dipped the bucket into the clear pond. In the days when he first started doing this, he was paranoid if water had been infected in some way, but it was either this or nothing. He and his daughter hadn't been ill so far, thankfully. He knew that other lakes, ponds that were situated in cities were probably in a terrible state, but the area he was in and the area where he lived wasn't directly hit. Buildings were still standing and the trees had leaves on them. In some ways they had been lucky, but most days they didn't feel lucky.

"Okay," said Simon to his daughter. "That's me finished. Time to go back."

"Hey!"

Both Simon and Imelda turned when they heard the stranger's voice call out to them.

A man stepped out of the woods that were situated behind the pond and began waving at the two of them. He walked around the pond and Simon was in two minds what to do. Should he see what the man wanted or ignore him and make his way back to the farm? At first he thought the voice belonged to Dicko, but this was a different guy. This individual had long grey hair, tied in a ponytail, and looked to be in his fifties.

"Where are you staying?" the stranger asked as he reached the pair of them.

"A farm," Imelda blurted out.

"Babe, be quiet," Simon snapped.

"I think I know which one you're talking about." The man revealed a wide grin, revealing his decayed teeth, unnerving Simon.

"Anyway, we're going now," said Simon and held up his hand. "See you later, mate."

He grabbed Imelda by the wrist, picked up the bucket and walked away from the pond.

"Hey!" the man yelled. "Where're you going?"

"We need to get going." Simon could feel his heart beating out of his chest and took a quick look over his shoulder, seeing if the man was following the pair of them.

He was.

"For God's sake," Simon muttered under his breath.

Imelda had now looked over her shoulder and cried, "Daddy. That scary man is following us."

Simon stayed quiet and was unsure what to do. He stopped holding hands with Imelda and put his now-free hand in his pocket and felt for the handle of the knife. He took another look behind him and saw that the man was following them with quick steps and was only twenty yards or so away.

"Stay away!" Simon turned around and yelled, his heart almost beating out of his chest. "I'm warning you!"

"You're gonna be needing a lodger at that farm," the man laughed. "I've got a feeling it's a big one, plenty of room!"

"Daddy, I'm sorry I told him we were at a farm," Imelda said with tears in her eyes. "I wasn't thinking. I..."

"Don't worry about it, babe," said Simon, taking another look over his shoulder, noticing that the man was getting nearer. "It's not your fault."

"Daddy, I'm scared."

Me too.

Simon could now see the farm up ahead in the distance and guessed that it would take possibly ten to fifteen minutes to get there. But they had a problem behind them that needed taking care of. He took a long breath in and placed the yellow bucket of water on the grass.

He turned to Imelda and said, "Keep walking and don't look back."

"But, daddy—"

"Just do it!" he snapped.

She did as she was told and Simon turned around to face the annoying stranger. Simon pulled out the knife and hid both his arms around his back.

"Leave us alone!" he said with a snarl in his voice.

"No chance," the man snickered. "That farm can house more than two people, and I bet you got food in there, haven't you?"

"Just fuck off!"

Simon was frightened, but told himself that if the stranger with the grey ponytail approached near enough, he was going to attack him. Was this it? Was this going to be the first person that Simon was going to kill? But what if *he* was the one that was killed? Imelda would be all on her own; left alone with this strange man. Perish the thought.

He wasn't going to come out of this situation second best; he couldn't. He had Imelda to think of. He then wondered if the man was carrying a weapon. If he was, why hadn't he pulled the thing out yet?

"I'm warning you," Simon snarled but could feel his face shake. "Stay away!"

"Warning me?" the stranger cackled at the shaking Simon. "Look at the state of you. You're shitting yourself."

Simon gulped and said, "Go away, please."

"*Go away, please*?" the man mocked and lunged at Simon. Simon closed his eyes and lashed out with the blade. The man with the grey ponytail fell to the floor, screaming and holding his bleeding face.

Simon stood in shock and looked down on the man. He was holding his face, his hand covered in crimson, and was writhing around on the floor like a snake on fire.

"Cunt!" the man screamed. "You fucking cunt! You're gonna pay for this. You hear me? You're gonna fucking pay!"

Simon didn't hang around for long and ran away.

Imelda turned around, but told her to face the front and keep walking. He had caught up with her and put his stained knife back into the pocket of his black combats and picked up the bucket.

"Was that a bad man?" Imelda asked.

Simon sighed, his heart still beating out of his chest. "I'm not too sure he's bad ... exactly. He's just..."

"What?"

"Desperate. Remember what I told you before?"

Imelda nodded slowly, but it was clear that she had no idea what her father was talking about. It was clear on her face.

"People aren't the same anymore," he tried to explain whilst constantly looking over his shoulder, making sure the now injured man was not following them. "Some of these people could have been lawyers, teachers. They could have been people that we passed in the town or street, but ... they've changed. They're doing what they're doing to survive."

"Will that man come looking for us?" Imelda cried. "He now knows where we stay."

"He'll be too scared to come to the farm."

"Are you sure, daddy?"

"Of course." Simon nodded.

He wasn't sure. *I fucking hope so.*

CHAPTER TEN

Hours had passed since the frightening incident at the pond, and Imelda had spent her time at the kitchen table, drawing with a pencil and paper that Simon had found in a cupboard. Both were still affected by what had happened at the pond, but neither spoke about it any further.

Simon had been outside boiling water on a fire he had made, whilst Imelda was preoccupied drawing. Two jars had been filled, whilst the rest of the water in the bucket was placed on top of the sink for another day. It was a matter of waiting for the water to cool down before they could drink the stuff. Simon had promised Imelda that he would put some cordial in hers. She hadn't been to the toilet in days and he was growing concerned for her and her constipation.

Simon could see Imelda was still drawing and went over to her. He stood behind her and kissed her on the top of her head. He gave her hair a little sniff and decided that the next time they went to the pond he was going to wash her hair with one of the soap bars he had in his rucksack.

He peered over her shoulder and could see that she had drawn four people and a car. The four people were obviously Tyler, Diana, himself and Imelda. There was Imelda and her dad on one side of the car, the dead on the other side, and her mummy and brother were up in the clouds.

"Why have you put mummy and Tyler up in the clouds?" Simon asked her.

She stopped drawing and pointed at the picture. "That's Tyler and mummy in heaven."

Simon gulped and took a step back. He could feel his throat harden and felt for his little girl. She stood up from the table and told her dad that she was tired and needed a lie down.

"Don't you want something to eat?"

She shook her head. "Just a sleep. That's all I need."

"Fancy a snuggle on the sofa? Me and you?"

She gave her father a rare smile and nodded. With their shoes still on, they headed for the couch. Simon lay on the couch and Imelda lay next to him; she put her arm across his chest and lay her head on it, closing her eyes.

Simon stroked his daughter's hair and kissed her gently on her clammy head and asked her, "You sleepy, babe?"

She nodded once.

He kissed her head again and stroked her hair like he used to on an evening when the world was normal, when Simon had a job, and Imelda had a school to go to the next day.

Back in the old world, after reading her school book with her, Imelda would sometimes ask Simon if he could stay for ten minutes and give her cuddles. Most days he would say yes.

"I was thinking about when we were all together," she began, then followed the sentence with a moan.

"Oh?"

"I was thinking about when we went to the circus. Do you remember?"

Simon smiled and said, "Yes, I remember."

Simon almost laughed when a flashback of a conversation between him and Tyler entered his head. Both father and son had the conversation whilst the place was filling up with people, before the first act.

Tyler was going through a horror movie phase and liked to draw vampires and werewolves. Simon had been the same when he was that age.

In the circus, Tyler had asked Simon, "Dad will there be any animals in the show?"

Simon replied, "Yes, of course."

"What about jugglers?"

"Yes, there should be jugglers as well."

"What about clowns?" his son asked him.

"I think there's one clown in this show."

Tyler then paused for thought and finally asked, "Will he be carrying an axe?"

Simon found the scene just as comical looking back as when it first happened a couple of years ago. There were many other stories, but that was his favourite.

When Simon's mum and step-dad visited them, Simon's mum told Tyler that her mum had passed away. Tyler then asked his grandma if she had been killed by a big lorry, causing Simon and his mum to burst into fits of laughter. When they first bought their guinea pigs, Alvin and Ham Sandwich, Tyler told Diana, his mother, that when they die he would like to give them a kiss.

The final one that Simon could remember was when their goldfish Bruce had passed away, floating lifelessly in the tank. Before Diana put it into the toilet and flushed it away, Tyler asked if he could 'have a go' at stabbing it.

Simon began to chuckle quietly, forcing tears to run down his face.

He then turned to the side and could see his daughter sleeping. The man by the pond then plagued his thoughts and he lost his smile. Simon slowly got up and tried his best not to disturb his daughter. He grabbed his coat that was hanging over the armchair, and placed it over her. He walked out of the living room and into the kitchen, looking over to the door to double check that it was bolted. He took a swig of warm water from the jar and glared out of the kitchen window, which was the same direction where the pond was. He wondered if the man dared to show his face again.

Simon never meant to harm him like that, and hoped it had frightened him enough not to seek them out. The stranger knew where the farm was, but Simon was hoping that the altercation earlier was enough to scare him off. Or would he be seeking revenge?

His mind was beginning to conjure up all kinds of scenarios that probably would never occur. What if the stranger decided to turn up during the night, whilst they slept?

Simon walked around the ground floor of the house, made sure the doors were all locked again, and went upstairs to check the bedrooms. He was sure that everything was fine, but thinking about the incident at the pond had fuelled his paranoia.

Once he checked the first floor, he made the slow descent back downstairs and sat in the armchair, hoping to get forty winks. He wanted to sleep for an hour or so, just in case the man by the pond *did* turn up during the night. He was certain that if he did fall asleep during the night and someone tried to get in, he would wake up, but he wanted to try and stay awake for one night, just this once.

He leaned his head back on the chair and closed his eyes. He began to think about Diana and Tyler.

Twenty-one minutes later, Simon had fallen asleep and began to dream about Diana and Tyler, but it wasn't a nice dream.

*

Simon's dream felt more like a flashback. It was a horrific flashback. It was an incident that he would never forget to his dying day, and neither would poor Imelda.

A gang of individuals had raided their home and Simon and Diana had decided that it was for the best to flee their place and go north, somewhere where it was safer.

Simon went outside and stared at the carnage in his barren and lifeless street and put on his car tyres, trying to ignore the smell of death in the air. Once the tyres were on and the petrol was put back into the vehicle, they were ready to go.

He reversed out of his drive and left the street, telling Tyler and Imelda to close their eyes. Dead bodies and body parts were present and Simon guessed correctly that these bodies had been there since the early days, before Stage Two. He had no idea how long it had been since the Canavars arrived, but he guessed that it had only been a month or so since the bombs had stopped. He drove along the desolate road and gazed up at the murky skies. The sky looked different, unusual ... polluted.

The plan was to hit the motorway and head north, but they had only been on the road a matter of minutes when a Canavar shambled out into the road. Simon hadn't seen the thing in time and hit the creature. Diana, Tyler and Imelda screamed, Simon lost control of the car and veered off the road, the car crashing into a hedge. The car had stalled and Simon desperately tried to start the car. That was when he woke up in the armchair and could feel a pain in his finger.

He quickly sat up, and realised he had fallen asleep with his knife sitting on his lap and had pricked his finger, which was why his dream had been cut short.

He looked over to see that Imelda was still sleeping and then thought about the rhyme/song that Tyler had made up to tease Imelda with. Even in dark times, his son still managed to conjure up a rhyme, which highlighted to Simon that his son wasn't frightened when the early days of Stage One were in progress. Tyler hardly showed signs of anxiety when it was happening. Yes, he missed his friends, but he saw it as a big adventure. He couldn't go back to school, he had to stay indoors, and he spent a lot of time watching out of his bedroom window in morbid fascination. It didn't seem to bother him as much when the power went, which was a surprise to his parents, as he loved playing on his phone.

Apart from peeping out of his window and teasing his little sister, Tyler spent his time at the dining table with paper and pencils. He drew pictures and made up some stories and incorporated some rather gruesome pictures to accompany the words he had written. He also made up comics and spent hours thinking up dialogue and colouring in the pictures. The one that Simon remembered was one called Tragedy. It was clearly a rip off from Jaws, a film that Tyler had secretly watched in his room. His story was nearly fifty pages long, something that impressed Simon, and was about a Hammerhead shark terrorising holidaymakers in Jamaica. He was impressed that his young son had written something like this, however, was slightly disturbed that the content was rather bloody.

Simon raised a smile when looking back. He remembered some of the sentences as he had read the book a couple of times out of sheer boredom. Tyler would spell picture as picher, Saturday as Saterday and library as lybrarie.

Simon then heard his little boy's voice scream inside his head "Daddy, don't leave me!"

Simon would never forget those words. Ever.

It was the last words his son had said to him, and the heartbreaking thing about it was that the words were coated with fear.

He took another look at his bleeding finger and began to suck the blood. He stood to his feet and began to walk around the house again, stretching his legs.

Simon decided to abolish the idea of staying awake through the night. He was a light sleeper anyway, and thought that it wouldn't be good for him, mentally, to try such a thing.

Tonight, he was going to sleep downstairs.

CHAPTER ELEVEN

Simon had been pacing the floor for the last fifteen minutes. Adrenaline coursed through his veins and he couldn't stop thinking about the man by the pond. He looked over at Imelda and decided to wake her. If she slept any longer, she would struggle to sleep on a night.

He went over to the sofa and crouched down. He began to gently shake his little girl and she began to stir and mumbled, "I don't want to go swimming, mummy."

Simon could feel his eyes filling when she said this, and he wondered if he had disturbed a pleasant dream that Imelda was having. Her blue eyes opened and gave her daddy a thin smile, the same way she would when trying to hide disappointment.

"Were you dreaming?" he asked her.

She shook her head and he knew that she was lying.

"I'm sorry if you were, but if I leave you any longer, then you won't sleep tonight."

"Daddy?" Imelda sat up and rubbed her eyes. "Tell me about when me and Tyler were born."

Simon smiled and was a little too jittery and impatient to be telling stories. "I'm not sure—"

"Please."

His daughter looked at him with pleading eyes. How could he resist?

"Okay," he sighed, "but after that I need to check the outside of the house."

He sat next to Imelda and put his arm around her shoulder. He began, "When you were born—"

"Start with Tyler," she said. "Then me."

"When it was time for Tyler to be born, we went to hospital and seven hours later he popped out. Just like that. Well, *popped* is probably the wrong word; it was more difficult than that. He was eight pounds and seven ounces and I was the first person to touch him."

Simon paused and could feel his throat beginning to harden. He swallowed hard and continued, "We thought he would be our only child and then suddenly you came along."

"Was I a nice surprise?"

"Of course." Simon smiled, groaned and rubbed his hand over his face. "You were both nice surprises."

"Tyler always used to tease me and tell me that he was the favourite because he was the first to be born, and I was..." Imelda couldn't find the words to finish her sentence.

"You were both special babies," said Simon.

Simon didn't want to tell Imelda the truth. Why do that now?

She said, "Daddy?"

"Yeah?"

"I love you."

Simon kissed his daughter on the head and sniffed her hair. "You mean the world to me. You *are* my world."

A rattling could be heard from outside, making Imelda gasp.

"It's okay." Simon stood up, trying to act in control, but he couldn't hide the fact that he looked panicky.

"What is it, daddy?" Imelda stood to her feet and wrapped her arms around Simon's waist.

"It's probably just another dog, an animal or ... or the wind." He turned so that he was facing his daughter and said, "I want you to go upstairs and hide under the bed, just in case."

"Not again."

"Please," Simon begged. "Just do as you're told."

"But daddy," she cried, "I don't want to leave you."

"Just do it. And don't move from under that bed until you hear my voice tell you to. Understand?"

Imelda glared at her father and remained motionless.

"Understand?" he tried again.

She nodded the once.

"Right, go upstairs. I'll call you once I'm done checking outdoors."

She gave her dad a hug, and then headed for the stairs and went up to the first floor with reluctant feet. He could hear footsteps above him, telling him that she was now in the room. He went in the kitchen and took his knife and the claw hammer from the side. He placed the hammer in his deep pocket and held onto the knife. He placed his hand on the bolt of the door, ready to slide it back, and took a long intake of breath.

He slid the bolt and slowly opened the door. He shut the door behind him and was aware that he couldn't venture far. The door was unlocked and could only be locked from the inside because the bolt was all there was. He made a decision to walk round the house, and then head straight back in.

As soon as he approached the first corner of the house, he was grabbed and thrown to the floor. Simon dropped his knife and was kicked in his side as he tried to get to his feet. He looked up and could see it was the same man by the pond. His face was badly scarred from the cut, but wasn't bleeding anymore, and he bent down and picked up the steak knife that Simon had dropped, and a wide beam stretched across his face.

Simon took another kick and groaned, now coughing hard and unable to find his breath.

"You should have taken me in," the man with the grey ponytail growled.

Simon reached inside his pocket and pulled out the hammer as his assailant, now holding Simon's steak knife, brought his leg back to kick Simon once again.

Simon took another kick to his side, but grabbed a hold of the leg and wrapped his left arm around. Aware that the man now had a blade, Simon began hitting the hammer against the man's right knee. The assailant screamed out and fell, clutching his knee, and Simon scrambled to his feet and struck the man again. He aimed for the head, but he missed and struck the man on the top of his shoulder.

He wanted to kill him.

Fuck it. He knew this day was going to come one day and he had the safety of Imelda to think of. If this man was quite willing to kill another human being to get a roof over his head and whatever supplies were in there, what could he do to Imelda? It wouldn't bear thinking about.

Simon tried to hit the man once more, but his attacker stabbed him in the hand. The knife didn't go in far, half a centimetre at the most, but it was enough to make Simon yell and drop the hammer. He took a step back and was now clutching onto his bleeding left palm.

The attacker grabbed the hammer and stood up. He was now holding the knife in his right and the hammer in his left, smiling devilishly, like a clown.

Simon ran towards the door of the house, trying to escape, but felt the hammer hit him in the back, making him collapse to the floor.

The man with the grey haired ponytail bent down and looked down at Simon who was now on his back, gasping for breath.

The stranger growled, "Don't worry, son. I'll make this very quick."

The man then gasped, stood up straight and had a look of confusion on his face, making Simon equally as confused. The man dropped the knife and hammer at the same time, then fell to his knees. Simon could now see another man standing behind the pond guy, blood running off of his trench knife.

It took Simon a while to realise that the pond guy had been stabbed by the other stranger from behind. The man with the grey ponytail fell to his side, gasping for air, and Simon stood up and took a few steps back as the man by the pond continued to gasp.

For reasons he didn't understand, Simon never turned away when the man behind bent down and dragged the blade of the trench knife across the front of the pond guy's neck to finish him off.

Blood gushed out of the pond man's throat and the killer stared over at Simon and said, "Hello again, Simon."

Simon nodded once. "Hello, Dicko."

CHAPTER TWELVE

Simon had told Dicko to come inside the house. Dicko had saved his life, so it was the least he could do.

Dicko told Simon that he'd be with him in a few minutes and that he needed to move the body in case the 'little one' saw it. Simon knew he was referring to his daughter and thanked Dicko for his considerate behaviour. Dicko had given the man from the pond a brutal death, but it was either Simon or him.

Dicko had stepped inside the house and could see that Simon was nowhere to be seen. He then returned from upstairs with his little girl, both entering the living room, and both father and daughter sat on the couch.

Imelda gasped when she saw Dicko, but Simon told her that the stranger was okay and had 'helped' daddy, but never went into detail how.

Simon felt relaxed around Dicko this time round, despite witnessing what he was capable of, and offered him a drink of water.

They talked and Dicko tried to explain to Simon about his recent past.

"I've been staying in a wooded bit. I saw that guy heading to your farm, so I went to the side of the fields and kind of followed him," he said. "I didn't know he was a danger until you two started to fight."

Simon admitted, "I had a confrontation with him before."

Dicko sat back and clasped his hands together. "Oh?"

"He wouldn't leave us alone, so I lashed out." Simon took in a deep breath and continued, "There was a little tussle between the pair of us and I slashed his face, albeit accidentally."

"You have a daughter to protect." Dicko nodded. "You did what you had to do. You also need to think about yourself. If anything happens to you, she's gonna suffer being on her own."

"I know." Simon huffed and felt uncomfortable talking like this in front of his little girl. He went into the kitchen and gave her some blackcurrant juice and asked her to go upstairs for a while.

She nodded and smiled, and surprisingly went back upstairs without protesting, knowing that the two men wanted to talk about grown up stuff. Her and Tyler used to get asked to go upstairs once in a while if ever her mummy and daddy needed to talk or argue about something.

"She's a sweet girl, beautiful," Dicko remarked. "I take it you want to know my story, but you don't want her to hear it. You don't want her scared."

Simon nodded. "That's right."

"I get it." Dicko laughed softly and added, "But there's nothing to tell. I'm just a guy that just so happens to be still around."

Simon took an intake of breath and asked his guest, "What did you kill that man with?"

Dicko smiled and stroked his dark beard. "This," he said. From the brown leather holster on his left, he took his right hand and whipped out a six-inch blade with a D-shaped knuckle skullcrusher. "This is Trevor. I never leave home without it."

"So, what's your story?"

Dicko smiled and placed the knife back into the holster. "What's yours?"

"You're my guest, and I asked first."

"And like I said earlier ... my story is very dull, very boring."

"Tell me anyway."

Dicko smiled and shook his head. "I am your guest. I'm not your prisoner, so I don't feel compelled to answer your question. And let's not forget that I saved your life."

"What's wrong, mate?"

"There's nothing wrong." Dicko sat back in the chair and placed his arms on the rest, looking more than comfortable. He said, "The past is the past. What matters is now."

"But didn't you have a wife ... or children?" Simon didn't understand why his guest was being so secretive. "Who did you lose?"

"I don't wanna talk about it." Dicko bit his bottom lip and added, "Talking about the dead cannot bring them back."

"If you don't talk about your story, then I won't be giving any secrets away."

"Good," Dicko began to snicker, "because I don't think the old life is important anymore. Talking about the old life is pointless."

"It's important to me. It's important to Imelda. Am I just supposed to forget about my wife and my son?"

"So you had a wife and a son?" Dicko rubbed his chin and added, "I thought you weren't going to tell me anything. What happened? How did they...?"

"Doesn't matter now."

"How did you get up here?" Dicko asked.

"What do you mean?" Simon seemed baffled by Dicko's query.

"You're not from around these parts. You're from the south."

Dicko sighed, "Okay. If you don't want to talk about yourself, that's fine. I've got no problem with it. But I'll tell you what me and my daughter have been through."

Dicko glared at Simon, waiting for him to start.

"I moved up here when I was in my twenties. Me and a pal of mine went to Turkey for two weeks and I met this girl. We kept in contact and she eventually moved down to where I stayed for eighteen months."

"Why just eighteen months?" asked Dicko.

"She couldn't settle. She had a big family and she was missing them, so I quit my job as a forklift driver, applied to some colleges up here, near where she stayed, and managed to get in one. Then the pair of us moved up, got married, had kids, blah, blah, blah."

"And you lived happily ever after," Paul said with a smile. "Until the dead arrived."

"The Canavars." Simon nodded.

"That's what they seem to call them around these parts."

"So you're not from around here either?"

Dicko shook his head. "I'm many miles from home. I've heard many names for these creatures since this thing has started, but I simply call them the dead."

Simon released a sad breath out and shook his head. "I can't believe how quickly it spread. I mean, what was our army doing, for Christ's sake?"

Dicko could see Simon getting worked up and said, "Those questions are pointless now. They're the questions that we asked ourselves during the period when the dead were here in their thousands."

"Me and my daughter call it Stage One."

Dicko smiled and nodded the once. "And I take it when the bombs fell..."

"That's Stage Two."

"Of course it is," said Dicko. "I never witnessed any bombing myself. I came from a village and was there for months after the announcement. I think the cities and some large towns were bombed, to reduce the dead population, but I didn't even know places had been bombed until I was told by someone."

"Why did you leave this village of yours?"

"I had no choice," said Dicko and his face developed into a sombre one. "It was a shame. I left a few friends behind."

Simon opened his mouth to ask more about the stranger's past, but decided not to push him too far. He had got more out of him than he thought he could.

Dicko ran his fingers through his dark greasy hair and had a look around the living room. "You certainly hit it lucky finding this place."

"We did," Simon agreed. "Not before time. We had spent most of our time going from one place to the next. The woods, fields and a garage. We had spent the night in a shed before we came across this place."

"And that little thing upstairs..." Dicko said, followed by a thin and sympathetic smile. "How's *she* coping?"

"Better than you'd think for an eight-year-old, but she has her wobbles."

"A shame. She must be missing her mum and..."

"I had a son called Tyler. They were both taken at the same time, mother and son."

Dicko lowered his head and said, "I'm sorry."

Simon could feel a dull sensation in his chest and could feel it moving up to his throat. He was beginning to feel numb and tried to get rid of the feeling by clearing his throat very loudly.

He said, "What's been happening..." He cleared his throat once more and tried again. "What's been happening over the last year has been beyond surreal. Sometimes I feel like I'm in a dream."

Dicko smiled. "I suppose that's understandable."

"I just don't know how long we can carry on like this." Simon looked crestfallen and put his hands behind his head. "I just wonder how the other countries have suffered across the globe."

"I think they've suffered, but the colder countries have probably got an advantage. The dead are slow as it is, without having to wade through inches of snow, or trying to balance on a sheet of ice."

"I just don't understand how a country, the world, could come to a halt from things that are so slow. It just doesn't make sense."

Dicko nodded in agreement with Simon and could understand his frustration. "It's quite simple when you put your mind to it."

"Simple? How?"

"Think about it," Dicko began. "After just three weeks trade had stopped. Now, once petrol stops being delivered to supermarkets, other dominoes start to fall. Even gas stations that we get fuel from have to be replenished twice a day. After three or four weeks, due to staff shortages, power stations start to fail. We then lose power. ATM machines stop working, but the shelves are empty anyway in the shops, so we resort to robbing to feed our families. Then the water stops running and the toilets stop working. Eventually people start dying from cholera, starvation..."

Simon grunted, "Well, I suppose when you put it like that..."

"Daddy?"

Both men turned in the direction of the opened door that was situated near the main door and the bottom of the stairs. Imelda was standing by the door and looked concerned.

Simon beckoned her over. "What is it, babe?"

"I was scared, being up there on my own."

"Of course you were." He beckoned her over. "Come here."

She walked over to her dad and sat on his lap. She lay down, resting her head on his chest. Dicko smiled and seemed touched by what he saw. Simon observed this, and was certain that Dicko had had a family once upon a time.

Imelda whispered to her daddy, "When is that man leaving?"

Dicko had overheard the pretty little thing and began to laugh.

"We were just talking," said Simon. "In fact, I was going to ask him to stay for something to eat. What do you think about that?"

She shrugged her shoulders. "Okay."

Simon looked over at Dicko. "Is that okay for you, mate?"

Dicko nodded. "I'd be honoured."

"Good," said Simon. "I hope you like leftover dog."

*

After an hour of more chat and some nibbles, Dicko excused himself from the table in the living room. Before Simon could ask the man where he was going, Dicko gave the man a wink and told him that he had stuff to sort out outside. He had moved the body earlier, but wanted to make sure it was completely out of sight.

Simon nodded and thanked the man, knowing that he was getting rid of the body. He didn't know how he was going to do it, though. Was he going to bury the body? Or put it in the empty barn? As far as Simon was aware, the man didn't have a shovel on him. Hide it? But where? Under one of the trees or in the small barn?

Simon and Imelda had exchanged no words in Dicko's absence, and once they had finished their meal, Dicko had returned. He had only been away for seven or eight minutes and sat back down at the table. Simon didn't ask the man where he had put the body, but thanked him by gesturing with his head, and then asked what his plans were.

"My plans?" he cackled.

"Yeah." Simon looked at his guest's hands and noticed that they were dirty. "What are you gonna do, mate?"

Dicko hunched his shoulders. "Do what I've been doing for months: Survive. I *do* have plans, though."

"Oh?"

"Well, there has to be some kind of—"

"Daddy?" Imelda spoke up and lowered her head.

Simon sighed, "You shouldn't really interrupt adults when they're speaking, babe."

"I'm sorry, daddy," she whimpered, "but I feel sick."

"It's not important anyway," the man that called himself Dicko reached over, smiled and patted Simon on the shoulder. "You see to your little girl."

Simon stood up and said, "Come on then, babe."

Both father and daughter exited the house at the front, walking down the path and Imelda bent over the grass and released some white vomit. Simon stood by her side and rubbed her back. She vomited a little more, and then coughed and spat a couple of times to get the lumps out of her mouth.

"You okay now?" he asked her, still rubbing her back.

"Uh-huh."

Back in the old days whenever Imelda had vomited in the house, usually during the night, Simon and Diana would go to the bathroom and find her crying after the ordeal.

On this day there were no tears. This had been the first time she had been sick since they had been out on their own, which was surprising, considering what they had to eat and the uncertainty on how filtered the water that Simon collected actually was.

She had complained that she had felt nauseous on a few occasions, but this had been the first time she had been sick.

"Do you want to stay out here and get some air? Or do you want to go back inside?"

She never answered his question. Instead, she said, "Daddy?"

"What is it?"

"Is that man staying with us tonight?"

"Erm..." Simon paused for thought and was unsure how to answer. Dicko had never asked to stay, but the thought had crossed Simon's mind. If Dicko *was* a threat to him and his daughter, then why on earth did Dicko save Simon's life? That thought alone was enough for Simon to be sure that Dicko was a good guy, although brutal when he could be.

"Well?" Imelda was waiting for an answer.

"Well what?"

"Is he staying with us?"

Simon shrugged his shoulders and said, "I don't think so. Why?"

"No reason," she said.

"We don't even know him. How do we know he's not a bad man?" Simon was sure that Dicko was okay, but said it to his daughter anyway.

"I don't think he is," the young girl said with confidence. "I like him."

Simon smiled. *So do I. How can I not like him? He saved my life.* "Come on." He playfully nudged his daughter and kissed her on the top of her head. "Let's go back inside."

CHAPTER THIRTEEN

NEXT DAY

The morning was a dull one, and Simon was the first to rise. He wanted to sleep on the sofa, but Imelda didn't want to sleep alone so she slept on the sofa and Simon nodded off in the armchair. With everything that had happened with getting a beating and then Dicko killing Simon's assailant, he found it difficult to sleep. His mind wouldn't switch off.

He walked into the kitchen, his knees cracking as he did this, and felt his sides. He lifted his black T-shirt up and couldn't see any bruises as such, but he did feel tender in that area, and then it hit him.

He could have died yesterday. Imelda would have been on her own.

Or even worse.

That man could have gone into the house, after killing Simon, went upstairs to where Imelda was sleeping... *No! Don't even think about it!*

He owed Dicko, or whatever his name was, and he owed him big time. Which was why he decided to finally pluck up the courage to ask the man if he wanted to stay the night. Dicko had politely declined Simon's offer and said that he had plans, but he'd see them both in the morning sometime.

Dicko was a vague character and didn't give much away as far as his past was concerned, but Simon liked him.

Simon decided to take a step outside and gazed around at miles of fields. Maybe tomorrow he was going to have to take another trip to the pond.

He remained standing and closed his eyes as the wind tickled his face. It was peaceful, and it was days like this that he was glad to be alive. He looked up to the murky sky. It looked similar to what it looked like after the bombs fell.

Simon felt something touch his hand, and he gasped and jumped at the same time. He turned to his side and saw his little girl staring up at him.

"You frightened me," he said with a smile.

"Sorry, daddy."

"You okay?"

She nodded her head, but she wasn't convincing her father.

"What is it?" he asked her.

"I was thinking about our guinea pigs."

Simon smiled.

"Do you remember, before school," she began with a rare smile on her face, "that me and Tyler had to clean out the cage, then feed them after it was clean?"

"Of course I do." Simon stroked Imelda's soft cheek on the right side of her face with his finger. "I used to pay you and Tyler ten pounds a week and give you the money every Saturday."

"That's right. Tyler was always messing around and he let me do most of the work, but he would still get paid."

"He used to put the bags in the bin," Simon said.

"Yes, but it was me that picked up the poo and scooped up the hay that Alvin and Ham Sandwich had peed on." She lowered her head and added, "Tyler used to pull my ponytail when I was trying to clean out the cage."

"I know, babe. He used to tease you terribly."

She lowered her head and said in a quaver, "I would give anything to have just one more morning like that."

"Oh, Imelda."

Simon turned and crouched down so that he was eye level with his little girl, and the pair of them hugged. He rubbed his hand up and down her back and they both slowly broke away from the embrace. He looked at her and could see two trails across her plump cheeks where tears had fallen.

He kissed her on the forehead and said, "I love you, Imelda."

"I love you, daddy."

Both father and daughter could hear dragging feet coming from the side of the house. Both looked at one another and froze, unsure what to do. Simon patted his pockets and realised that he had no weapon on him. He grabbed Imelda and they began to make their way towards the back door into the house, but a figure had already appeared from around the corner. It was Dicko.

"Morning, folks." He held his hand up, making Imelda smile and Simon sigh with relief.

"Thank God," Simon gasped.

Dicko looked at both of their faces. "Sorry, I didn't mean to scare you both."

"What're you doing ... creeping up like that?"

"I didn't think you'd be up so early and outside. What's up?" Dicko snickered, "Did you shit the bed or something?"

Simon rubbed his face and groaned. He was in two minds whether to reprimand Dicko for talking like that in front of Imelda. Dicko had saved Simon's life only yesterday, so Simon decided to keep his mouth shut and let him away with this one. But any more cussing in front of

Imelda, and he would have to have a polite word. Imelda began to moan that she was hungry and Simon told her to go inside and see what was in the bag.

"I think there's a tin of sardines in the bag. A few tins of beans as well."

"Ew," Imelda moaned and added as she went inside the house, "I think I would rather starve."

"We're not far off it," Simon murmured.

"I was going to talk to you about that, funnily enough," Dicko spoke up.

Simon narrowed his eyes. "About what?"

"I'm going to disappear for a while."

"What for?"

Dicko rubbed his dark beard in thought and said, "I don't know how far I need to go or how long it's gonna take me, but I'm gonna try and get a set of wheels."

"Isn't that a bit dangerous?" Simon questioned. "If people, desperate survivors, hear the engine, you're opening yourself up to be attacked. It's one of the main reasons why I—"

"We're in the countryside," Dicko began, interrupting Simon's rant. "But we're only a couple of miles from Silverburn, the shopping centre. There's a supermarket next to it. There could be an endless amount of supplies there. I don't know about you, but I'm sick of living off scraps."

"I can't see there being anything for us, especially after this length of time."

"You never know."

"Even if we did get stuff," Simon began, unsure about Dicko's plan. "It's not going to last forever."

"I know. That's why we take a trip to the homestore first, the one in Darnley, a couple of miles from Silverburn."

"Why do we need to go to the homestore?"

"Why do you think?" Dicko chuckled. "What are in these places?"

"Erm..." Simon thought for a few seconds and shrugged his shoulders. "Paint, lawn mowers, kitchen units..."

"And they also sell packets and packets of vegetable seeds and the tools that we need to make vegetable patches possible, like forks, spades..."

"Wait a minute." Simon scratched his head. "We only met yesterday, and you're talking about making vegetable patches."

"True, but I have a deal for you."

"Deal? What kind of deal?"

"You and Imelda trust me, right? I can see that. Let me stay near here and we can share the land. If we make this trip to the homestore, set up patches somewhere in the back, we may have something special here. It's spring. It's the perfect time to grow ... shit."

"Grow ... shit?" Simon smiled at Dicko's remark.

"Okay, so I'm no Alan Titchmarsh. Also, if we get thugs coming here to rob or kill us, I'll come in handy. You know I can handle myself. Oh, and I also saved your life, so you owe me one."

"Jesus, mate. Talk about emotional blackmail."

Dicko scratched at his hairy chin and Simon knew he wanted to say something further, but seemed reluctant to do so.

"If you're going out there, then I'm coming with you," said Simon.

"That's not going to happen." Dicko shook his head. "What about the house, Imelda?"

"I'm not sitting about here while you're out there busting your arse for us two. It's not fair."

"You're giving sharing land with me. It's my way of paying you back."

"It's not even my land," Simon said with a chuckle, but then his face turned sombre. "I've been walking these streets for months. There's nothing out there. I'm coming with you."

"If I go on my own, there'll be more room in the car to put supplies in."

"And if I go with you, we could load up the car a lot quicker."

Dicko rubbed his forehead and thought for a minute. He shook his head and asked, "What about Imelda? You can't leave her here."

"She's coming with us. If she's going to be living in a world like this from now on, she's gonna have to get used to it. Besides, I'm her dad. I won't let anything happen to her. And if other survivors see us and we have a young girl in tow, we'd look like less of a threat, don't you think?"

"Erm..." Dicko couldn't think of anything else to say. He agreed with Simon about his less of a threat theory, and was also convinced that it would be a simple journey, going through wastelands and barren roads to get where they wanted to go, but Simon also had a point about leaving Imelda on her own.

Simon asked Dicko, "So when're you thinking about going?"

"Easy, Tiger," Dicko snickered. "It might not be until tomorrow. If we're gonna do this, it's best to have the whole day so we have plenty of daylight to play with."

Simon nodded. "Okay."

"But I need to get wheels first." Dicko playfully punched Simon on the top of his arm and walked away, going in the same direction he had come from. "Wish me luck."

CHAPTER FOURTEEN

Simon and Imelda shared a tin of beans whilst Dicko was out looking for a vehicle. Eating the last tin that he had in his bag was tempting, but he held off. Imelda was moaning that she was still hungry, so he reached into his rucksack and handed her the packet of out-of-date Frosties. If they came back empty handed from the trip to Silverburn, they would have to go elsewhere to find food, even if it was just a trip to the woods to see if it had berries, mushrooms, or even an orchard somewhere. A hydrated human could last weeks without food, apparently, but Simon's growling stomach was in no mood to put that to the test.

After the beans and a small drink, Simon told Imelda to relax on the couch until Dicko came back.

"I'm always relaxing," she moaned and pouted out her bottom lip, clearly bored.

"Have a lie down." Simon sat in the armchair and took out the paperback book from his bag. He had forgotten where he was in the book and couldn't remember the last time he read it. He opened it in the middle, but Imelda spoke up before he could start a sentence.

"Is that a book about a shark?" she asked, gazing at the front cover. "What's it called?"

Simon smiled and said, "Didn't we have this conversation a few weeks ago?"

"I don't know." Imelda hunched her shoulders. "Did we?"

"It's Jaws. Daddy's favourite film. It was the first book I ever read."

"How old were you when you read it?"

"I don't know. I read it when I was little." Simon hunched his shoulder and scratched his dark beard as he began to think. "I think I was about eight … or nine. I'm not sure."

"Why did you take it with you when we left the house?"

"I began to read it again. I started reading it at work, during my break times. I used to take the rucksack to work. It must have been at the bottom of the bag when I packed some clothes and food, before we left."

Simon began to read the page and only had two minutes of peace when Imelda asked him another question.

"Daddy?"

"Yes?"

"Could I read it after you're finished?"

Simon clocked the words 'yawning vagina', near the part where Matt Hooper was about to sleep with Chief Brody's wife. He cleared his throat and said, "It's not for your eyes, babe."

"Oh?"

"Maybe when Dicko comes back with a car and we get to Silverburn, we'll try and pick up some reading books and colouring books as well."

"Silverburn?"

Simon smiled and realised he wasn't going to tell his daughter until Dicko arrived. Maybe it was better to tell her now. At least it would give her time to get used to the idea. He had no idea how she was going to react. She could freak or...

Simon puffed out a breath and mumbled, "Sod it." He stood up, leaving the paperback on the arm of the chair, and went over to Imelda and sat next to her.

"Dicko has come up with a plan that could keep us alive for a long time," Simon began. "Dicko has gone out to get a vehicle, then when he comes back we're going to take a trip to Silverburn, where that supermarket is, and fill the car up with supplies."

"Do *I* have to go?" Imelda asked.

"Yes."

"But why?"

"Dicko needs me to go, and I'm not leaving you here on your own. We can't just let him do all the work and then eat and drink what he's brought back with a clear conscience."

Imelda looked confused by Simon's ramblings and said, "But we gave him dinner last night."

"Yeah, but he saved my life."

Simon hadn't told Imelda what had happened outside the house and Dicko killing that man, and wanted to keep it that way. Thankfully, she never pressed him about how Dicko had saved his life.

"If we have to go with Dicko," Imelda began. "Does that mean we have to leave the farm empty?"

"I suppose it does." Simon had never thought of that. He looked at Imelda's confused face and said, "I don't like doing this, especially because we can't lock the doors when we leave, but food isn't going to just turn up and land on our doorstep."

Imelda lowered her head and Simon placed his arm around her shoulder. "Are you okay with that?"

She nodded.

"Are you scared?"

"A little," she admitted. "But I'm sure I'll be fine if you and Dicko are with me."

"Yes, you will." Simon smiled.

Imelda smiled and dropped her head and said, "I was thinking about that scary man by the pond."

"Oh?"

"What if he comes back?"

"He won't."

"How do you know for sure?"

Simon leaned and kissed the top of Imelda's head. "I just do." He went back over to the armchair, sat down and closed his eyes. "I'm just gonna rest my eyes for a while."

Imelda never responded.

*

"Daddy, I can hear a noise coming from outside."

Simon sat up and widened his eyes. He had dropped off and was immediately angry with himself for doing so. He had had a terrible night's sleep, but with an eight-year-old girl to care for it was no excuse.

Simon rubbed his eyes and groaned, "What kind of noise?"

"Not sure." She screwed her face up and tried to think.

"Was it an animal or…?"

"Sounds like a car."

Simon walked over to the front window and peered from behind the curtains. He saw a Mazda turn up the drive, at the side of the house. Simon smiled and knew who it was, despite not seeing the face of the driver.

He headed to the back door, to greet the man that bizarrely called himself Dicko.

"Where're you going, daddy?" Imelda's eyes followed her daddy's frame as he walked to the other side of the house.

"Stay there."

"Who is it?"

"It's Dicko," Simon announced. "He's back."

CHAPTER FIFTEEN

Dicko had told Simon that he had seen the car on the drive and broken into an abandoned house. He'd only been away for an hour or so, but both men agreed to start their venture the next day. Fortunately, the owners had left the car keys in one of the kitchen cupboards.

Simon had asked Dicko if he wanted to stay the night for the second time and this time he agreed. Dicko told Simon that he'd sleep on the couch; he also joked that he wouldn't be offended if Simon barricaded his bedroom before he and Imelda went to sleep.

Simon and Imelda had turned in over an hour ago and Dicko had helped himself to some water from the kitchen. He sat in the armchair and closed his eyes. Tiredness was beginning to creep up on him once more. A small sound from outside made him open his eyes wide, like plates, but nothing else was heard afterwards. He began to relax again and had a look around the dusky living room area.

Dicko released a yawn, stretched his arms, and began to groan. He scratched the chin area of his beard and then placed his hands on his lap, closed his eyes and tried to fall asleep once again. He could hear a thudding noise coming from upstairs and wondered what it was. Had Simon got up to go to the toilet? Had Imelda fallen out of bed?

Gentle thuds could be heard above him, and those thuds seemed to be moving. Dicko opened his eyes once more, and puffed out an annoyed breath as the footsteps began to make their way downstairs, down to the first floor of the farmhouse. The footsteps had reached the bottom of the stairs and had stopped. Dicko stared at the door and when it finally opened, Imelda walked through into the dusky room.

"Hello, there," he greeted the young girl. As soon as he clocked the little girl, any frustration that he had had evaporated.

She smiled and said, "Hello, Mr Dicko."

Dicko laughed, "Just Dicko will do."

Imelda was wearing a dressing gown that was far too big for her, and Dicko guessed correctly that it was something that the previous owners of the house had left behind.

"It's a bit cold tonight, isn't it?" he said.

She nodded.

"What's up, honey? Can't you sleep?"

"Not really. Daddy's snoring doesn't help."

Dicko tried to joke, "You should give him a nudge; tell him to turn over."

"I didn't want to disturb him. He never slept very well last night."

"That's very sweet of you." Dicko smiled and her concern for her daddy warmed his heart.

Imelda began to scan around the dim room and was thinking of something else to say.

She didn't feel uncomfortable with the silence. She knew that Dicko was a good guy, and if her daddy trusted him ... that was good enough for her.

Dicko cleared his throat. "You better get yourself back to bed. If your daddy wakes up and you're not there..."

"He won't," she said with confidence. "Mr Dicko?"

"Please, just call me Dicko."

"If you had one wish ... what would it be?"

"That's easy," Dicko snickered. "I would wish for things to go back to normal."

"It has to be something more realistic, otherwise the wish won't work. You can't wish for the old world or loved ones to still be alive."

"Wow." The man blew out his lips and puffed out a breath. "That makes it more difficult. I don't know." Dicko shrugged his shoulders. "A water-well in the back of the farm would be good. Am I allowed that?"

"Yes." Imelda nodded.

"What about you?" Dicko stroked his dark beard and smirked.

"What about me?"

"What would you wish for?"

Imelda went quiet and lowered her head, staring at her lap. Dicko wasn't sure if she was doing this because she was upset or because she was thinking of an answer.

"Imelda?" Dicko pushed.

She looked down and he felt the sadness in the room.

He persisted, "What would you wish for?"

"I don't know." She hunched her shoulders. "I suppose..."

"Yes?"

"What I'd really like ... is to see my daddy happy again."

Her voice began to quiver and her statement made Dicko's throat swell. Poor little thing, he thought. Living in a world like this.

"I'm certain that *you* make him happy," Dicko said.

"I'm not sure." Imelda tucked her blonde hair behind her ears and added, "He used to be happy, when mum and Tyler were alive, but now..."

"The situation we're in is horrendous, Imelda," Dicko began. "Your dad isn't happy because he's worried. He's worried about you, this situation we're in ... everything."

"We were staying at a house a few weeks ago," Imelda began, "and I got up during the night and realised daddy wasn't in the bed; he was downstairs. I left the room and sat on top of the stairs. I was thinking about going down, but I changed my mind."

"Why?" Dicko narrowed his eyes and leaned forward. "Were you scared?"

Imelda shook her head. "No."

"Well, what was it then?"

"I think my dad needed some time alone."

"Oh?"

Imelda licked her lips and seemed reluctant to tell Dicko the next sentence, as if it was a secret. Imelda's big blue eyes began to fill and Dicko thinned his lips as his heart began to break for the child.

Dicko said softly, "You can tell me, Imelda. You can tell me anything."

"I didn't go down because daddy was crying, really loudly. At first I thought there was a wolf downstairs. It sounded like howling. But I stayed on the top of the stairs and realised that it was daddy. I think he was crying for mummy and Tyler."

Dicko gulped, trying to remove the swelling from his throat, and asked her, "What happened to your mum and brother, if you don't mind me asking?"

"Erm..."

Both of them looked above when they heard quick footsteps across the ceiling. The panic-filled footsteps ran downstairs and a couple of seconds later Simon burst through the living room.

"Jesus!" Simon exclaimed and placed his hand on his chest, now relieved that he could see his little girl.

"She was just keeping me company." Dicko smiled.

Simon kept his hand on his chest and panted, "I nearly had a bloody heart attack when I woke up to find you weren't there."

"I'm sorry, daddy," Imelda whined. "I couldn't sleep."

Simon held out his hand and urged his daughter to take it. "Come on back upstairs. Give it another try and leave poor Dicko alone."

"That's okay," Dicko laughed. "She was no bother."

Imelda walked past her dad, not taking his hand, and said, "Goodnight, Mr Dicko," before making her way back to the first floor.

"I'm sorry," Simon apologised to his guest. "Did she wake you up?"

"No," Dicko snickered.

"Good night." Simon grabbed the handle of the living room door and was about to shut it behind him and go upstairs, but Dicko had called after him and temporarily stopped Simon from progressing to the first floor.

"What is it?" Simon asked him.

"Your daughter is a little angel, and..."

"And?"

Dicko sighed, "I'm sorry you lost your wife and son."

Simon looked at him strangely. He wasn't sure if he had already told him what had happened to Diana and Tyler. He thought that he did, but revealed very little detail. Maybe Imelda had said something more. She had always been terrible at keeping secrets. Diana used to say that Imelda couldn't even hold her water.

Simon gulped and nodded at Dicko, thanking him for his words, and said, "Me too."

CHAPTER SIXTEEN

NEXT DAY

It had been a restless night's sleep for all three individuals of the farm, but neither one complained when they woke up.

Imelda was the last to wake up, which didn't surprise her father. She usually *was*, even back in the old days. During the week, when the kids had to attend school, Simon would be the first to wake up. He would get up about seven, sneak down the stairs and make himself a coffee. He would then make up Tyler and Imelda's lunch for school, which would contain a sandwich, a packet of crisps and some fruit. He'd also make sure they took a fresh bottle of water with them and mid-morning snacks that would include an apple or tangerine and a croissant or a small packet of cookies.

After making their lunches, he would top up his coffee with more hot water and then sit down and watch the news up until half past seven. It was many minutes of peace he savoured every morning, and by half past seven he would go upstairs and wake everybody up. Even with her dad shaking her and her curtain open, Imelda would struggle to get out of bed every morning.

All three members of the farmhouse were dressed, and the last tin of beans had been shared by father and daughter. Simon had offered some to Dicko, but he claimed that he was okay and didn't like eating breakfast when the world was a normal place, let alone now. Simon guessed that Dicko was lying and was just being nice, but he never pushed the man.

"Right, guys." Dicko clapped his hands together. "The car's outside, so are we ready?"

Both Simon and Imelda nodded. Simon was wearing his usual black boots, black combats and T-shirt. Of course, food and water were the main reasons why they were heading to the supermarket after the homestore, but he was hoping there'd be something left in the clothes section.

Dicko ran his fingers through his bushy beard and said, "Okay, good. Now, there's only half a tank in the car, but it'll be more than enough to get us to where we're going. If it's clear when we get there, inside the place and outside, then I'm gonna make a second trip on my own. We'll empty the car when we come back, and I'll go back out straightaway."

Simon was about to open his mouth and say something, but Dicko held up his finger to stop the man. "If the journey is hazardless, then I should be fine on my own. The Mazda is a small car, so I'll need the extra room for the second journey. Besides, we don't want to be leaving that house empty and unlocked for a long period of time, do we?"

Simon thought for a few seconds and then nodded in agreement. Then Dicko went outside and father and daughter followed him.

"Let's go," Dicko said with a smile, and pointed over to the vehicle.

"I'll sit in the back with Imelda," Simon said.

"Sure thing."

"And we're definitely doing the homestore first?"

"I think it'd be best to get it out of the way." Dicko nodded, then asked Simon, "Are you okay with that?"

Simon nodded.

Dicko fired up the engine and pulled away. Imelda began to put her belt on and her daddy asked if she was okay.

She nodded. "I think so."

"It should be okay," said Simon. "And if it's not we'll come straight back. We can try the next day."

Overhearing Simon's talk with his daughter, Dicko looked at the pair of them through the rear view mirror and said to the little girl, "I reckon the places where we're going should be quiet. I think most people have either fled the area or..."

"What about the bandits, daddy?" she asked. "Will there *be* any?"

"I've no idea, babe. Hopefully not."

Dicko took a left at a junction and began to enter a place that used to be a residential area. Simon recognised where he was now. So did Imelda. Houses were to either side of them, the road was barren and there was no sign of life.

Simon shook his head and asked nobody in particular, "Where did all the survivors go?"

He received no answer.

They entered a town called Darnley and was greeted with bodies strewn across the roads, seven in all, with three abandoned cars, one burnt out. Simon was going to tell Imelda to keep her eyes shut until they arrived at the homestore, but this was the world she was living in now, and she was going to have to get used to it.

It was hard to tell if the dead were victims of bandits. He guessed that they were. If the Canavars had got a hold of them, there'd be nothing left of them.

Dicko made a right and went straight ahead at the roundabout, which told Simon that he had been here before. He seemed to know where he was going. He made a left, and then a left again, into the almost empty car park.

"There're a few cars here," Simon remarked. He counted seven. It wasn't many, but where were the owners? Had these cars been abandoned? If so, was it during the Stage One period?

Dicko pulled up the vehicle by the main doors and all could see that the doors were open.

"Have you done this kind of thing before?" Simon asked the driver.

"I've taken cars before and visited supermarkets in the past. I've never bumped into much danger."

"Much?"

"I had one recent incident," Dicko looked sheepishly at Simon, hesitant to say anything in front of Imelda.

Simon said, "It's okay. Just ... not too much detail."

Dicko nodded and began, "Most places I've visited, mainly in the Paisley area, were reasonably clear, more or less."

"Reasonably? More or less? You're a bit vague, Dicko."

The driver smiled. "Anyway, I went into a place in Elderslie and came across a few undesirables."

"Were they bad men?" Imelda asked the man.

"Well ... in a way." Dicko was unsure how to answer the young girl. "Some of these people are desperate, mentally unstable. A lot of people have seen some terrible things, especially when the monsters were here, the Canavars. I suppose Stage Two, as you guys call it, only affected major cities and some towns in an attempt to kill off the Canavars."

"That's enough," Simon intervened.

"Anyway, back to this supermarket I visited." Dicko rubbed his face before adding, "I took a few tins from a shelf and could hear people arriving. They were on motorbikes. I think there was about six of them, but they were definitely people you wanted to avoid."

"How did you know?" Imelda asked him.

"I dunno." Dicko shrugged his shoulders. "You just ... do. Anyway, these guys came in and I hid. Eventually I was spotted by some of them and they chased me. I dropped the car keys while I was running, but I knew they'd catch me up if I ran back for them."

"What happened?"

"I headed for the countryside and have been on foot ever since."

"So cars can be a nuisance," Imelda said. "Is that what you're saying, Mr Dicko?"

"Just call him Dicko," Simon groaned.

"To be honest, cars nowadays are great for what we're doing today, but it's risky. If survivors are desperate and they hear a vehicle coming their way, they could hide or may even attack you for the wheels. I think getting here is the most dangerous part."

"So what do we now?" she asked.

Dicko switched off the engine and put the keys in his pocket. "It's time to go shopping."

CHAPTER SEVENTEEN

All three entered the building with Dicko leading the way. He told them that they should take only a few garden utensils, like shovels and forks, and concentrate on packets of seeds and even gas canisters, if there were any. If there were supplies aplenty, another journey could be made in the future. Dicko assumed that all the canisters had probably been taken, but hoped there were some left. Most of the room in the car was going to be used for the supermarket trip.

From what they could see, the establishment was empty, tidy, and although some shelving had been emptied, there seemed to be supplies left. Dicko could see an abandoned trolley by one of the checkouts. He went over and grabbed the trolley and left it by Simon's side.

"Wait there," Dicko instructed father and daughter.

"Why?" Simon held out his arms and shrugged his shoulders.

"I'm going to check down all twenty aisles before we start. I don't want any nasty surprises coming round the corner when we're filling up the trolley."

Simon and his daughter waited around nervously as their new friend started to check down the aisles. Once he returned, he announced that it was clear, grabbed the trolley, and told Simon and Imelda to follow him.

They travelled nearly twenty yards and turned into Aisle 6. The aisle looked untouched and this forced a smile from Simon and Dicko.

"There we go," Dicko announced a little too loudly, his voice eerily echoing in the empty place. "Garden utensils and seeds in the same aisle. We should be in here for no longer than ten minutes."

Simon parked the trolley up halfway down the aisle, and told Simon that they were only going to take a few utensils, but every packet of seeds that was available. They could see the packets and there was a lot on offer. Carrot, broccoli, beetroot, potato ... they were all there.

"Once we get back to the farm," said Dicko, "we can make a start on an allotment. Don't forget the green fly spray."

The whole process had taken no more than eight minutes, and now the three of them were leaving the homestore with a trolley full of goodies.

They had emptied the supplies into the boot of the car and now it was time for the short trip to Silverburn, where a Tesco supermarket was also based right next to it.

A five-minute journey along the desolate road was achieved with no incidents, and once Dicko turned right at the roundabout, they were in Tesco's empty car park.

They could see to their right the huge shopping mall that was Silverburn, but that could be tried another day. Maybe at a later date. Silverburn hosted many restaurants, clothes shops and a cinema, but food was their primary target. Food would probably be available in some of the restaurants' kitchens, but the supermarket was first and they only had a small car.

All three were out and made the short walk to the entrance of the place. They all stopped and peered inside. The place looked like it had been ransacked more than once, blood was smeared on the floor. All three winced when their noses sensed the horrendous smell. They were unsure if the smell was from rotten fruit, meat, death ... or a mixture of all three. Simon and Dicko looked at one another, both unsure what to do.

"Let me go in first," Dicko said, and pulled out his trench knife from the leather holster. "Me and Trevor will sort this out."

Simon shook his head at Dicko because he had given his knife a nickname, and Imelda gasped on seeing the blade and was given a reassuring squeeze on her shoulder by her daddy.

Dicko treaded carefully, making sure his boots didn't step in any blood or accidentally kick one of the few scattered tins on the floor, and began to walk along the checkouts and look down the aisles for any danger. Simon and Imelda waited patiently and watched as Dicko walked past over twenty aisles. They continued to watch as he turned on his heels and slowly headed back towards them, gazing down the aisles for a second time.

"It seems to be clear," Dicko announced when he reached father and daughter. "There's a bit of a mess in some of the aisles, but surprisingly there's still food."

For twenty minutes, Simon and Dicko filled a trolley each with tins, bottled water and sodas, as well as items of clothing from the upstairs. The rickety trolleys were pushed to the Mazda and at first Simon wasn't sure they'd be able to get it all in.

"There's a bit of room left," Dicko said and clocked that there was a small gap inbetween the driver's seat and the passenger seat. "I think we could get a few more bottles of juice in there, easy."

"Can't we just go," Imelda moaned. "I'm tired."

"Me and Dicko will go in," Simon suggested. "You stay in the car. Stay down."

To Simon's surprise, Imelda said okay and sat in the passenger seat. Dicko shut the door and locked it, then both men headed back to the entrance of the supermarket. Dicko took a basket and told Simon to do the same. The men knew where they were going. They had already been to the soda and water section, and headed for the ninth aisle in silence.

They both stopped at the aisle where they needed to be and Dicko gave Simon a little nudge. "I bet there's more stuff in there." He pointed over at a door that led to a warehouse at the back of the establishment. "I bet they have pallets of drink and food in the back."

"We only have the Mazda with us," Simon said nervously, desperate to get out of the place and go back to the farm. "Let's just take what we've come for and get the fuck out of this place."

"I think that's the first time I've heard you swear," Dicko laughed softly.

Simon smiled and began to lighten up. "That's because Imelda is usually with me."

Dicko grabbed more bottles of water and slipped them into the basket. Simon took water and some cordial juice for Imelda.

"You enjoying yourself there, guys?" a voice called out from behind them.

Simon and Dicko turned and could see a man dressed in dark clothing and wearing a Burberry cap. His face was covered with a ginger beard, matching his hair, and had a menacing grin. Despite it being two on one, in Simon and Dicko's favour, the ginger guy looked confident.

"There's plenty to share," said Simon.

"Is that right?" said the ginger male. His six-foot frame straightened up and now folded his arms, slowly losing his smile.

"Yeah, that's right." Dicko placed down the basket and added, "Do you have a problem with that, ginge?"

"Look," Simon grabbed Dicko's shoulder, "We don't need to be so hostile."

Dicko hunched his shoulders. "I'm not the one being hostile."

Ginger began to laugh and shook his head. "Why don't you two turn around and head out, and I'll even let you have the stuff that you took earlier."

Dicko and Simon slowly turned and glared at one another.

Dicko turned to Ginger and said, "You ... You've been watching us?"

Ginger grinned. "You were spotted when you left the premises. To be honest, you should have been spotted earlier than that. I had to leave my watch, because when you need a shite..."

"Charming."

"I can't believe you came back for..." Ginger looked down at the two baskets of water and juice, "...a few bottles of liquid."

"I'm sorry," Simon said, "But we're desperate. You see, I have a daughter, and—"

"Spare me the sob story," Ginger growled.

"So ... is this your place?" Simon asked.

"This is Orson's place."

"Who's Orson?"

Ginger never answered Simon.

"I think I know what's going on here," Dicko spoke up and pointed at Ginger. "Fanta Pants here is a guard of some kind, and he answers to this arsehole ... Orson ... whatever the fuck the name is."

Simon scratched his head and turned to Dicko. "I don't understand."

"These guys have a base somewhere. This supermarket is being guarded. What happens is that every day food is transported from this place and to where they're based. This continues until the supermarket is cleaned out, then Orson's men go elsewhere, maybe find another supermarket, and do the same."

Ginger began to clap his hands and said with derision, "You got some bits right."

"Look, mate," Simon began, and could feel his arms shaking with fear, "we had no idea that this place belonged to someone."

Ginger said, "What you've taken is nothing compared to what we have in the back. No one will notice. Just you guys be on your way. I'll have a word with Nathan. Make sure he keeps his mouth shut." Ginger pulled out a walkie-talkie and began to converse with Nathan.

Simon scratched his head and muttered, "Who's Nathan?"

Ginger turned, walked away from the two men and added, "Just make sure you don't come back here again. That's the only warning you're gonna get. You see, if Orson found out that I had disappeared during a watch, as well as allowing strangers to steal some of our food, my guts would be ripped from my belly."

"Why are you doing this?" Simon asked.

Ginger turned around, smiled, and said, "I had a daughter ... once."

"I'm sorry."

"Just go."

Simon and Dicko, baffled by the bizarre experience with the big ginger fellow, bent over and picked up their full baskets. They walked away, heading for the exit, still confused about the meeting. And who the fuck was Nathan?

The wind wasted no time and tickled the men's faces as soon as they stepped out. Dicko looked up, over at their vehicle, and placed his free hand on Simon's chest before he had chance to look up. Simon turned and faced Dicko, asking him what was wrong.

"Don't freak out," Dicko said with clenched teeth. "Don't run. Play it fucking cool, okay?"

Simon didn't know what Dicko was talking about until he turned and glared over at the Mazda.

A man was standing by the car and mockingly waved at the two men. Simon wanted to desperately run over there and see if his little girl was okay, but he adhered to Dicko's words, although it was a struggle.

Dicko smiled at the Nathan character as they both approached, "Thanks for looking after the car," Dicko derided, making the Nathan character lose his smile. "There're some bad people about."

"You have no idea," Nathan growled.

"Oh, I think you'll find that I do."

Both men glared at one another, each one refusing to back down. Ignoring the two, Simon knocked on the passenger window and waved at his frightened and confused girl. He gave her the thumbs up and this seemed to have settled her a little. Dicko opened the door and shoved past Nathan to get into the driver's side. Simon jumped into the back passenger seat, next to his daughter, and they both hugged.

"I was worried," she said.

Simon smiled. "Nothing to worry about."

Dicko started the engine, took off the parking brake and pulled away. Nathan sarcastically waved at Dicko, who returned the gesture with his middle finger.

"You should ignore him," Simon scolded. "What if some of Orson's men come to the farm?"

"Why would they?" Dicko responded. "These thugs seemed to be monopolising the supermarkets. Anyway, I've met worse than these lot."

"Yeah?"

"Yeah," Dicko sighed.

Simon said, "I'm surprised the stores weren't raided during the Canavar period."

"Me too."

"Daddy?" Imelda interrupted the men's brief chat.

"What is it, babe?"

"Who's Orson?"

"Doesn't matter," Simon sighed.

Simon was relieved to be on his way back to the farm after the frightening episode. Dicko looked unruffled by the previous incident and Simon put it down to experience of being out there, surviving, and having to do things that Simon hadn't asked about yet. He wasn't sure if he wanted to know about the things Dicko had done to survive, to still be here.

Simon placed his hand on his daughter's lap. She placed her silky hands on top of Simon's and both gazed out of the window, their eyes clocking the empty streets. He hated doing this, taking Imelda into unknown territory, but his pride wouldn't allow Dicko to do all the work whilst he sat on his arse.

Simon suddenly snapped out of his gazing once the vehicle began to slow down. Dicko had slowed to ten, then put the vehicle in second and turned and went down the drive of the farm that went by the house, pulling up near the back.

"Daddy, I'm tired," Imelda said.

Dicko turned to face Simon and said, "That's okay." He then winked at Imelda. "You get this little cutey to bed for an hour and I'll start moving the stuff. I think I'll give the second trip a miss."

"Okay." Simon smiled. "I won't be long."

"Don't rush."

Simon opened the back door and stepped inside with Imelda holding his hand.

"Didn't you lock it, daddy?" she asked him.

"I couldn't, babe. There're no keys. We can only lock it when we're inside, with the bolts. That's how we managed to get in here in the first place."

"Oh."

They crept upstairs and Imelda began to yawn. Simon rubbed the side of her arm and gave her a kiss on the top of her head.

He told her, "As soon as you wake up, you'll feel great."

Simon put his hand on the doorknob and opened the door.

Imelda gasped and placed her hand over her mouth, "Daddy, what's going on?"

Simon gulped and shook his head. He had no idea.

There was somebody lying on their bed. It was a woman.

CHAPTER EIGHTEEN

Simon and Imelda continued to glare at the body on the bed and both stood still, frozen with alarm, and unsure what to do. The female groaned and turned on her back. Simon could see she was mid-twenties. She had a slim build and her hair was dark and quite short for a woman, and styled like one of The Beatles in the early sixties. Her trousers were green combats and she was wearing a brown T-shirt. Her black coat was lying on the floor.

Her eyes opened, making Simon and Imelda gasp, and the young female sat up with a start. She gazed at the father and daughter strangely and rubbed her eyes.

"Okay," she said, ruffling her hair with her right hand. "So this is a bit awkward."

Simon never said anything; he just continued to glare, lost for words.

"I saw a rucksack when I first came in," the female stranger began, looking at Simon. "Is that yours?"

Simon nodded.

She swung her legs to the side of the bed and stood to her feet. "Was this place *originally* yours, or...?"

"We came here a few days ago," said Simon, staring at her slim frame and her perked breasts.

"Ah," she giggled. "It speaks."

"I'm Simon."

The female smiled and nodded, "I'm Yoler." She bent down, placed her hands on her knees and smiled at Imelda. "And you, beautiful. What's *your* name?"

Imelda had become shy all of a sudden and shrugged her shoulders.

"You don't know?" Yoler said and teased lightly. "You've forgotten your own name? Now that's a little strange, don't you think?"

"No," Imelda giggled and already decided that she liked this person.

"Is your name ... Ariel, like The Little Mermaid?"

Imelda smiled and shook her head. "Nope."

Yoler scratched her dark hair and asked, sticking her tongue into the inside of her cheek, "Is it Rapunzel?"

"No," Imelda giggled, shaking her head. "That's from Tangled."

"What about Belle, like the girl in Beauty and the Beast."

"Not even close," Simon spoke up. "Her name's Imelda."

Yoler looked at Simon's morose face and cackled, "And you must be King Grumpyguts, by the look on your face."

Simon sighed, "I already told you that my name's Simon."

"Oh yeah." Yoler rubbed her face. "I'm still half asleep." She turned and bent over to pick a bag up. She threw it over her shoulder and thanked Simon for the use of the bed, even though he had no say in the matter, and she told them both that she'd be on her way. She took one step forwards to the door, but one word from Simon Washington made the young woman stop in her tracks.

"Wait," Simon said softly.

"What is it?" Yoler asked.

"Have a drink with us downstairs before you go. What do you say?"

Yoler looked moved by Simon's gesture and said, "Thanks. That's very kind. But can I ask one question?"

Simon nodded. "Sure."

"How have you managed to survive for so long?"

Simon was unsure about her question, and the look on his face confirmed that. He said, "I don't understand."

"There are survivors out there butchering one another for food and shelter. I've seen it with my own eyes. And you're offering me a drink? Your act of kindness is a rare thing these days."

"It's the right thing to do, as far as I'm concerned."

"Doing the right thing might get you killed one day, Simes."

Simon was becoming a little annoyed with the uninvited guest. He knew she was right, and he knew he had to toughen up, but he wanted to hold on to the Simon Washington of old, despite what had happened. He didn't want to change.

He huffed, "You wanna drink or not?"

"Alright, alright," Yoler giggled. "What's up with you, King Grumpguts? You look like someone has stabbed your cat."

Simon shook his head and walked away. He began the descent to the ground floor and realised that Imelda wasn't by his side. He stopped moving and turned around. He was about to yell at Imelda to get a move on, but she was already close behind him, holding onto Yoler's hand, the two girls walking downstairs together.

He entered the living room and saw Dicko sitting in the armchair. "I've only just sat down," said the man. "All the supplies are put away, cupboards are full..."

He stopped talking when Yoler entered the room, holding Imelda's hand.

"What the...?"

"I found her sleeping in one of the bedrooms," Simon began to explain. "Her name's Yoler. And she—"

"Alright, Simes," she cackled. "I can speak for myself, you know."

"I was about to say that she's got a bit of a mouth on her."

"Charming," she said. "Anyway, where's this drink you promised me?"

Dicko stood up and it was clear he was instantly attracted to the young female. "We have some water left, but we've just come back with sodas and—"

"Sodas?" gasped Yoler.

"We're just back from a supply run," Simon said. "Could have turned nasty, but we got lucky."

Yoler smiled. "Bumped into a few ... undesirables, shall we say?"

"You could say that." Dicko went into the kitchen and returned with a small plastic bottle of coca cola. He passed it to Yoler and her face lit up, thanking the man for the generous offer.

"Probably not the best drink for hydration," she said, "but it's been a while since I've had a coke."

She unscrewed the bottle and began to swallow the substance down.

"So, where're you headed after here?" Dicko questioned her, but never got an answer straight away. She was still downing the bottle of coke. As soon as she was finished, she twisted her face and rubbed her chest, releasing a loud and long belch, making Imelda giggle.

"That was the absolute tits," she said with a smile, then turned to Imelda and apologised for her choice of words.

She turned to Dicko and said, finally answering his question, "I have no idea where I'm gonna go. I was thinking of staying here for a while, if you fine gentlemen would let me. I could be very useful."

"There's enough in here as it is," Simon spoke with zero hesitation, deflating Imelda and Dicko who had quickly taken to the woman.

Dicko gazed over at Simon and said, "Can I have a word?"

"Sure." Simon nodded.

"Upstairs."

"Erm..." Simon looked at Imelda, then Yoler, and was reluctant to leave the girls alone.

"Oh, seriously," Yoler snapped and pointed at Imelda. "Don't worry. Nothing's gonna happen to her."

Dicko left the living room and Simon followed him upstairs to the landing. Simon turned around and before he had a chance to speak, Dicko had already begun.

"I like her," Dicko announced. "I think we should keep her here."

"I don't know." Simon placed his hand over his mouth and pondered. "I've only been here a few days and we could already have four people living here. When's it going to stop?"

"I did save your life," Dicko said with a cheeky smirk. "Let her stay, and if she fucks up, it's on *my* head. Imelda seems to like her as well."

"We don't know her. She's been here for a matter of minutes."

"Aw, come on."

"For Christ's sake." Simon shook his head. "You fancy her. You just want her to stay to see if you can bone her."

"That is offensive." Dicko pointed at Simon and added with a straight face. "How could you think of something like that, in the state this country is in?"

"So it's never crossed your mind?"

"Can't get it out of my head," Dicko began to snicker.

"Imelda *does* seem to like her," Simon began to ponder. "And I do think she's generally a good person."

"Is that a *yes* then?"

"Okay." Simon nodded. "But that's it. Four people is the max."

"I think we should take turns on watch, now we have a few numbers," Dicko suggested, and could see Simon already agreeing to it. "Three people have been to the house in the last few days, including myself, Yoler, and that arsehole that tried to kill you."

"I agree."

Dicko clapped his hands and rubbed them together, wearing a smile that stretched across his face. "Shall we go down and tell her the good news?"

"Yes," Simon sighed in defeat. "I suppose so."

CHAPTER NINETEEN

Yoler had been fed and briefly told Simon and Dicko about her story of survival. She was vague about her tale and never mentioned losing family members. It was a simple story of staying at random places, scavenging for food, and hiding from a gang of men that she had come across on a couple of occasions.

With four individuals present, Simon had decided to go to the pond and collect more water. He trusted Yoler, and asked her if she didn't mind looking after Imelda.

"Why don't I come with you?" she suggested.

"Erm..." Simon didn't know what to say.

"If you run into trouble, you might need some help."

Dicko was sitting in the armchair and although secretly he would have rather have gone out with Yoler, he said to Simon, "I'm happy to stay here with Imelda."

Simon remained silent, lost in thought.

"I can handle myself, if need be." Yoler began to laugh, "How the piss do you think I've lasted this long?"

"Okay," Simon sighed. "I think there's another bucket under the sink. What I do is fill the bucket, then we come back here, fill the jars in the kitchen—"

"Simes," she said and ruffled her moptop hair. "I have filtered water before, and I ain't picked up cholera so far."

"Okay." Simon flushed and lowered his head.

"No matter how much you filter and boil it," she remarked, "it still tastes like cat's piss, though, doesn't it?"

"It doesn't taste the best, but you kinda get used to it."

Imelda was upstairs, playing with an old cuddly toy that had been found. It was a lamb and she had called it Lambie. Simon went upstairs to tell her he was going out, but she didn't seem bothered when he told her. She seemed more troubled that he had interrupted her fantasy playtime by announcing that he was going out and trying to keep her hydrated.

Simon told Imelda he loved her and left the bedroom to go downstairs. He entered the living room and saw Yoler and Dicko chatting. The conversation looked very flirtatious and Simon raised a smile. He went into the kitchen and picked up the yellow bucket that was sitting on the side of the sink; he then went into the cupboard for the other one. He definitely saw two when he first came here.

He pulled out a red bucket and popped his head into the living room and said, "Sorry to interrupt your chat, but are you coming, Yoler?"

She laughed, "Sure." She jumped up to her feet, gave Dicko a playful wave, and followed Simon outside.

"It should be pretty straightforward," Simon began to explain, "although Imelda and I did run into a bit of trouble—"

"I know," she interrupted. "Dicky Boy was just telling me, when you were upstairs with your daughter."

Their feet hit the grass and were now heading straight, towards the pond. "Did he tell you everything?"

"Yeah," she said. "You'd slashed his face and the guy returned, and then Dicky Boy turned up and killed him." She said the sentence as if it was nothing.

"And what do you think about that?" Simon gulped and looked at Yoler.

She smiled and shrugged her shoulders. "Not a lot. Shit happens, Simes."

*

Carrying both empty buckets, Simon strolled across the field, heading to the pond with Yoler by his side. Simon wanted to take the time to get to know the girl better, but she decided to sing Beatle songs all the way there. Halfway through *Strawberry Fields Forever*, she stopped once they were at the pond.

She looked around and asked Simon, "Is this the only source of water you have?"

"What do you mean?" Simon placed the buckets on the floor and wasn't sure what the young girl meant.

"Any streams nearby or...?" She nodded towards the woods that were in front of them. "Streams are clearer and the water, once filtered, tastes better, too."

"I don't think so." Simon hunched his shoulders.

"You don't think so?" she smiled and mocked his southern accent. "This pond looks a bit murky, like King Kong has shat in it."

"We've never gone into the woods. Dicko has been in there, but says there ain't much where he had been."

"But he hasn't covered every square inch of the woods, has he?"

"The man that attacked me and Imelda came from the woods." Simon rubbed his nose before adding, "He came to the farm afterwards. He must have been desperate, so I take it there's nothing in there that could help somebody survive."

"I think we should go in there and check the place out anyway."

Her comment made Simon judder with nerves. He shook his head in disagreement.

"I'm collecting the water," said Simon, "and then I'm going back to the farm to see my little girl."

"You're piss scared." Yoler nodded. "I understand."

Simon was about to protest that he wasn't scared, but he'd be lying. Instead, he grabbed one of the buckets and asked Yoler, "Are you gonna help me or not?"

He walked into the pond a few inches, feeling the water getting into his boots, and dipped the bucket in. Yoler did the same and was standing by his side. Once the buckets were filled, the pair of them made the walk back to the farm. Simon could feel Yoler gazing at him and immediately asked what was wrong.

"I was wondering..." she said.

"Wondering?" he snapped. "Wondering what?"

"I was wondering what it'd be like to sleep with you."

Her comment made Simon almost gasp and he took a quick glance at her, making sure she wasn't joking.

"Jesus," he said. "You're not shy, are you?"

"No," she giggled. "Never have been. I always used to say to my friends that life was too short. Now, after what's happened, that statement has never been so true."

"Erm..." Simon smiled, but his lips quivered with nerves as he stared at the young beauty. "My wife..."

"That's okay. You just let me know if you change your mind." Yoler looked him up and down and cackled, "Oh yeah, I could ride you into the ground, no bother."

*

Hours had passed, Yoler and Simon were back at the farm, and a conversation began to take place in the living room.

Dicko had mentioned that there was an orchard half a mile from the place, and also a visitor centre. Dicko had told Simon that he had been there before, but had to flee the visitor centre because he had 'company', but didn't go into much detail after that.

Simon and Dicko had agreed to check it out, as Yoler was going to dig and plant the seeds that had been taken from the homestore. She had told the men that she had done it before, and both men agreed to let her get on with it.

Simon had an early night with Imelda and had informed Yoler that she could stay. Dicko said that he and Yoler would take turns on watch during the night, and Simon thanked the pair of them.

Imelda had been asleep for a few minutes and the man sat up in bed, curtains open to allow as much daylight as possible, but was struggling to read the paperback book that he had already read many years ago. He was at page 134 and decided to give in. He put the book on the side table and glanced over at his sleeping girl. He smiled and kissed her on the forehead. He lay down next to her, but shot up as he heard a noise from downstairs.

He knew that Dicko and Yoler were downstairs, but decided to check it out for peace of mind anyway.

He crept down to the ground floor and could hear groans as he reached the bottom. He put his ear against the door that led to the living room and could hear the unmistakable sound of two people having sex.

Jesus. She's doesn't waste much time.

He ascended to the landing, and realised he hadn't told the two where to sleep. Dicko had slept on the couch the night before, but there were now two of them.

"There are two extra bedrooms. I'm sure they can work it out for themselves."

The groans were now fading, and he went back to the bedroom, back to his little girl.

*

Simon had finally drifted off after spending half an hour staring at the ceiling, and dreamt about his wife and son. He didn't mind dreaming of Diana and Tyler, but on this particular night the dreams weren't so pleasant. The dream he had was more like a flashback, and it took him back to the time where he had lost both of them.

His dream took him to the time when he decided that they should leave the house. All four family members were travelling in the family car. Simon had turned left at the roundabout, lost control of the car and veered off the road. The car crashed into a hedge. The car had stalled and Simon desperately tried to start the car, and screamed out as the car was surrounded by a herd of Canavars.

There were so many surrounding the sides of the car and at the front, and he couldn't get the vehicle moving again. Imelda and Tyler were hysterical and couldn't stop screaming in the back passenger seats. Simon unbuckled himself and opened the sunroof. It only opened a few inches so he punched his way through and climbed to the top of the car. He pulled Diana out, Tyler, and then Imelda.

All four were now standing on the car roof, shaking with fear. There were about a dozen of the dead around the car, but Simon had noticed that there was a gap at the front of the vehicle.

He grabbed Imelda and yelled to his wife, "Grab Tyler and follow me!"

Simon stepped down off the roof, onto the bonnet of the car, and jumped down.

Cold rotten hands could be felt trying to grab him, but he slapped them away with his free hand and ran a few yards, pulling Imelda with him. A scream forced Simon to stop and turn around. He could see that the horde had lost interest in him and Imelda, and had turned their attention to Diana and Tyler.

Simon took a step forwards and called out for his wife, but Imelda screamed and tried to pull him back. Diana was taken down and disappeared into the crowd and Tyler was next. The little boy screamed at Simon, "Daddy, don't leave me!" before Simon woke up.

He sat up in bed and wiped the sweat away from his forehead and under his neck with the palm of his right hand. He looked to his left side and still could see his daughter sleeping. He took a gape outside and could see that the sky was a bruised colour and guessed correctly that it hadn't passed midnight yet. He didn't know how long he had been sleeping.

Maybe just an hour?

He stood to his feet and approached the window in the dark room. He placed his elbows on the windowsill and gazed out.

His mind began to drift, but not for long. He could hear Imelda stirring and moaning behind him.

He smiled thinly at his precious girl and walked back over to the bed with tears in his eyes. He sat down and stroked her head, gently shushing her as she continued to groan. Even with the little light that was left in the room, he could see her pouting lips, her chunky cheeks and little nose.

"No," she moaned.

Simon shushed her and stroked her head again.

"I don't want you to sing that song. Stop it, Tyler."

Simon shushed her once more. "It's okay, baby. It's okay."

"No, Tyler."

"Shh."

"Leave me alone. You're mean."

"Shh."

She moaned, "Tyler."

Imelda's eyes opened and glared at her dad in the room. She was confused and it took a few seconds to realise where she was.

"You okay?" Simon asked her and stroked her cheek.

"Daddy?"

"I'm here, baby."

She sat up slowly and rubbed her eyes. It was clear that she was still half asleep. Simon asked her to lie back down. She did, and he lay next to her.

"It sounded like you were having a bad dream," Simon said.

"I was." She nodded.

"What happened?"

"In my dream, Tyler was being mean to me." Imelda was becoming emotional and Simon stroked her cheek.

"Don't speak." He continued to stroke her cheek and added, "Just close your eyes, babe. Just close your eyes, my darling."

"He was trying to make me sing the Canavar song."

"Was he?" He smiled. "Naughty Tyler."

"I know."

"I remember the song well," Simon said. "I remember getting him into trouble for teasing you with it."

"Why are boys so mean?"

"I don't know," Simon snickered softly. "I was just like Tyler when I was a kid. I was a real pain in the butt. Put your head on my chest and close your eyes."

She did as she was told, and rested her head above his heart and put her left arm across his chest. He stroked the back of her head and heard her moan once more.

"Daddy? Remember when mummy used to call me Le Bossy?"

"Of course," he released a small chuckle. "You were always telling people what to do, just like your mother, and we realised your name sounded French, so we teased you now and again and called you Le Bossy."

"I miss that," she said with sadness in her words.

"Me too, babe."

"Daddy?"

Simon sighed softly. "I thought I told you to go to sleep."

"Just one more thing, and then I'll be quiet."

"What is it?"

"I really miss Tyler." Imelda took in a deep breath and released it out. Her silky warm hand rested on her dad's cheek. "And mummy, too."

"So do I, babe."

"Do you?"

He kissed Imelda on the top of her head and could feel two tears fall out of each eye. They ran down his cheeks and were soaked up by his daughter's blonde hair.

"Yes. I miss them every hour of every day."

The young girl sighed and grumbled, "Good night, daddy."

He looked at the palm of his hand where the steak knife had pricked, when he had that tussle with the pond guy, before Dicko had killed him, and could see it was healing up. "Good night, my princess."

CHAPTER TWENTY

NEXT DAY

Breakfast had been served. It consisted of cold spaghetti hoops for Imelda, baked beans for Simon and Dicko, but Yoler had opted to not bother. She told the other three that she wasn't hungry, which Simon and Dicko thought was a lie, and decided to take the occasional swig of orange juice instead.

The two new people were sat on the couch; Simon was in the armchair, whereas Imelda was sitting by the table, drawing with a pencil and some paper that had been found a few days ago.

Simon could see that Yoler and Dicko were occasionally flashing each other glances and then smirking.

Simon sniggered to himself and decided to have a little fun on their part. He looked over his shoulder before making his tongue in cheek statement to Yoler and Dicko.

"So…" Simon began and couldn't help a cheeky smile. "I heard a lot of groaning last night. Was one of you ill? Sore tummy, perhaps?"

Yoler began to giggle, but Dicko's face flushed red.

Dicko was the first out of the two to respond. "I think Yoler was moaning when she was tired, when the two of us were keeping watch. Erm…" Dicko struggled for more words. He was looking uncomfortable, but Simon wasn't finished with his harmless ribbing.

Simon said, "I'm pretty sure at one point I could hear the *pair* of you moaning."

"Really?" Dicko scratched his head and his face reddened.

"Yeah." Simon nodded. "I was thinking about coming downstairs to see if you guys were okay."

Dicko gulped and hunched his shoulders. "I don't remember making any noises."

Yoler's face was lacking emotion until the corners of her lips elevated slightly. She turned to Dicko and patted his thigh. "Relax. He's taking the piss, aren't you, Simes?"

Simon was unmoved and Dicko scrunched his face up and said, "What?"

"He heard us at it last night, playing hide the sausage," Yoler laughed and took a quick glance behind her, making sure Imelda wasn't picking up on the conversation. "And it's a good job you didn't walk in on us, Simes. I can't imagine how embarrassed you would have been to see Dicko's hairy arse going up and down while he was balls deep in me and destroying my lady garden."

Dicko burst out laughing, and this time *Simon* had flushed red.

"Just for the record," Dicko held his hands up to Simon, "I used protection. On our supermarket trip I picked up a couple of packets of condoms, and—"

"Alright, alright," Simon huffed. "You're adults. I'm not your father, you know. Anyway," Simon sat up straight and cleared his throat, "when are we going to this orchard, or whatever it is?"

"As soon as you're ready," said Dicko. "It's about half a mile walk. If we go by car, it could attract thugs, plus I want to save as much petrol as I can. What I had planned was to check the place out on foot, and if there's a lot of stuff there and no people, we go back for the car."

Surprisingly, there was no protest from Simon; he nodded in agreement to Dicko's plan.

"There's other fruit there as well," said Dicko.

Simon asked, "Like what?"

"Well ... there's bushes with blackberries, mushrooms, strawberries. Better take a couple of bags with us."

"Seems a bit daft walking all that way for some fruit. What we got from the supermarket should do us for a while."

"There's other stuff there."

"Other stuff?" Simon screwed his face after his query.

"There's a visitor centre not far from the orchard. There's a play park there. A restaurant, a kiosk where they used to sell chocolate, sweets... I think it's worth checking out. I would have checked out the place further when I passed it, but like I told you before ... I ran into some trouble."

Simon suddenly clutched onto his chest as a pain went across. He then began to feel short of breath and stood up.

Dicko looked at Simon strangely and asked if he was okay.

"I'm fine," Simon stood up and added, "I'll be back in a sec," before going upstairs.

Simon felt light-headed and struggled to reach the landing. He turned around and sat on the top step and put his head in his hands. "What's wrong with me?"

Simon felt like he couldn't breathe and tried to suck a deep breath in, held it for a few seconds, and then slowly released it. He still felt short of breath and placed his two fingers from his right hand on his neck, feeling for his carotid artery. He could feel his pulse and placed his left hand on his chest where his heart was. He was trying not to panic. He knew that panicking would make it worse, whatever *it* was.

Simon heard the door open downstairs and could see Dicko looking up at him.

Dicko called up, "You okay, Simon?"

Simon nodded. "I think so."

"What's wrong?"

"I don't know. Just give me a minute, will you?"

"You don't have to go. I can take Yoler."

"No, I want to. I can't continue in this world with my head in the sand. I need to man up, for Imelda's sake."

Dicko nodded once and went back into the living room.

CHAPTER TWENTY-ONE

Simon and Dicko said their farewells to the girls, left the house and walked to the front of the place, now heading down the lane. There were trees on both sides of the road and both knew that an ambush of any kind could occur. Dicko seemed relaxed as he strolled, but his partner walking next to him was jittery and was twisting his neck from left to right every second, gazing into the trees.

Noticing this, Dicko released a chuckle and told Simon to relax.

"Relax?" Simon shook his head and felt his right pocket to make sure the steak knife was still there. "I can't do that."

"It'll be fine. I've walked lanes like this and nothing has happened for miles. If you don't go out, fear will keep you inside. Staying inside with no supplies makes you hungry."

"We *have* supplies."

"I know we do." Dicko nodded. "But this place could be a little goldmine. I didn't have chance to stay long because of that gang turning up."

"What did you do?"

"I did what any sane man would. I ran. I didn't see them, and they didn't see me, so I don't know what they look like. Probably miles away now." Dicko smiled to himself and said, "Maybe many months ago I would have stayed and faced the gang."

"Really?"

Dicko nodded. "I was in a bad place for many months, did some bad things. Maybe I lost my mind for a while, I don't know, but I came back."

Simon sighed and wiped his clammy hands on his jeans. "What if there're other people there today?"

"We approach this place with caution," Dicko said. "If there're more than three of them, then we leave."

Simon seemed perplexed with his companion's statement. "So ... what do we do if there's three of them ... two of them, even?"

"We talk to them, if they seem okay. The gang I mentioned earlier ... you just knew were bad news."

"Talk?"

Dicko chuckled and put his arm around Simon, but Simon felt like shrugging it off. He felt like Dicko was being patronising.

"We can't just assume that everybody we come across are bad people," said Dicko. "If we see other survivors, we need to get to know them, unless they turn on you. We need to help each other out. Look what you did for me and Yoler."

"You told me not to trust anyone a few days ago," Simon said with his face screwed up. "Make up your mind."

"I said that?"

"You said that friends and good people don't exist anymore."

"Did I?" Dicko chuckled. "Am I allowed to change my mind?"

Simon never answered and shook his head with confusion.

"I know you had that experience with the man by the pond, but there are some good people out there as well. There're a lot of people out there that are hungry, have lost family members, and this has turned some of them into psychologically damaged individuals."

"It's just so..." Simon could feel tears filling his eyes.

"What?"

"Fucked up."

Dicko smiled and sped up a little, noticing that Simon was moving ahead. "It is what it is now. Nothing we can do to change it."

"I'm dreading the next winter."

"Don't worry about winter. Worry about now."

Dicko veered left and stepped into a wooded part. He looked up at the trees and swivelled three-sixty, making himself a little dizzy. They were at the orchard and there were many apples hanging from the branches above them.

"Now what, mate?" Simon asked.

"Now, I climb." Dicko smiled, took off his bag and threw it at Simon's feet. He then climbed the nearest tree. For fifteen minutes Dicko had climbed and picked apples, then threw them at Simon, who then placed them in the bags. It had gone better than the two guys thought it would. Both of the bags were full of apples and there wasn't any room for anything else.

"We'll check out the visitor centre," Dicko said. "If it's clear, and there's supplies there, we'll go back and get the car."

"We should have done that in the first place," Simon huffed.

"Can't be too careful, Simon. Being in a vehicle makes us more of a target when they're people around. We could be heard from hundreds of yards away."

The two men hit the road once more, followed the bend in the road and Dicko pointed up ahead, to a crossroad, at a brown tourist sign. The visitor centre was two hundred yards to their left. They weren't far now.

"This way." Dicko beckoned Simon to follow him through a cluster of trees.

Simon seemed confused and could see the sign for the entrance up ahead.

"If there's someone there," Dicko began to explain, "then I don't want them to see us coming."

"Fair enough." Simon nodded.

"We'll sneak in here," Dicko pointed in the wooded area, "and if there're people here, too many of them, then we're gonna have to scarper."

The two went as quietly as they could as their feet shifted through the bracken, and Dicko held his hand up to stop Simon from progressing any further. Simon stopped behind Dicko and both could see they were coming to the edge of the wooded area.

Dicko took another step forward and could see the visitor centre, the car park and the play park. He could also see the kiosk and restaurant from a distance that was situated behind the play park. The place looked barren.

"It seems quiet enough," Simon remarked.

Both men were crouched down, scanning the area.

Dicko nodded in agreement. "Looks that way. Probably best if we get a proper look, then we can go back and get the car."

The two males emerged from the wooded area and strolled over the play park. A lot of effort had been put into the park. All climbing frames, swings and other props were made from wood, and even the large ground area they were walking on was covered in wood chipped bark.

Simon's right shoulder was getting sore with the heavy bag of apples and he swapped shoulders. Despite his skinny frame, Dicko walked as if he didn't have a heavy bag on at all.

They reached the visitor centre and both looked around. The whole area was surrounded by trees, and Dicko told Simon to wait where he was whilst he took a walk round the small wooden building.

Two minutes later, he was back and told Simon the place was locked, but he couldn't see any sign of life around the area.

"We'll check the kiosk and restaurant," Dicko suggested. "If the places have already been raided, there's no point coming back."

They could see that the wooden kiosk was nothing more than a small wooden hut. It was a place that would have sold ice creams, served coffee and sandwiches. The shutter at the front of the kiosk was down and Dicko suggested going round the back. They could see a wooden door and see that it was shut, but there was no padlock. It seemed like it was a simple matter of sliding the bolt to get inside.

Dicko did just that. His trench knife, Trevor, remained in its holster, so he was confident that there was nothing inside. He pulled the door open and peered inside. He turned to Simon and said, "We're definitely coming back." He opened the door wider and Simon had a look inside. It wasn't what someone would call healthy food, but what was on offer was products hard to ignore.

The kiosk had many chocolate bars, soda drinks and crisps. Some of the shelves had been emptied, but there was still plenty left. Definitely worth going back to the farmhouse and bringing the car back, Dicko thought.

"We'll check the restaurant and then go and get the car," was Dicko's comment.

Simon agreed and nodded the once.

Dicko shut the door to the kiosk and slid the bolt back.

"It's quite tempting to just dump the apples and take this stuff instead," Simon said.

"It is," said Dicko, "but we're not going to." He slapped Simon on the shoulder and said, "Come on. Restaurant, and then home."

The two men left the kiosk and approached the restaurant, with their paranoid eyes scanning around.

Dicko was the first to approach the main glass door and tried the handle. They looked inside and both could see the restaurant was empty and immaculate looking.

"Looks empty," Simon remarked.

"Just need to check the kitchen." This time Dicko *did* put his bag down and pulled out his trench knife from his holster. "You wait there."

"Okay, mate." Simon never argued with Dicko. The man knew what he was doing. He certainly had more experience than Simon.

Simon waited patiently, but the paranoia was strong. He looked from left to right, into the woods, with shallow breath, but he kept his knife in his pocket. Dicko had only been away for a couple of minutes, but each minute felt like an hour for Simon Washington.

Dicko returned and Simon noticed that the man was panting and also had dark blood on the side of his cheek.

"You okay?" Simon looked startled. "You seem a little..." Simon couldn't find the words, but Dicko certainly didn't seem himself.

"There's nothing in the kitchen," Dicko panted. "Nothing that's edible ... anymore."

Simon nodded and scrunched his face at his companion. "You seem different. You look... You look kind of excited."

"Do I?" Dicko cackled.

Simon nodded.

Dicko beamed and beckoned Simon inside. "Come and take a look."

Simon refused to go in and waggled his head. "Tell me what it is first."

"It's a Canavar," said Dicko. "Haven't seen one of them in weeks."

"In weeks?" Simon added, "I haven't seen one of them in months."

"It came at me when I entered the kitchen. It was the only one there. It must have been stuck or something."

"Had it killed anybody?"

"I didn't see any blood or remains anywhere. It was just shambling about, looking lost and disorientated. You wanna take a look?" Dicko revealed his stained knife, and put it back into his holster. "I had to stab it in the head."

"No, I'm okay."

"Are you sure?"

"I'm positive. Let's just get the hell out of here."

"*Let's just get the hell out of here*," Dicko mocked. "You do realise we're coming back, don't you?"

Simon nodded.

"Something like this," Dicko pointed at the kiosk, "is a rare thing after nearly a year into this catastrophe. We've got the stuff from the supermarket, the apples, and now this confectionery. And then when that produce starts growing round the back of the farm, we'll be set up for the rest of the year."

Simon clenched his teeth together and said, "Okay, so is that the lecture over with?"

Dicko smiled. "I'm just saying."

"Let's go back."

CHAPTER TWENTY-TWO

"Should take us twenty minutes to get back," Dicko announced. "Maybe a bit longer."

Simon never said anything. He took a quick glance at his companion and realised they were dressed the same. They both had an all black look. They had black boots, combats and a black coat over their black T-shirt. They looked mean, two guys that looked like individuals you didn't want to cross, but Simon didn't feel very mean or brave at all.

Every ten seconds or so he was moving with his bag from one shoulder to the next. The more he walked, the heavier the bag became. He was getting tired.

"Simon?" Dicko looked to the side of him, at his companion. "Are you okay?"

Simon nodded, but not convincingly.

"What's wrong?"

"Just tired, mate."

There were still trees to either side of them, and the two men reached a bend in the road and they both recognised it. They were halfway to the farmhouse.

Dicko took another glance to the side of him and could see that Simon was struggling with the bag, puffing out impatiently, and wiping his forehead with the backs of his hands.

"Won't be long now," Dicko spoke up, trying to raise Simon's already crushed spirits. Maybe he didn't sleep well the night before, thought Dicko.

The road straightened up the more they progressed, and the pace of both men increased as the realisation sank in that their place wasn't very far away now.

"About what you saw in the restaurant..." Simon began but never finished.

"Yes?" Dicko looked to the side and now both men were staring at one another.

"Keep it to yourself."

Simon's comment sounded like a threat more than a request, but Dicko tried not to let it rile him. He was aware that he had bigger balls than Simon and would win in a fight if ever the pair of them fell out, so he didn't take Simon's rude comment to heart.

"Yeah?" Dicko tried to play it down. "And why's that?"

"I told Imelda that they were all gone." Simon lowered his head and kicked the ground. "I told her that the bombs had got most of them, and that the rest had wilted away."

"Why did you tell her that?" Dicko had a feeling why Simon had told Imelda this, but asked anyway.

"After we lost Diana and Tyler she ... we both were ... I don't know how to explain it."

Simon stopped walking and Dicko did the same. Both bearded men looked at one another and Dicko waited patiently for his companion to finish off his explanation.

"We were both shell shocked, but Imelda struggled to sleep and wet herself for weeks after my wife and son were taken."

"I'm sorry." Dicko placed his hand on Simon's shoulder and added, "It must have been rough."

"Still is."

Simon dipped his shoulders and allowed the bag to slowly fall off and land by his feet. He placed his hands over his face and took Dicko by surprise by sobbing like a child. Dicko never hesitated. He took a step forward and put his arms around the man he had only known for a few days and both men hugged. The embrace was short, and Simon soon broke away and took a step back and began to apologise.

"There's nothing to be sorry for," said Dicko. He scratched at his long dark hair that hadn't been cut in a while. The fringe was down to his eyebrows, and his hair at the sides covered his ears.

"She's all that I have left." Simon wiped his tears away with the palms of his hands and lifted his bag back over his shoulder. "If anything happens to her, then that's me finished. I don't even know why I'm putting the pair of us through this."

"You want your daughter to live, right?"

"Of course. But what kind of world is she going to spend her adult life in?"

"If she sticks with you, me and Yoler, that girl of yours will be a true warrior."

"I don't want her to be a warrior. I want her to be like a normal girl, going to dance classes, doing gymnastics, going out with her friends—"

"Those days are gone," Dicko snapped, bringing Simon back to the harsh reality. "And they won't be coming back."

"I know," Simon sighed. "It breaks my heart to think what she'll be missing out on."

"She'll learn to survive, if she sticks with us," Dicko said. "She'll learn other things as she gets older, and..."

Simon had noticed that his companion had paused. "And?"

"If anything happens to you..."

"Yes?"

"I'll take care of her. And hopefully Yoler will be around still."

"Thanks ... I think." Simon wasn't sure how to take Dicko's statement. "I have no plans on going anywhere, but thanks, mate."

"I'm serious, man." Dicko nodded and flashed Simon a smile. "I know I've only known you guys for a few days, but she's a great girl. I couldn't leave her on her own if anything happened to you. I won't leave her to fend for herself."

*

They weren't far away now, and Dicko told Simon that once they were back at the farm they would empty their bags and dump the apples in the sink, have a few drinks and have five minutes. Then they would take the two bags with them, take the car, and head back to the visitor centre and empty the kiosk.

"Sounds like a plan," said Simon. "I can't remember the last time Imelda had some chocolate. I should have grabbed a few bars when we were there and put them in our pockets."

"Already did," Dicko snickered.

He put his hands in his pockets and pulled out four Dairy Milks. "One each." He handed one to Simon. "You want yours now?"

"Why not?" Simon grabbed the chocolate bar. "Can't wait to see her face when you give her hers. She just loves chocolate."

"Doesn't every female?"

"We'll just tell them that we need to go back to get some tins and stuff," suggested Dicko. "When we return with a car full of chocolate and soda drinks, Imelda will love you forever, and Yoler..."

Dicko suddenly stopped and realised he was getting over excited.

"What about Yoler?" Simon asked with a smirk. "Would *she* love you forever?"

"Up yours." Dicko snickered and both began to laugh. "You know, she's the first woman I've been with since..." Dicko paused and dropped his head.

"Since?"

"Doesn't matter."

Dicko had a quick look at Simon and was glad that he was feeling better. He had only known the man for days, but he liked him. He was a good man, and a good father. Imelda was lucky to have him.

Their eventual arrival was spotted by Yoler. She opened the main door and greeted both men.

"Any luck?" she asked.

Both men nodded and stepped inside. Imelda was at the table in the living room and gave her daddy a smile. There was no hug; he had only been away for an hour. She simply looked up at Simon, flashed him a smile, and then lowered her head and continued to draw. He noticed that her long blonde hair was in a ponytail. He assumed that she or Yoler had found an elastic band from somewhere.

"What're you drawing?" Simon walked over, bag still over his shoulder.

Imelda put her arm around the picture and covered it up. "It's not finished yet."

"Sorry," Simon laughed.

He went into the kitchen and Dicko followed him in, and then both men emptied their bags into the empty sink. Yoler walked in and flashed a smile when she saw the sink full of green apples.

"Excellent, guys." She put her arm around Dicko and kissed him on the cheek. "Was that all there was?"

Simon took a quick glance and felt a twinge of jealousy. He wasn't jealous because he was attracted or had feelings for Yoler. He missed the affection from an adult female. He missed his wife.

"There was more," Dicko spoke to Yoler, "but we came across a kiosk full of confectionery." Simon pulled out two bars of chocolate from his pocket. "One for you and Imelda. And there's much more where that came from."

"Nice one, rent-a-gob," Dicko huffed. "Remember the surprise we were talking about?"

"Shit," Simon laughed. "Sorry."

"Chocolate. Wow, Dicky Boy." Yoler flashed both men a wide grin. "Multiple orgasms in a wrapper. I haven't had a chocolate bar since I broke into a newsagents in Shawlands. I think that was a few weeks ago."

"Well, there's plenty more," Simon said. "Dicko was going to keep it as a surprise, but I messed that up, didn't I? Anyway, all this chocolate is the reason why we're going back."

"*I* can go if you want," she volunteered.

"No, it's okay." Dicko rubbed his eyes and said, "This shouldn't take as long. We're taking the car this time, now that we know for definite that the place is clear. Well ... it was kind of clear."

"What do you mean?"

Remembering what Simon had told him, Dicko lowered his voice so Imelda couldn't hear and said, "I came across one of the dead."

"Not a big deal." Yoler shrugged her shoulders. "They're still out there."

"Yes, but..." Dicko took a step back and took a peep in the living room to see Imelda with her head down at the table, still drawing. "Simon has told her that they're no longer around."

"Why? To protect her?" Yoler looked at Simon.

Simon nodded. "We hadn't seen any for months, and even *I* believed that they had gone for good. It's been nearly a year. I thought the ones that weren't killed by the bombs surely must have rotted away and fallen to pieces by now. After all, they're dead, aren't they?"

"Nice theory, Simes," Yoler began, "but they're still out there, and some look quite ... fresh, new."

"These things have scarred her, mentally," said Simon, "especially as they killed my wife and son. I suppose I thought it would help her, psychologically."

Dicko shook his head and huffed, "Until she sees one for herself."

"I think a lot of them are pretty much gone, but not all." Yoler nodded, and then took a look over her shoulder to make sure that Imelda was still in her own world, drawing at the table. "Just hope for your sake you don't come across any. Or you'll have some explaining to do, daddy-o."

Simon and Dicko took a drink of water, then Dicko took the car keys from the kitchen worktop and both men said farewell to the girls for a second time.

"Be careful," Yoler called out as they both left through the back door and headed for the Mazda.

Imelda had now left the table and stood next to Yoler. The vehicle moved away and both females waved. Simon blew Imelda a kiss and she caught it, and then the vehicle turned on the country road.

CHAPTER TWENTY-THREE

"There's a lay-by up ahead," Dicko had announced; he dropped the vehicle into third and slowed the car down. "It's just past the orchard."

It had been an uneventful short drive back to where they were before, but Simon and Dicko weren't complaining. He finally brought the car to a stop in the lay-by.

"What are we stopping here for, mate?" Simon asked. "Why don't we drive right into the visitor centre car park and get this thing over and done with?"

"Just being cautious," Dicko said, and couldn't believe Simon's naivety. "We need to park the car in a reasonably hidden place, and you *know* why. Also, if people have arrived at the visitor centre while we were absent, then they won't be able to hear us coming."

Dicko turned off the ignition and reached into the back passenger seats. He grabbed both of the empty bags and handed one to Simon.

"Ready, soldier?" Dicko snickered.

Simon sighed, "I suppose. Do you think we'll get most of the stuff in the back of this car?"

"I don't see why not." Dicko began chewing the inside of his mouth in thought. "I don't particularly want to go back to the farm and then come back here again, do you?"

"No, I fucking don't," Simon huffed and ran his fingers through his beard.

Dicko opened his door and stepped out, with the bag over his shoulder and his trench knife still in its holster. Simon stepped out and kept his knife in his pocket after seeing that his companion was relaxed enough to walk to the centre without a blade in his hand. Simon had the hammer back at the house, as well as other tools since the homestore raid, but he preferred the knife. If a Canavar did appear, he knew the blade would be the less messy of kills compared to the hammer.

The two men walked along the side of the desolate road, trees to either side of them, and went over to the same cluster of trees they went to before entering the premises of the visitor centre. They crept through the woodland and Simon stopped walking when Dicko had stopped and held his hand up.

Both men were near the edge of the group of trees and could see the play-park and kiosk from where they were crouching. They remained silent for a minute or so, and then Dicko asked Simon if he was ready to go over and start filling his bag.

"No time like the present," Simon said.

Dicko took a quick look and realised that Simon was trying to put on a brave face, albeit not very successfully.

Dicko led the way, with Simon close behind.

Over a twenty-five minute period, Dicko and Simon had made three journeys to the car and had dumped a lot of confectionery and drinks in the back seat.

"There isn't much left in that kiosk now," Simon panted. "I'm getting knackered. One more journey?"

"I think one will be enough to clear the place out." Dicko nodded, sweat running down the arch of his back. "Come on. When we get back I'm gonna have to have an afternoon nap."

"Me too, mate," Simon chuckled.

A snap of a branch made both men hold their breaths and freeze. They gaped at one another and Simon was the first to break the silence.

"What was that?" Simon whispered.

Dicko shrugged and tried to laugh it off. "Maybe it was a bear or something."

"We don't get bears in this country. Well ... apart from what's in the zoos."

"If there're any zoos left."

"Maybe we should just go back to the car."

"Nah." Dicko shook his head. "One more trip."

Both men walked over to the kiosk with tired feet and stopped in their tracks when a figure came from behind the small building.

It was a female.

The woman was in her thirties, had dark greasy hair tied back in a ponytail, and her face was a little blotchy. She wasn't unattractive to Simon and Dicko, but she certainly wasn't in the same league as Yoler.

"Hello there," she greeted.

"Where the hell did you come from?" Dicko asked her.

Simon could see that his companion was a little jittery and rested his hand on his knife holster.

"My name's Clare," the woman said. She took a step forward and held out her hand. Neither man shook it.

"Oh." She lowered her arm and placed it by her side, and then took a quick glance over her shoulder.

The woman clearly looked embarrassed and Simon felt a little sorry for her.

"You didn't answer my question," Dicko said sharply, making the woman, and even Simon, feel uneasy. Dicko was a nice guy, but Simon had seen for himself that he was more than capable of taking a life if he had to.

Simon decided to step in. "Look, love," he began. "We're all just a little on edge, that's all." Simon put the palm of his hand on his chest. "I'm Simon. And this is … Dicko."

"Pleased to meet you both." The woman smiled and glanced over her shoulder again. "I just came from the woods. Been living rough, but haven't we all?"

"You on your own?" Dicko questioned her with a hard stare.

"Yes, I am." She smiled.

"Then why do you keep looking over your shoulder?" Dicko elevated his eyebrows and quizzed further, "Expecting someone?"

"No," she snickered. "Of course not."

"Are you sure about that?"

Before she could answer, two men appeared from around the corner and stood either side of the female.

"We don't want any trouble," Simon said immediately and raised his hands in the air.

"What the fuck are you doing?" Dicko growled at Simon. "Put your hands down. We've done nothing wrong."

"You muppets have taken from our shed!" the man on the right yelled. "You've completely emptied it."

The man that had spoken was surprisingly clean-shaven, unusual these days, and the man next to him had short grey hair and a grey beard to match his hair.

"Shed?" Dicko snickered. "What shed? You mean the kiosk?"

"You know what I mean, funny fucker," snapped the clean-shaven individual.

"Where did you put the stuff?" the man with the grey beard asked.

"What?" Dicko wasn't sure what the man meant at first.

"Did you hide it somewhere … or do you have a vehicle?"

The woman spoke up and said, "What's going to happen is that you guys are going to take us to where you've put our stuff."

"Then what?" Dicko laughed.

"Then we're gonna bring it back to our shed, sorry … kiosk, and you two gentlemen can be on your way and never come back."

Simon shook with nerves and turned to Dicko. "That sounds fair. We now have a sink full of apples, and we have enough produce back at our place anyway."

"Don't be naive, Simon," Dicko laughed. "These three aren't going to let us out of here alive."

"That's not true," said the woman with the greasy ponytail. "Deep down, we're good people."

"Bullshit." Dicko smiled and reached for his knife. "We know where you're based now, so in your eyes we're a threat."

"Don't listen to him." The woman glared at Simon. "All I want you two to do now is put your weapons on the floor so we can sort this predicament out peacefully."

"Come on." Simon turned to Dicko. "Let's just do what they say."

Dicko shook his head. "It's not happening. As soon as we unarm ourselves, they're gonna kill us." Dicko then nodded over to their bulging pockets. Each one had a knife. "They're all carrying. All three of them."

"So are we, aren't we?"

"Look," the woman placed the palm of her hand on her head in thought. "Why don't we see if we can come to some kind of arrangement?"

"What kind of arrangement?" asked Dicko.

"Well," she began; her eyes moved to the side and this was noticed by Dicko. "What we can do … is … sit down and talk and…"

She seemed to be trying too hard to make conversation and her eyes slightly looked away again, this being noticed by Dicko.

Shit.

He quickly turned around and saw a large man with short dark hair, holding an axe. As soon as Dicko had spotted the man, the man ran at Dicko and raised the axe.

Dicko dropped his bag and ran at the axe-man as Simon stood in shock. He straightened both legs and went to ground, taking the man's legs from underneath him. Simon left his empty bag and ran away from the scene as the other three ran over to the two men that were fighting; all had their blades out.

Dicko called after Simon, but the father of one disappeared into the wooded area. Dicko decided to make a run for it as well, now that the three were near him, and the fourth man with the axe was scrambling to his feet. Dicko ran through the wooded area, after Simon, and knew that Imelda's dad was heading for the car. Where else would he go?

Dicko had exited the other end of the cluster of trees and ran as fast as he could. He had always been a quick runner, even as a child, and appeared to be making good ground and leaving the four assailants behind, but he needed to get back to the car and pull away before they reached them. He needed to be ten seconds ahead of them, at least, giving him time to get inside the vehicle and start the engine. He turned left and ran into the lay-by where the car was, but there was no Simon.

"Oh no."

He gazed at all the products in the back of the car and was aware that the four individuals from the visitor centre weren't far behind. He took his keys out of his front pocket and got inside. He started the engine and pulled away. His driver's side window was being slapped and he quickly looked to see that it was one of the men from the centre trying to slap and punch his way in. The car reached twenty in seconds and Dicko could see that the man, and the other three, had stopped trying to pursue the vehicle. The car took a bend and Dicko had shifted the vehicle into fourth and was now doing thirty. He then slowed down and pulled in at the side.

He couldn't go back to the farm without Simon. He couldn't have left the vehicle either; otherwise the four individuals would have taken back the products as well as the car.

Dicko was in a hopeless quandary now. What was he to do? He had to drive round the country lanes and hope Simon would jump out and flag the car down. But what if the four that they had stolen from ambushed him? That was the risk.

He flirted with the idea of parking up the vehicle once more, somewhere secluded, and trying to search for Simon in the woods on foot.

"Stupid prick," Dicko huffed, thinking back at what Simon did.

Simon Washington had left Dicko to his own devices. Without warning, he just ran, leaving Dicko to fend for himself. He wasn't sure if he should have been angry with Simon. Maybe preparing to fight was stupid on Dicko's part, but he was certain that they were going to be killed even if they both yielded.

Simon had Imelda to think of, so Dicko knew his reason for fleeing, but he was also a coward. That was going to have to change. *Simon* was going to have to change, just like Dicko did.

Simon and his daughter had survived the Canavars, the bombs, but as far as human savagery was concerned, this was just the beginning. It was going to get a hell of a lot worse than this.

Simon had told Dicko that he and Imelda called the plague of the dead Stage One. When the bombs fell, Simon called this Stage Two. Maybe survivors killing other survivors was Stage Three.

Dicko punched the steering wheel in frustration. Maybe he should return to the farm without Simon, at least then he could empty the car and the girls would have treats to munch on, and then he could go look for him.

"Fuck it."

The man that called himself Dicko pulled away and took a left at a junction. He was going to drive for ten to fifteen minutes, and then he was going to go back, with or without Simon Washington.

He couldn't think of anything else to do.

CHAPTER TWENTY-FOUR

Dicko came to a junction and took a left. He kept the vehicle in third, at twenty, and pulled out his trench knife and sat it on the passenger seat, just in case. With the tall intimidating trees on either side of him, he turned his head from left to right, smothered in paranoia.

"Come on, Simon," he moaned. "Where the fuck are you?"

Seconds after his groan, Simon Washington was seen coming out of the woods on the right, thirty yards up ahead. Dicko flashed the car's lights at him and the man on foot stopped. He stared for a few seconds, and then ran towards the car that was heading his way. Dicko stopped and Simon entered the passenger side without saying a word.

Dicko moved away and took quick disapproving glances at his shamefaced passenger as he went through the gears. Dicko decided to drive back to the farm in silence, waiting for Simon to speak.

He had been in the car for two minutes and Simon finally spoke, "I'm really sorry for what happened," he said. "I panicked."

"No shit," the driver mumbled.

"I'm a coward. What can I say?"

"You left me there to die, Simon."

Simon flashed the driver a quick look and said with a frown, "Now you're being melodramatic."

"Oh really?" Dicko slammed on the brakes and pulled the parking brake up. He turned to Simon with a vicious glare, making his passenger jump, and said, "You need to grow some fucking balls, and pretty soon. Those four pricks weren't there to give us a spanking, they were going to kill us."

"Wait a minute. I have a daughter to think about. If I die..."

"You still need to grow a pair, daughter or no daughter. In fact, you'll need to grow some for the *sake* of her. If you two ever end up on your own again ... I'll never know how the fuck you've lasted this long."

Simon snapped, "Don't forget who gave you a roof over your head."

"And don't forget who saved your life. As for the roof over my head ... you honestly think I couldn't take that place for myself if I really wanted to, if I was a real heartless bastard?"

Simon screwed his eyes at Dicko and could feel his blood boil. "What are you saying? You would have hurt me and my little girl to get that house for yourself?"

Dicko sighed and sat back in his seat, his head resting on the head restraint. "Let's just go back, before we say anything else that we'll regret."

He moved away and was driving for a matter of seconds, and then both men could now see the axe bearer from the visitor centre step out of the woods from almost twenty yards away. The man began yelling into the woods that he had spotted the car. It was obvious that he was speaking to his three friends who hadn't appeared yet, and he had been the first of the four to have stepped out from the condensed woodland.

"Hold on," Dicko said to his passenger.

By the time Dicko had reached forty in fourth gear, he was near the axe bearer. He turned the steering wheel slightly to the right, aiming for the individual, and saw the other three step out seconds before he made impact. The Mazda struck the man and a huge clatter was made as the individual hit the bonnet of the car and went over the roof. Dicko never stopped the vehicle and took a quick peep in his rear view mirror and could see the man lying in the middle of the road.

"Holy fuck!" Simon gasped and looked around, staring out of the rear window. "Do you think he's dead?"

"More than likely." Dicko nodded.

"Well, I don't think we should be going back to that area again. Especially with the other three hanging around."

"Doesn't matter where we go. There will always be the possibility of danger. We were lucky with the homestore. Even the supermarket had been claimed. There is *one* good thing to come out of all of this," Dicko said.

"Yeah? And what's that, mate?"

"The only travelling we need to do for a while is to the pond and back. We have those bottles from the supermarket, so we can get them filled once we've drunk them. No more buckets."

Simon nodded. "And if Yoler gets this allotment up and running at the back of the house, things will be looking up. But the winter ..."

"Don't worry about the winter." Dicko slowed the vehicle and took a sharp bend to the left. "A few more minutes and we're nearly home."

CHAPTER TWENTY-FIVE

Yoler had spent an hour digging a plot. It was small, but she was going to extend it day by day. The first seeds that she was going to plant were the potatoes. She told Imelda that this time of the year was almost perfect for planting potatoes. They planted the King Edward seeds in loamy soil and had put pre-planting potato feed in first and forked the soil. They had many others to plant, but the digging process and the planting of the potatoes alone had taken up most of the morning.

Yoler could hear the sound of an engine. She looked up and could see the two men returning from their trip to the woods.

*

Hours had passed, and Imelda had decided to have an early night. She helped as best as she could, helping the three adults to empty the car. It was a great feeling for everyone. The cupboards in the kitchen were full of sodas, tins and chocolate bars, the potato seeds had been planted and there was going to be more to follow.

Yoler sat down in the armchair, opposite Simon, and Dicko was in the kitchen, filtering the last of the water from the yellow bucket. With the sodas available, all agreed that they were in no rush to take another trip to the pond. Tomorrow they were going to play it by ear.

"So..." Yoler said and revealed a smile. There were signs of some decay in some of her front teeth that Simon hadn't noticed before, but that was understandable considering the world they were living in now. Thankfully, toothbrushes and toothpaste were something else that they had taken from the supermarket. Despite the decay, Yoler was still a beautiful woman.

"So?" Simon scrunched his eyes in confusion. "What is it?"

"Now that Imelda is in bed," Yoler began and spoke loud enough that Dicko could also hear her. "Are you two gonna tell me what happened when you went out?"

"I don't know what you mean." Simon shrugged his shoulders. Even though Yoler didn't know Simon well, she could tell he was lying.

"Come on, Simes," Yoler snickered. "You and Dicky Boy have hardly spoken to one another since you've got back. You two haven't had a Brokeback Mountain episode while you were out in those woods, have you?"

"No," Simon sighed.

"And those dents on that car weren't there before."

"Oh, you saw them?"

"Yep."

Simon puffed out a breath and clocked Yoler gazing at him with those wonderful large dark eyes of hers, waiting for the truth to spill out of the man's mouth. Simon decided to tell the truth.

Dicko remained in the kitchen as Simon informed Yoler what had happened. He told her about the four individuals turning up, his cowardice, and that he had left Dicko in a precarious position. He flushed as he told her how he had run and was eventually picked up by Dicko. And he informed the twenty-six-year-old female that one of the gang was purposely run down on the way back to the farm.

"Dead?" Yoler asked.

"Possibly." Simon nodded. "It was a hell of a hit."

"Fuckity fuck."

"I know."

"Jesus Christ on a cross." She shook her head and sighed, "What was Dicky Boy thinking?"

Simon shrugged his shoulders.

"Let's hope to piss they don't find this place."

"That's what I was thinking." Simon rubbed his eyes. It was time for a nap before doing a few hours guarding during the night. Dicko was going to do most of it.

Yoler remarked, "You look tired."

Simon smiled. "I was gonna try and get an hour before doing my stint."

"Good idea."

Simon rose to his feet and held his hand up at Yoler. Dicko emerged from the kitchen and stepped into the living room.

"Simon!" Dicko called out.

Simon stopped and turned around.

"No hard feelings." Dicko held out his hand. "Let's wipe the slate clean and start again tomorrow."

Simon looked relieved, produced a thin smile, and shook his hand. "I'm sorry I let you down. It won't happen again."

"Forget it."

Simon lowered his head and turned on his heels. He went though the living room door and slowly made his way to the first floor. He opened his room and could see that Imelda was fast asleep, still dressed in her day clothes. It was still light outside and he could see her face perfectly. He lay next to her and kissed her on the head. He sniffed her hair and decided that he would take her down to the pond and get her washed the next day, despite deciding earlier that he wasn't going to bother.

His daughter smelt a bit stale.

He kissed her again and then sat up to take his boots off. He sat at the side of the bed and kicked them off, then noticed an A4 piece of paper sitting to his right on the side table.

Simon picked up the piece of paper and his heart sank when his eyes clocked the drawing. It was the same drawing that Imelda had been working on before Simon and Dicko had left.

The drawing was in pencil. In the middle of the picture, at the bottom, Imelda had drawn a car. On the left side of his car were six bodies, standing up with their arms out. Simon guessed correctly that these were Canavars, and on the other side of the car was a man and a girl, Simon and Imelda. Tyler and Diana had been also drawn, but Imelda had placed them at the top of the paper, in the clouds, in heaven.

The picture had been worked on and the little girl had added extra details, compared to when Simon had seen the picture for the first time. Where Imelda had drawn Diana and Tyler in the clouds, she had added four more individuals and Simon guessed that she had put her grandparents there, Simon and Diana's parents. There was no evidence that his or Diana's parents had died, but he was convinced they were gone. What filled his eyes was the speech bubble she gave Tyler who was in the clouds with his mummy and grandparents. In the speech bubble Imelda had written: "Daddy, don't leave me!" which were Tyler's last words before those dead bastards took him down.

In the picture, Tyler was saying those words when he was in the clouds, when he was dead. But in reality, he screamed those words to Simon when he was still alive, before he experienced the first bite, but Simon was hardly going to tell his daughter that the picture wasn't a correct account of what really happened. She was only eight years old, for Christ's sake!

My poor baby girl.

Simon lay down next to his daughter once again and put his arm around her. She was snoring gently and her red lips were pouted.

He had a short cry to himself, and then he nodded off for half an hour.

CHAPTER TWENTY-SIX

NEXT DAY

Yoler and Simon were up early, sitting in the living room. Imelda was still in bed and Dicko was now sleeping in one of the rooms after doing most of the guarding during the night.

Yoler was sitting in the middle of the couch and Simon was opposite her, lounging in the armchair. She could see he was crestfallen and had every sympathy for the man, especially that he had another soul to look after as well as his own.

"You okay, Simes?" Yoler asked. "You look like somebody has jizzed in your Corn Flakes."

"I'm okay." Simon took in a deep breath and groaned, "Just sick of shitting in a bucket."

"At least we managed to get all that toilet and kitchen roll from the supermarket," said Yoler.

Simon never responded and Yoler smiled and rose to her feet. "I'm gonna take a look outside."

She went into the kitchen and unbolted the door. She stepped outside. It was cloudy but dry, and the temperature was reasonable enough not to need a coat.

She began to inspect her handy work from yesterday, and quickly turned around, noticing Simon was now exiting the house to take in some fresh air.

Simon scratched his dark hair and could see that Yoler had filled some buckets with soil as well as creating a large square patch for other products due to be planted.

"You've done well," said Simon, smiling at the woman.

"Thanks."

"You really busted your arse over this, haven't you?"

"I've had some help, Simes."

Simon rubbed his stomach and could feel a little pain where his colon was situated. He was constipated earlier and it had been the first time he had evacuated any faeces in days. He put it down to lack of hydration as well as eating, and stuck by his decision to take another trip to the pond. They had plenty of fluids now, but Imelda needed a wash, but it wasn't something he wanted to do with just the two of them. Not after what happened before.

"When you've done all that," Simon said to Yoler, "do you fancy a walk to the pond? I need to get Imelda washed."

"Sure." She nodded.

"If you want a rest, I'll understand."

"No, it's fine. I could do with a change of scenery."

Simon smiled and was about to say something further, but Yoler had beaten him to it.

"I was thinking about our sanitation issue earlier, Simes," she began.

"Oh?"

"Yeah." She nodded. "I was thinking about another method, now that toilets don't really work."

"Like pit latrines?"

"No." Yoler shook her head. "Pit latrine is a good idea, but they have some serious drawbacks, the first being that they stink."

"Then what?"

"A composting toilet."

"What's that?"

Simon looked up and waited for an answer off of Yoler, but he was staring out, down to where the trees were, where the pond was behind.

"What's up?" Simon stood next to her. "Did you see something?"

"I don't know."

Simon looked up to the sky to see that, despite the murky clouds, the sun was desperately trying to shine from behind them. "Maybe it's just the glare."

"Maybe." Yoler nodded. She then turned around when Imelda stepped out. She had clearly just woken up and went over to Simon and wrapped her arms around her daddy's waist.

"You okay, babe?"

"I woke up," she moaned, "and you weren't there."

Simon rubbed her back and felt her arms tightening around his waist.

"Listen," Simon began. "Me and Yoler are going to the pond for a wash, and you're coming as well."

Yoler said, "Why don't we kill two birds with one stone and get some water as well? You can never have enough."

"I don't want to kill any birds, Yoler," said Imelda.

"Relax," Simon chucked. "It's just a saying."

"I'll go and get the soap," Yoler spoke up and added, "I could do with a bit of a clean myself. I'm beginning to smell like a fish market down in the nether regions, know what I mean?"

*

Dicko was now awake. Yoler had woken him up before she left the farm with Simon and his daughter.

The walk to the pond was a pleasurable experience for Simon Washington. The day was still murky, but at least it was dry and humid, and he closed his eyes and moaned every time the wind gently stroked his face. Alongside him was Yoler, singing *Dear Prudence*, and to his other side was little Imelda. Most of the walk had been made in silence, with the exception of Imelda singing a Katie Perry tune every now and again.

Yoler was carrying a bag with six empty bottles that were going to be filled. Simon told her that they had more than enough fluids for the time being, but Yoler insisted. She also had a bar of soap and a towel stuffed inside and insisted on carrying it before they left. The bag was light, but the empty-handed Simon still felt guilty.

"We need go through those trees and the pond should be there," Imelda said to Yoler.

Yoler smiled, and didn't have the heart to tell the eight-year-old that she knew where the pond was. She had been there before.

The three of them walked through the trees, but Yoler's steps were more careful than the father and the daughter's.

"Why are you taking your time?" Simon turned around and could see that the female was a few yards behind Imelda and himself. Yoler was walking on her tiptoes through the long grass, like she was barefoot and trying to avoid broken glass.

Yoler never answered Simon's query, so he asked her the same question, hoping that the second time round he'd get an answer.

"Doesn't it worry you that there could be spring coil animal traps in here?" Yoler said, still staring at the ground and stepping ever so carefully. "There could be traps that have been here for months, left by poachers, before the shit hit the fan."

Yoler could see Imelda looking at Simon, knowing that the little girl was shocked to hear the *shit* word.

Noticing this, Yoler apologised and said, "When I said ... *shit hit the fan* ... I meant when the dead arrived."

"Me and daddy call it Stage One," said Imelda.

"Oh."

Simon continued to walk, but was more careful where he put his feet after Yoler's announcement. Did Yoler have a point? Dicko was a survivor and never mentioned the threat of traps as such.

Once they were out of the trees, they made the short walk to the pond. All three stopped by the water's edge and gazed at the water.

"It's beautiful, don't you think?" Yoler dropped the bag on the ground and placed her hands on her hips, looking around the area. Trees surrounded the water and the pond itself was like a large mirror.

"I suppose." Simon hunched his shoulders. "Never really thought about it, to be perfectly honest with you."

Yoler bent over and began to take the empty bottles out of the bags. She threw Simon a bar of soap and a towel, and Simon and Imelda walked ten yards around the pond and began to take their shoes and socks off. They held hands and walked into the pond. Once the water was up to their ankles, Simon told Imelda to stop walking and took her top off and his as well.

"We'll just wash our top half today," he told his daughter. "We can come back down here tomorrow."

"The water's cold," Imelda moaned and began to shiver.

"It'll just be for a few minutes." Simon pointed by the water's edge where the towel sat. "And then we'll dry off straight away."

"Okay."

Simon said, "Ready?"

Imelda nodded, her lips still quivering with the cold. "Are you going to wash my hair as well?"

Simon nodded, and then bent down and dipped the soap in the water and began rubbing the soap on his hands. He soaped his body, bent over and dipped his head in the water. He rubbed some in his hair and beard and then dipped his head again. He passed Imelda the soap and she began to also wash her body and her hair. She wouldn't be able to wash it like the old days, but it'd have to do.

On bath nights, on a Thursday and Sunday, Diana would wash Imelda's hair with shampoo and then conditioner. She would then dry off and go to her parents' room to blow dry and brush her hair. As a special treat, Diana would sometimes straighten Imelda's hair with the hair straighteners. But now, a bar of soap and a cold pond was the best that was on offer.

Simon looked to his left and could see that Yoler had almost filled the bottles. He had been washed, but was waiting for Imelda to finish washing her hair. He wanted Imelda to use the towel first. If he used it first, she would be left with a damp towel to dry herself off.

Simon went back to the grass and stood shivering, patiently waiting for his little girl to finish. Finally, Imelda had finished and made her way over to her dad. He picked the towel up and handed it to his little girl. She dried her body first, put her T-shirt back on, and then wrapped the towel around her head.

"Should have brought two towels," Simon muttered.

Simon picked up his black T-shirt off the ground and put it back on his damp body.

"I'm sorry, daddy," Imelda said, realising she was hogging the towel.

"I was almost dry anyway," Simon began to laugh and turned to Yoler. He called over to her, "What about you? You having a wash?"

"What are you trying to say, cheeky prick?" Yoler had her hands on her hips and glared at Simon.

"Erm..." Simon decided to be brutally honest. "Well, I don't think you've washed since you've been with us. And didn't you say you smelt like a fish market?"

"Am I starting to smell?" Yoler snarled. "Is that what you're saying? I'm beginning to stink like a monkey's arse?"

"Erm..." Simon gulped. He was in two minds whether to reprimand Yoler for saying *prick* and *arse* in front of his daughter, but he thought: What's the point?

"Relax," Yoler began to snicker. "I'm just pulling your pisser. Throw me the soap over, you clown."

Prick, arse and now pisser. Simon shook his head and still kept his mouth shut.

He took the soap and threw it over to Yoler, then took the towel and walked over this time and placed it on the grass, near where Yoler was. She kept a hold of the soap and took her top off. Simon turned away when he realised she wasn't wearing a bra and began to put his shoes and socks back on, helping Imelda with hers.

"That's me finished," Yoler announced some two minutes later. "Everything cleaned: Armpits, buttocks, and even managed to soap up the growler while you weren't looking."

Simon shook his head. "For God's sake."

Yoler walked over to the bag and put the soap in, followed by the towel. She then took the bag and went over to where the bottles were lying and put them in the bag. She bent down and zipped the bag up, ready to go, and then stood up as she threw it over her shoulder.

"Are you two ready to go?" she asked them.

Both father and daughter nodded.

Imelda looked up and gasped, pointing ahead of her and exclaimed, "Daddy! Who's that?"

CHAPTER TWENTY-SEVEN

All three stood and stared in silence. What they could see in the distance was a boy, no older than ten, walking at the other side of the pond.

"Where the hell did he come from?" Simon muttered.

Yoler shook her head. "Bollocksed if I know."

Simon raised his hand and waved at the boy. They could all faintly hear that the boy was crying, and guessed that he was lost.

"Poor thing," said Simon. "Let's go round and see what we can do for the little guy."

"His guardians can't be too far away," Yoler said, and was now following Simon and Imelda, who were both walking around the pond to meet up with the boy.

"You think?"

Yoler could feel the heavy bag slipping off her shoulder and moved the strap back up. "There's no way a child that age could survive on its own. He's either run away or his guardians have ... well, you know."

As they got closer, it was clear that the boy was frightened. He was wearing a pair of red shorts and a matching top, with trainers on his feet.

Simon, Yoler and Imelda approached the boy and stopped a few yards away from his presence. He looked nervous and teary, but Simon thought without Imelda's presence the boy would be more terrified.

"Are you okay, little fellow?" Simon asked the infant and crouched down to his level.

The boy began to cry and wailed, "I'm lost."

"Where're you from?" Yoler asked the boy.

The boy pointed into the woods and Yoler and Simon gaped at each other briefly.

Yoler asked another question. "And what's your name?"

"My mummy said I shouldn't talk to strange people."

"Yoler's not that strange," Simon tried to joke.

Yoler stood up straight and looked at Simon. "Shall we take him back to his home?"

"Home?" Simon blew out his lips and moaned, "We don't even know where his home is."

"Well, we can't leave him here, can we?"

Simon stood and thought for a moment, unsure what was for the best. There were only two options he could think of: Take the boy back to his home, wherever that may be. Or take him back to *their* place and hope that the boy's guardian decided to look for him at the farm so they could be reunited. Leaving him wasn't an option.

"We should try and take him back to his … home. Shall we take Imelda back to the farm first?" Simon asked Yoler.

"No, I don't think that's a good idea," she responded with no hesitation. "If we return this kid to his guardians and we also have Imelda by our side, the people will know we're not a threat. And more importantly, we won't be attacked."

"Do you think the people where this boy stays are … bad guys?"

Yoler laughed at Simon's naivety, which he took offence to. She stopped giggling and raised her hand at Simon as a way of apologising to the man.

She said, "I'm sorry. You say *bad guys*, but maybe *we're* the bad guys to other people."

Simon ignored Yoler's comment and turned to the frightened boy. The little man was a cute thing with dark hair and large brown eyes. "Do you know exactly where you stay?"

"In the woods," was his vague answer.

"If he knew exactly where he stayed, Simes," Yoler snickered, "he wouldn't be lost in the first place, would he?"

Simon rubbed his chin in thought and knew that Yoler had a point. Maybe taking him back to theirs was the only thing to do.

Voices could be heard in the distance, from within the woods. It sounded like two or three different voices, and they were all calling the name *David*.

"You recognise those voices?" Yoler asked the little man.

For the first time, the little boy had managed a wide smile and said, "Mummy's one of them."

"Good." Simon smiled. "So you must be David."

The little boy nodded.

"We can wait here and let them come to *us*."

"Is that definitely your mummy's voice," Yoler asked little David as the voices continued to bellow through the woodland.

David nodded rapidly and continued to smile; the relief could be seen on his innocent face.

"Then you should call her, so that she knows where you are."

David did as he was told, whilst Simon, Yoler and young Imelda took a step back.

The woman's voice yelled, seconds after David called out for his mum, "David! Oh my God! David, is that you?"

"I'm by the pond, mummy!" David cried.

"Straight ahead!" the woman's voice yelled to her companions.

Simon and Yoler didn't know exactly whom she was talking to, but they'd soon know. They could see three figures in the trees heading their way. Yoler and Simon gazed into the trees as the excited yells continued, but they still couldn't see the faces of the three individuals that were approaching.

David took a step closer to the trees and ran in once he clocked his mum's face.

Both mother and son hugged from around twenty yards where Yoler, Simon and Imelda were standing, and could see his mother break away from the embrace and look at the three of them with suspicion. So did her other two male companions.

Simon and Yoler could hear the little lad say to his mum, "It's okay, mummy. They're my friends."

Friends. Bless his innocence. Simon smiled. *He doesn't even know us.*

Simon took in a deep breath as the four individuals, including David, began to walk forwards. They were heading out of the trees and around the pond, heading for Simon, Yoler and Imelda.

The people from the woods practically stepped out at the same time. The first person that Simon had clocked was a woman in her late thirties. It was David's mum. She was in tears, had dark bobbed hair, brown eyes and was very pretty in the face. She was a little heavy, but Simon thought that she was very attractive.

The woman walked over to Simon and gave him a hug. "Thank you," she cried. "Thank you so much."

She broke away and wiped her eyes. She took a step backwards and put her arm around her son. The two other people that were with her were men. There was a man in his thirties, with dark hair, attractive and slim. There was also a scary looking individual, bald, thin, and looked to be in his early forties, and he stood next to the thankful woman.

The pretty woman placed her hand on her chest and said, "My name's Helen." She then pointed at the scary bald man to her side. "This is Donald. He's our leader." She then turned and pointed at the younger man with dark hair. "And this is Gavin."

Simon smiled and introduced Yoler and his daughter to the three of them.

Neither party shook hands or even spoke to one another. They simply gave a nod of the head once they were introduced. There was an awkward silence between the two groups, forcing Yoler to say, "I'm glad you have your boy back. We better be off."

"Of course." Helen smiled. It was such a pretty smile, Simon thought.

"Right," the bald man standing next to Helen growled, "crisis over. Let's get back."

"Back to where?" Yoler asked politely.

"None of your fucking business," the bald man snapped. "That's where, darling."

Yoler took a step forward, narrowed her eyes and said, "The last guy that called me darling got a knife in his gut."

"Donald," Helen scolded, "don't talk to her like that. These are good people."

"Its okay," Simon laughed. "I suppose we're all a bit paranoid … and maybe a little overprotective."

"Mummy?" David spoke.

"What is it?" Helen bent down and David whispered in her ear. As this was going on, Helen glanced over at Imelda a couple of times.

Once David had finished his whispering, Helen stood up and said, "I'm not sure that's a good idea, David. I think we better go back and leave these people in peace."

"What's up?" Simon asked. He had an idea what the short conversation was about, but asked anyway.

"David would like to play with Imelda for a while." Helen blushed and scratched the back of her head. "It's been a while since we've seen someone of similar age."

"Same here." Simon looked at Yoler and thought for a few seconds before saying, "I'll tell you what. Why don't you come to ours for a couple of hours? We also have another person back at the farmhouse you should meet."

"You live on a farm?"

Simon nodded.

Helen looked at Donald. "How did we not come across that?"

"I knew it was there all along," the bald man growled. "We're better off in the woods, and not out in the open, exposed."

"Anyway," Simon continued before an argument broke out between Helen and the volatile Donald. "Come to ours and we'll walk you back to yours later on. What do you say?"

Donald and Gavin looked at one another and shook their heads. They didn't approve.

"Don't worry, guys," snickered Simon. "I meant just Helen and David." Simon then flashed the two men a cheeky smile and gave the pair of them a wink. "You're not invited."

"I don't want this prick knowing where we're staying, you dig what I'm sayin'?" Donald pointed a menacing finger over at Simon.

Helen sighed at Donald and said, "He's taking us to his place first. Calm down. And he saved David."

"Well," Simon began, "I'm not sure we *saved* the boy. We just stood about for a bit."

"Anyway," Helen grabbed David's hand and said to Donald, "We won't be long."

"We'll bring them back in one piece," Yoler spoke to the bald man and gave him a little wave.

The man called Donald Brownstone bit his lip and huffed, "Fine. Do what you fucking want!"

"Now, now," Helen sniggered. "Language in front of the kids."

Simon waved goodbye to Donald and Gavin. Donald just glared, but Gavin waved them off as Helen, David, Simon, Yoler and Imelda began to move away from Gavin and Donald and around the pond, heading back.

Helen, David and Imelda were walking ahead as Simon and Yoler lagged a few yards behind.

"Well, he seems delightful," Simon said to Yoler, referring to the Donald character. "Charming, wasn't he?"

"Charming?" Yoler scoffed and said in a whisper, "More like a cunt. The younger guy seems okay. I wouldn't kick him out of bed for farting."

Simon said, "I don't think that Donald fellow likes you."

"Doesn't like me? That's fine. He can take a seat with the rest of the bitches that are waiting for me to give a fuck."

CHAPTER TWENTY-EIGHT

Dicko was outside and admiring Yoler's handy work. He folded his arms and stared at the soon-to-be vegetable patch, and at the buckets where she had planted the potato seeds. Originally she was going to plant the potatoes in the patch, but had changed her mind. Yoler told Dicko that it would take between two to three months for them to be ready, as well as the other produce. Thank goodness they had raided the supermarket and the kiosk at the visitor centre, Dicko thought.

Dicko could hear voices from behind him. He turned around, his hand resting on the leather holster where the trench knife rested, and took a few steps forwards, looking down the grassy hill.

Five figures could be seen approaching from a fair distance. He knew three of them, but the female and the little boy were a mystery. *What's this? More survivors? Two more mouths to feed?*

He stood with his hands on his hips and waited for the first person to approach. When they were only twenty yards away, he was greeted with smiles and a wave from Imelda. Dicko raised his hand and said to Simon, "What's this?" He nodded over to Helen and her son.

"They're guests," Simon began to explain. "We've actually managed to bump into people that are decent for a change."

"Apart from that Donald geezer," said Yoler. "He's a bit of a bell end."

"Donald's okay," said Helen. "He's just a bit grumpy." Helen held out her hand and introduced herself and her son to Dicko.

"I'm Dicko," he said.

Helen never batted an eyelid and accepted Dicko's name without making any wisecracks.

"Go inside," Simon urged mother and son. "Have a look around."

"Come on." Yoler took Imelda's hand and said to the guests, "I'll show you about."

They disappeared inside and Simon told Dicko what had happened once they were left alone.

"And they're only visiting, right?" Dicko asked Simon, looking concerned. "I don't want this place ending up like The Little House on the Prairie."

"Don't worry, John Boy," Simon laughed and said further, "They already have a place in the woods. We met two others. They seem ... okay, kind of. Two guys."

"You don't sound so sure," Dicko began to snigger.

"Anyway," Simon sighed. "We're gonna take a walk over to their place once Helen's had enough here."

"She seems quite nice." Dicko began to smile and winked at Simon, playfully nudging him in the side.

"She *is*, so keep your filthy mitts off her." Simon gave Dicko a glare, but Dicko could see that he couldn't keep a straight face. "Anyway, we don't even know her background. She could be a widow. She could be grieving."

"She could also be choking for it," Dicko laughed.

"You're a very bad man." Simon tucked in his top lip and began to chew it in thought. He turned to Dicko and said, "About yesterday..."

"Let's not go over this again." Dicko shook his head. "Forget it. *I* have."

"Admittedly, I left you in the shit, and I'm sorry." Simon ran his shaky fingers through his beard and continued, "Imelda and I have spent most of our days hiding. We've had to."

"You don't have to explain. Seriously." Dicko placed a comforting hand on Simon's shoulder and could see he was beating himself up over the incident. "I understand why you did it. Your experience of violence and confrontations is minimal, and not only that..."

"What?"

"Like you've mentioned before ... If anything happened to you..."

"Just the thought of her being alone for one day, after all she's been through, kills me inside."

"Okay." Dicko smiled and scratched his nose. "Let's just say that you die tomorrow. Do you honestly think me and Yoler would up sticks and abandon that little girl?"

"Probably not." Simon lowered his head like a child after being reprimanded by its parent.

Changing the subject, Dicko cleared his throat and said softly, "So what's the purpose of this trip to their small camp?"

"I don't really know." Simon hunched his shoulders. "When Helen decides she wants to go back, I thought it'd be best if just me, Yoler and Imelda went. Is that okay with you? Don't wanna be leaving this place unguarded."

"It'd be interesting to see what kind of set up they've got." Dicko nodded in agreement.

"It will," Simon agreed.

"Besides, I'll probably get to see it another time."

"Of course, and there're a few new characters to meet."

"But what's the point? To make new friends?"

"I suppose just knowing that there are good people about kind of dampens paranoia we have in survivors in general. Maybe in the future we could help each other out, regarding food, and anything else that pops up."

Dicko nodded, but wasn't too keen on the idea. Helen and the boy seemed nice, but he was concerned that if these survivors came across rough times and needed a place to stay, then their own food supply would suffer. If things got so bad, would they feel obliged to put these people up? If that were the case, then that would mean more mouths to feed.

Simon could feel his tooth throbbing in the back of his mouth again. He winced, gave his mouth a quick rub and then nodded down at the made patch of soil, ready for seeds to be planted. "Are you gonna add to that while we're away?"

"I did say to Yoler that I could give it a go, but I don't think she trusts me." Dicko chuckled gently and added, "Maybe she's a control freak."

"Or maybe she thinks that you'll fuck it up," Simon laughed.

"More than likely."

Yoler exited the house and onto the back garden, smiling at Simon and Dicko. Helen wasn't far behind her.

"Where're the kids?" Simon queried Yoler.

"Upstairs," she said. "They can have half an hour and then we're gonna take Helen and David back."

Helen smiled and said, "Thanks. They seem to be getting on really well. It's good for the pair of them."

"I agree." Simon nodded. "It's been a while since she's had company around her own age. We should definitely do this again."

Dicko yawned and was growing tired of the small talk. He looked over at Helen and asked, "So Helen, what's your story? Are you still married, or...?"

Both Yoler and Simon verbally blasted the man for his rude question and gave him a cold glare.

"What?" Dicko held both of his hands up as if someone was pointing a gun at him. "I'm just intrigued, that's all. Just trying to make conversation with our guest."

"It's okay," said Helen, and gave off a little giggle. "I'm not offended." She took in a deep breath and told them all, "It's just me and David. My husband died before it all happened."

"I'm sorry," Dicko said.

"He died of a brain haemorrhage four years ago," she said sadly. "David doesn't even remember him. He says he *does*, but I think he just says that so he doesn't hurt my feelings, bless him."

The group fell silent and Helen turned and looked at the opened back door and through into the kitchen. She saw Imelda and David running out, both giggling, and both of them stopped running once they reached the four adults.

"That's the first time for a long time I've seen Imelda smiling," Simon said, looking at David.

Helen nodded. "Same here."

"Right, you two," Yoler clapped her hands loudly to get the attention of the two youngsters. "I hope you two have been to the toilet, because we have a camp to go back to ... wherever it is Helen and David stay."

"Are we going now, mummy?" David moaned. He was clearly having a good time at the farm, and now these adults were about to ruin it.

"I'm afraid so," his mum replied, "but Imelda, her dad, and Yoler are walking us back. They've showed us round their place, so we're going to do the same."

"Are we ready?" Simon looked over at Helen and smiled.

She nodded.

CHAPTER TWENTY-NINE

The five of them slowly walked down the grassy incline and headed for the small cluster of trees.

Once they were on flat land and were near the trees, Yoler spoke up. She said, "I like this walk. I could get used to this."

"You like this walk?" Simon narrowed his eyes at Yoler. "Why?"

"It's just a nice change, Simes. I'm used to walking through barren streets, going through homes that are abandoned, stepping over bodies that have been dead for months. It's like the lands, streets and towns are now full of ghosts, rather than people."

They walked, all side by side, and Simon spoke up and mentioned that Yoler had told him about animal coil spring traps.

"Well, we've never come across any where *we* are," Helen remarked. "And we've lived in the woods for a while."

"Okay," said Simon and turned to his daughter, "but you're still walking behind me and following my lead. I'm not taking any chances."

They entered the small cluster and were out at the other side and near the pond in minutes. Yoler was now leading the way and went right to walk around the pond. Helen, Simon, Imelda and David were close behind, but they all stopped once Yoler held her hand up, like a captain to his platoon, and everybody remained motionless and quiet, patiently waiting for an explanation from the twenty-six-year-old female.

"I thought I heard something." She turned and gazed at the two adults, and then the two children. To their credit, both kids looked relaxed and were behaving impeccably.

"Like what?" Simon put his hand in his pocket and was getting ready to take out his knife. He didn't want to do this. He didn't want Imelda to see him carrying a knife.

"Movement," was Yoler's short answer.

The rustle coming from the woods was to their right, at the other side of the pond, and the noise was growing, getting louder. Whatever was inside, it was getting close to revealing itself, or themselves.

Yoler pulled out her knife and took a few steps forward, and then they all saw what was in the woods. An Alsatian dog stepped out of the wooded area and growled as soon as its eyes clocked the five humans. Its black and faded red fur was matted in old blood, and the adult members of the group were certain that the blood was from other living things that the dog had attacked.

"Don't move," said Yoler, raising her arm to the people behind her. "This has happened a few times before with me."

"We had a couple of them in our camp a few weeks ago," Helen whispered to Simon.

"What happened?" he asked her nervously, dreading the answer.

"Donald and some of the others managed to chase them away?"

"Will it go away?" Simon called out to Yoler.

"Maybe," was her short vague answer. "Just keep still."

The dog cautiously stepped towards the group, snarling and gnashing, saliva running from its mouth.

"What's wrong with it, daddy?" Imelda groaned. "Is it ill?"

Simon placed his arm around his daughter and could feel her whole body shuddering. "It's not ill, babe. It's starving."

The canine took a few more careful steps further and stopped once Yoler stood up and made herself tall. The snarling and gnashing began to subside and the animal retreated, taking two steps back, then turned around and trotted off back into the woods with the greenery eventually swallowing the animal up.

All five relaxed and released relieved breaths out. Helen asked both minors how they were feeling and their responses suggested that they were both okay.

"Half the time we come this way, something seems to happen," Simon moaned.

"It was just a dog." Yoler shrugged her shoulders. "It's not what I'd call a major worry."

"No? What would *you* call it then?"

"It's a normal way of life now," she said, shaking her head at Simon. "In one day I was attacked by a lone man, was attacked by two Canavars, and shot at by a farmer who claimed I had got too close to his land, and then he set his dog on me."

"In one day?"

Yoler nodded with a smile.

Helen placed her hand over her mouth on hearing the story from Yoler, and asked the young woman, "So what happened with the dog? Did you manage to shake it off?"

"The mutt caught up with me. It was very quick."

"Were you hurt?"

"Nope." Yoler flicked her hair, moving her fringe from tickling her eyelashes. "Fortunately it was just *one* dog. They're not so dangerous on their own, but if there were a pack of them..."

"So you killed it?" Helen asked.

Yoler nodded. "And it tasted delicious." She then began to move, heading to the woods. The other four followed.

Two minutes had passed, and the only words that had been spoken were strong words to the two kids. David and Imelda had been playfully poking one another with their fingers as they walked, unaware that the situation they were in could be dangerous. A minute had passed and the kids began to giggle behind the adults; this was followed by moaning about the walk and that their legs were tired. This resulted in David and Imelda being reprimanded by Helen and Simon.

It wasn't the time for horseplay, and it appeared that the dog incident had been quickly forgotten about by the two infants.

Yoler was still leading the way, listening to Helen's instructions where to turn, and the two kids were behind Yoler, Simon was at the back of the line and Helen was in front of him, behind the two children.

Simon asked Helen, "How do you know where to go? All I can see is trees and bracken."

"I don't know." She hunched her shoulders and giggled in unison. "I just do. We've made this journey a few times when we go to the pond and collect water."

"I suppose we would have met eventually, if that's the case."

"Probably." She turned around and smiled at Simon.

He then lowered his head, smothered with guilt. *What are you doing?* It was clear that she was attracted to him, but as soon as the thought of being with Helen for a brief second skated across his mind, the image of Diana and Tyler being taken down by the gang of Canavars polluted his thoughts. He whispered, "Sorry" to his wife and thought that there was no reason why he and Helen couldn't be friends without intimacy.

Helen smiled and said to Yoler, "We're nearly there."

"Really?" Yoler scratched her head and look confused. "I can't see piss all but trees."

Helen laughed, "Yes, we're well hidden. Just wait until you pass that huge sycamore."

As soon as Yoler did so, she saw a large bald guy standing next to four homemade huts and a large cabin. It was Donald. There were washing lines tied to trees, a fire with a pot on a metal grid, and a couple of people skulking about. The set up didn't seem as good as the one that Yoler and Simon had back at the farmhouse, but these people had made this from scratch. The farm was already there and Simon had just happened to stumble across it.

"I thought you'd got lost," Donald growled. "It'll be getting dark soon."

"Don't exaggerate," Helen chuckled, which seemed to have angered Donald.

Helen turned to Yoler and Simon and said, "Let me introduce you to everyone."

"Er ... okay," said Simon.

"You know Donald," she pointed at the miserable looking man and then clapped her hands. "Everybody come out! There're people here for you to meet!"

Seven people had gathered in the middle of the area where they stayed, some exiting the small huts that they were staying in. There were ten people in all, including Helen, young David, and the grumpy Donald Brownstone.

Yoler noticed that the small area had thin rope around the circumference of the small camp and had tins and chimes attached to the rope. There were small manmade huts, but there was also an impressive looking cabin that was to their side. Yoler guessed correctly that the cabin had already been there when the group had turned up to this particular part of the woods, and had built their small huts near it. The rope was tied around the trees and was at knee height. It had obviously been put there to warn the campers of any intruders, especially during the night.

Helen began introducing the people to Yoler and Simon, but there were far too many names to remember. It looked like a reasonably young crowd and it appeared that Donald was the eldest at just forty-three years old.

She reeled off the names to Yoler and Simon: Hayley Bertrand, Gavin Bertrand, Jason Martins, Harriett Henderson, John Duncan, Jamie Monk and Gary Monk.

A young woman approached them and asked them if they wanted some soup. She nodded over to the large pot that was sitting on the fire.

"No thanks," Simon politely declined her offer.

"Don't mind if I do." Yoler wandered over and another woman by the name of Hayley, another blonde, gave Yoler a bowl and began to serve the soup.

"What kind of soup is it?" enquired Yoler.

Hayley smiled and said, "It has a bit of everything."

"Of course it does," Yoler laughed and began to slurp the soup once Hayley had passed her a spoon.

"Sit down," Helen smiled and pointed at the others. "Sit around the fire, everyone. Let's get to know our new friends."

CHAPTER THIRTY

For many minutes they conversed with Helen's people, most of them sitting around the fire. Out of all of them, apart from Helen, Simon liked Gavin the best. He was a dark haired fellow, and was incredibly polite. His sister, Hayley, was also a nice woman. She had blonde hair and both had told Simon and Yoler that they had no kids and were both fortunately single when it all kicked off. Simon told them all about his own family and they seemed genuinely sorry for his loss.

"At least there ain't many of the dead about these days," Hayley said. "At least that's something."

Simon shook his head at Hayley and signalled her to keep it down. He looked over his shoulder and was relieved that his daughter was playing with David, out of earshot of what the adults were talking about.

"What's the matter?" Hayley asked.

"I told Imelda that they're not around anymore," he said softly.

"You told her that?" Donald folded his arms, began to snicker and shook his head. "What did you tell her that pish for?"

"Because we hadn't seen one in ages." Simon was getting annoyed with Donald Brownstone. "What's it to you anyway?"

"It doesn't matter whether you're seven years old or seventeen, a person should be told what's really happening."

Helen could see that Simon was getting annoyed and she tried to change the subject, but no one was listening to her.

"She knows what's happening," Simon snapped. "We were all cowering in my basement as we heard the bombs fall."

"But you do know what *really* happened, don't you?"

"Of course." Simon nodded, not entirely sure what Donald was getting at. "It started in that medical centre, in Newcastle. That was when the outbreak occurred. That was the start of the ... Canavars."

"I'm not talking about that. I'm talking about months after, when the dead roamed our lands, and every other nation was shit scared, paranoid of it spreading. So they left us to fend for ourselves, and people, *millions* of people, died. A lot of them reanimated and turned into those freaks, leaving us with an estimated ratio of ten to one, in the dead's favour."

"We're aware of this," Yoler scoffed. "Why are you telling us things that we already know?"

"Before I met up with this lot," Donald pointed at the people from his camp, "I was with a friend of mine and we met up with a stranger."

"A stranger?" Yoler queried.

"I don't know whether he was crazy or not, but he claimed to be a deserter from some regiment. He had heard that our major cities were nuked by the powers overseas, and the rest of our lands were bombed to nullify the danger. Then soldiers from NATO, or whoever the fuck it is, were going to go through our land and wipe out the remaining threat."

"I think you've been reading too many books," Yoler said with an imperfect smile.

"It's true."

"I don't believe that's what happened?" Yoler laughed. "Anyway, I don't think that nukes were used."

"I don't care what pish you believe, darling. I think it makes sense." Donald twitched his nose and added, "I was also told that escaping from the UK is impossible."

"Of course. The waters are freezing and the…"

"I'm talking about the English Channel. That's the only realistic way of escaping, especially from Dover to Calais. But the English Channel is swarming with boats. Any survivors escaping would be killed. Even the Channel Tunnel has been blocked up at both ends. Not that it makes any difference to us, being six hundred miles away."

"I think your information is bollocks." Yoler paused and then added, "Don't you remember the first week, when we had power, when this thing was global? Didn't you watch TV when it kicked off? It's not just a UK problem. This thing was … *is* global."

"I know that, but it's not as bad in other European countries, or so I've heard."

"Now, you seem to be guessing." Yoler shook her head at the bald forty-three-year-old. "And as for the nukes…"

"I'm telling you now," Donald snapped. "Our cities were nuked. I've heard stories from other survivors who witnessed the cities from afar getting hit. They nuked the cities because, obviously, the more populated the area, the more of the dead. Have you seen what it does to people? When the Americans dropped the bombs in Japan, the victims that were hit were burned instantly to ashes. And imagine what it was like for folk in this country who lived on the outskirts of the city, with the radioactive dust and ash created when a nuclear weapon explodes. Fallout may get entrained with the products of a pyrocumulus cloud and fall as black rain, which is rain darkened by soot and other particulates."

"But we don't know for sure if our cities were hit like that," said Simon. "Not for sure. Of course, I never saw anything like that because I lived in a small town, but I definitely heard bombs being dropped, but they weren't nukes, otherwise I wouldn't be here."

"I'm telling you, according to this soldier, that's what happened. Why would this man lie to me, you dig what I'm sayin'?"

"I suppose it could have happened." Simon began to scratch his head. "I lived thirty miles from the nearest city, so I wouldn't have known."

"The lingering radiation hazard could represent a grave threat for as long as one to five years after the attack," said Yoler. "So if what you say is true, then surely we should be suffering."

"Not necessarily." Donald shook his head "Predictions of the amount and levels of the radioactive fallout are difficult because of several factors. Beyond the blast radius of the exploding weapons there would be areas, hot spots, if you like, the survivors could not enter because of radioactive contamination from long-lived radioactive isotopes. That's why I don't like moving about. And it's certainly the reason I don't wanna go down south or anywhere else. Look at where we are. We're twenty-five to thirty miles away from Derby, our smallest city. And we're twenty-five to thirty miles away from Birmingham the other way. If nukes have been used, then Birmingham definitely got it."

"And on that bullshit light note," Yoler finished the rest of the soup and stood to her feet, "I think I might go and stretch my legs."

"It's not bullshit," Donald snapped.

"I think it is."

CHAPTER THIRTY-ONE

They had spent fifteen minutes chatting around the fire, and Yoler was having a little stroll around the area. Others had now decided to move away from the dying fire and Yoler clocked the dark handsome man that was called Gavin. She leaned against a tree trunk and smiled at the man. He smiled back. He stepped over to her and introduced himself, but she reminded him that they had briefly met at the pond. He was dark in features, handsome, and seemed polite, almost shy.

"How long have you been with this lot?" Yoler asked him.

He laughed shyly, making Yoler's heart melt, and said, "A while."

"He seems quite a character," she whispered and nodded in the direction of Donald. He was still sitting down and talking to Simon.

"Er ... yeah," Gavin cackled. "You could say that."

"Not too sure about his theory." Yoler glared at Gavin and was strongly attracted to him. "What are *your* thoughts?"

Gavin hunched his shoulders. He took a look over, as if he didn't want to be heard and was fearful of Donald, and said in a soft tone, "I think it's a global thing. I think *everyone* is affected."

"So what is he on about with nuclear hits on cities, boats along the English channel—"

"He has his own theory. Everybody has their own theory."

"And what do *you* think?"

"I go by what we were told in the first couple of weeks, until the power died, of course. But I think we're all fucked. Maybe NATO or the RAF did bomb certain areas in the beginning, but ... I think the world has changed for good. We're alone."

Yoler smiled and felt her face flushing. "So ... what's your story?"

Gavin looked perplexed and screwed his eyes up. "Story? What do you mean?"

"Come on," snickered Yoler. "Everybody has a story. We're almost twelve months into this ... whatever it is, and you don't have a story?"

"I suppose it's like everybody else's," said Gavin. He dropped his head and seemed reluctant to continue. "I had a family, a girlfriend, a mum and dad, but now they're gone. At least I have Hayley."

"That's your sister, right?"

He nodded.

"You don't give much away, do you?"

Gavin flashed Yoler a smile. "We've only just met, and anyway, you haven't told me anything about yourself."

"True," she laughed. She turned around and could see Helen, Donald and Simon talking about something and turned her attention back to Gavin. She opened her mouth, about to tell Gavin about her journey, but he had interrupted her and began talking.

"The first weeks seem like years ago now," he began. He folded his arms and leaned against a tree. "I suppose it started off the same way it did for most people."

"I know what you mean." Yoler nodded. "What did you do for a living, before...?"

"I don't think it matters now," Gavin sighed.

"And your girlfriend?"

Gavin shook his head. "She never made it."

Yoler opened her mouth to ask how she never made it, but then realised her question would be deemed as insensitive.

Gavin sighed and added, "We're from down south, Hayley and I," he began. "From Bristol. We thought the further north we headed, the better it'd be. We only managed this far."

Yoler nodded. "I thought your accent was different."

Gavin continued, "When we finally left ... me and my sister got as far as the next town and then we came across a horde." Gavin shook his head and a thin smile developed on his features.

"What's so funny?" Yoler asked him.

"You know, one on one, even two on one, those things are easy to take care of. When they're in numbers it's a different kettle of fish altogether."

"I hear what you're saying." Yoler nodded.

"Anyway," Gavin groaned. "We turned the car around and there was another horde, out of nowhere. They must have heard the engine of the car ... or something." He didn't seem sure.

"What happened after that?"

"There were fields to either side of us, and those Canavars, or whatever you call them, headed towards the car, quicker than we thought was possible."

"I think they call them Canavars because it was a term used when the media was still up and running. I think the phrase was coined by some Turkish scientist being interviewed by the BBC."

"I heard quite a few names, but Canavars seems to be the one that stuck the most."

"What other names do you remember?"

Gavin rubbed his chin and smiled at the female. Already, he was wondering what it would be like to sleep with her. He loved her hair. It was like one of The Beatle haircuts from the Rubber Soul album, and despite the fact that she had no make up on and probably hadn't showered in a while, he thought she was gorgeous.

"Erm..." Gavin finally answered. "The ones I can remember off the top of my head were Biters, Shamblers, Rotters..."

"My friend used to call them Shufflers, but with the amount of people I've come across I've heard other names like, Monsters, Lurkers, Crazies. Another friend of mine called them Snatchers."

A silence fell on the two of them and Gavin cleared his throat, looked down, and began to kick at the ground, desperate to think of something else to say. He didn't want Yoler to excuse herself just yet. He was enjoying her company.

"So..." It appeared that Yoler had decided to break the silence. "When are you going to take me out?"

"What?" Gavin burst out laughing and placed his hand over his mouth, apologising to Yoler for his insulting reaction. Her question was ridiculous and had also taken him by surprise. Take her out? Where on earth could he take her out? In this area? In this situation they were all in?

Gavin finally managed to compose himself and was thankful that Yoler was also laughing with him.

"Take you out?" he continued to snicker. "And where do you suggest I take you out? To an Italian restaurant? Out for a coffee? To see the new Tom Hardy movie?"

"Mmm, Tom Hardy." Yoler began to lick her lips. "Now there's a face I haven't seen for a while. I hope he's still alive."

"Probably not," Gavin said with a cheeky smile. "Anyway, back to this so called date of ours..."

"In a few days we can have a picnic by the pond," said Yoler. "Maybe even get up to some naughty stuff."

"Jesus," Gavin scoffed and his face flushed red. "You're not shy, are you?"

"Life's too short to be shy these days." Yoler leaned forward and rubbed Gavin's arm. "After you've seen what I've seen ... well ... you just don't know when your time is up."

"It's not as bad as it used to be, don't you think?"

"The dead have certainly dwindled in numbers." Yoler gently brushed her dark fringe from her eyes. "But a lot of survivors have become arseholes now."

"Arseholes?" Gavin questioned. "Or simply just desperate people wanting to survive?"

"Trust me," Yoler said. "Some of the stuff that I've seen has had nothing to do with survival. What has beating a man to death in front of his family have to do with survival? What has raping a fifteen-year-old girl got to do with survival? And what has killing a harmless family dog with a crowbar, even though the family allowed the men to go inside their house and take what they wanted, got to do with survival?"

Gavin gulped, stood up straight and took a small step away from the tree he was leaning against. "And you've seen all these things?"

Yoler nodded. "I have seen some human kindness as well. It's not all doom and gloom, but you don't know who to trust. Like Simon, I tried to avoid company, and now suddenly, for the last few days, I'm with a small group of people, *good* people, and loving it."

"Anyway," Gavin smirked. "Let's talk about this date of ours. You mentioned being ... naughty. How naughty?"

Yoler giggled and said, "As naughty as you like."

"But..."

"But?"

"What about...?"

"You need to start finishing your sentences, Gavin," said Yoler with a smile, her tongue planted inside her cheek.

"What about protection?"

"There're ways and means of doing things without me falling pregnant," she said with a smirk. "Anyway, a friend of mine brought back some condoms from a recent supermarket trip." She decided not to tell Gavin that this *friend of hers*, Dicko, was someone she had slept with and would probably continue to sleep with.

Gavin began to shake with nerves. There were a number of reasons why this was the case. He wasn't used to being around women so up front. Helen was all about the safety of her son and had never hinted or showed any signs of wanting any sexual activity. Neither did the other females in the camp. The other reason why he suddenly felt uncomfortable was because of guilt.

Gavin had kept himself to himself and had told the people in the camp very little about his past life. He had told Helen that he used to live with his parents and had lost them in the first week, but he never told them much about his girlfriend.

He kept in contact with his partner in the first week and both had agreed that they should stay where they were, despite only being half a mile from each other. After eight days of staying indoors, on June 17th, his parents' house was attacked by a group of the dead. Gavin had no idea how this had happened. They had kept the curtains and blinds shut and made very little noise, but something had stirred the couple and had made their way to the front door. There were only two of them at first, and then a day later there were dozens of them.

It took only hours for the ground floor windows to give way, and Gavin and his parents moved upstairs for good, but the danger hadn't stopped there. The dead crawled their way up the stairs and Gavin and his dad spent many hours killing these things as they reached the top. Gavin used a pool cue, whereas his dad had taken a rolling pin from the kitchen when they first went upstairs.

His dad was grabbed and pulled downstairs, where a sea of crawling dead devoured him in minutes. His screams were short. After this incident his mother just gave up and had taken an overdose whilst Gavin was at the top of the stairs, fighting some of them off.

He returned to his parents' room for a breather and found his mum on the bed, dead. She had written the word 'sorry' in lipstick, on her dressing table mirror. After a few minutes of crying, he texted his girlfriend to tell her what had happened and that he was coming over. She told him that she wanted to leave to go to a school where her friends were staying at, but her parents didn't want to leave the house. He told her to pack a few things and that they'd be leaving in her car.

Gavin went through his attic and climbed over his roof; he went down a drainpipe and reached the ground floor, then ran for his girlfriend's house. She was still there, and when they left, with her parents' blessing, they headed for the primary school where her friends were supposed to be staying. But they never made it.

Two of the dead had shambled out from behind a bush; his girlfriend hit the pair of them and panicked, and then ended up crashing into somebody's brick wall. The pair of them got out of the car, took the packed bag from the back passenger seat, and fled on foot. They stayed in an abandoned house for two nights, but his girlfriend was then killed when they both broke into a newsagents to grab some food, but one of the dead inside, presumably the owner, had grabbed her and took her down before Gavin could do anything about it.

He then took the short drive to Hayley's house and was relieved that she was still alive. The pair of them were on their own for many months, and agreed to journey north where they eventually met this group. Despite the quote that time was a healer, he was still hurting. There wasn't a day that went by when he didn't think of his partner, or his parents.

"Gavin?"

He snapped out of his daydreaming and looked up to see Yoler calling his name and playfully snapping her fingers in front of his eyes.

"Hello, Gavin." She continued to snap her fingers and giggled, "Is there anybody in there?"

"What?" Gavin yawned, widened his eyes and took a quick peep at Yoler. "What was that?"

"You were miles away," she snickered and slapped him on the shoulder. "What were you thinking about?"

Gavin shook his head gently and smiled thinly at Yoler. "It doesn't matter."

"An old flame?"

Gavin became irritable with Yoler's persistence. "I said ... it doesn't matter."

Yoler gazed at Gavin and said, "I'm sorry. I know I'm a bit full on some of the time, but..."

"You don't have to explain."

"I never used to be like this ... in the old world."

"You don't have to explain, I said."

"Okay."

Gavin excused himself from a confused Yoler and turned on his heels, ready to move away from the female.

"Is that our date out of the window then?"

Her question made Gavin pause and stopped him from making his first step. "Probably not a good idea," he said.

Gavin walked away and went over to the large cabin that had been there before they arrived. He placed his hand on the door handle of the place and Yoler spoke once more before he had a chance to go in.

"I had a partner once, when it all kicked off," she said. "If this situation has taught me anything—"

"I know, I know," Gavin snapped. "Life's short."

"It is."

Gavin lowered his head and looked to the side, over to Yoler. "I suppose I'll see you around, Yoler. Good to meet you. You're not exactly ... normal, are you?"

She shook her head and smiled. "I sometimes pretend to be normal, but it gets boring so I go back to being me."

She gave Gavin a wink and walked away, back over to Simon and the rest.

Gavin shut the door behind him and looked around inside the cabin. Supplies were getting low. They were always low, but they always somehow managed.

Gavin sat on one of the chairs, in the corner of the cabin, and looked up to the ceiling.

His thoughts went to Carla, his girlfriend of almost two years, and his mind went back to her demise. It scared the life out of him. He knew that hundreds of thousands, possibly millions, had gone this way, but it wasn't the way he wanted to go.

The Canavars had depleted in numbers as time passed on, but they were still around. For reasons he couldn't understand, he thought about their weekend trip to Rhyl. It was their last break before the apocalypse began. He remembered driving most of the way there whilst Carla slept.

He smiled as he remembered passing places like Prestatyn, Flint, Queensferry, Mostyn and Mold ye Wyddgrugg.

He wondered what condition they were in now. Were there any survivors?

He could feel his eyes filling, and allowed the tears to fall now that he was alone in the dusky place. He sobbed gently, and even began to think about his friends from the past, his work colleagues and even his ex-girlfriend, Jade.

He was too young when he went out with Jade Greatrix, and he treated the poor girl like dirt. Sometimes they would arrange to go out, only for Gavin to cancel at the last minute and go out with his pals instead. She dumped him after four months, and accused him of only using her for sex. She wasn't wrong.

He smiled and apologised to Jade under his breath. He hoped she had made it, but doubted it. The last thing he heard, she had moved to the West Midlands and got herself a job at a sports centre as a fitness instructor. But that was around a year ago.

He wiped his eyes and could hear voices being raised. He looked out of the cabin window and could see that the new people were getting ready to leave. He smiled, hoped he would see them again, and sat back down in the murky cabin.

CHAPTER THIRTY-TWO

The feet of Yoler Sanders and Simon and Imelda Washington trudged through the bracken. They exited the wooded area and were now at the pond, on their way back to the farmhouse. Simon looked up to the murky sky and was feeling tired. Another few hours and he and Imelda were going to retire to their bedroom for the night.

With Yoler leading the way, they went around the pond and headed for the cluster of trees that would lead them out to the field, leading them to the incline that would take them to the farmhouse. Yoler wiped the few beads of sweat on her head and turned around to see both father and daughter holding hands. This scene made her heart swell and she knew she was lucky. She had spent months after months scavenging, going from one place to the next. Now, she had found somewhere where she was happy, with people she liked and got along with. She just hoped that it was something that would last.

She had walked along the flat part of the field, was many yards in front of Simon and his daughter, and began to walk up the grassy hill, up to the back yard of the farm.

Yoler was the first to make it up to the farm and looked at a sleeping Dicko who was outside and sitting on a deck chair, head lowered and snoring heavily, like a hog with asthma.

Yoler walked up to him and gave him a kick, making the guy jump to his feet. He looked at Yoler with confusion, and then looked around the area, rubbing his eyes and beginning to groan.

"What's going on?" he asked with panic. "Anything wrong?"

"Some guard you are, Dicky Boy," Yoler scoffed and wiped her fringe away from her eyes. "Useless prick."

"It's all under control," said Dicko with a wide smile. "I'm a light sleeper anyway."

"You're bloody hopeless."

"So you don't want to spend time with me tonight then?" he snickered.

"I suppose it would kill a minute or two."

"Below the belt," Dicko laughed, and then turned to his left to see that Simon and Imelda had arrived.

"Everything alright?" Simon asked Dicko, once he and Imelda had finally cleared the hill and were now at the back of the farm. "No trouble?"

"Went like a dream," Dicko snickered and flashed Yoler a look. Simon understood that it was a private joke between the pair of them and decided not to ask any further questions. He went inside the house with Imelda and the pair of them grabbed a drink of water.

Simon stared at his little girl and could see that her face was sombre. He placed his hands on her plump cheek and asked if she was okay.

She nodded, but unconvincingly, and gave her daddy a small smile. "I'm a little bit tired after all the walking."

"Fancy an early night?"

She nodded and took a step forward and wrapped her arms around Simon's waist. She put the side of her head against Simon's stomach and released a heavy sigh.

"What's wrong?" he asked her. It was a stupid question. Everything was wrong.

"I want a cuddle."

"Why?"

She sighed, "Because I need it."

They hugged for a minute and once they broke away, Imelda announced that she was going upstairs for a lie down.

"You want me to come up with you?" Simon asked.

She shook her head. "I'd like to be on my own, daddy, if that's okay?"

"Of course." He leaned over and kissed her on the top of her head. "See you in a bit."

He watched her as she left the living room to go upstairs, and then headed for the kitchen. Simon stepped outside and saw Yoler and Dicko sitting down and chatting. Simon remained standing up.

Yoler turned to Simon and said, "I was just telling Dicky Boy about that Donald fellow. What a head banger he was."

Simon agreed and said, "He's rather highly strung."

"He *should* be." Yoler smiled.

"What do you think to his ... story?" Yoler asked Simon. "Load of crap, if you ask me."

"I don't know." Simon rubbed his face with both hands. "I'm not sure anybody knows for certain what really happened during Stage Two."

"I was thinking about the situation at the visitor centre," Dicko said.

"Let's not go through this again, please," Simon sighed and shook his head.

"I'm not talking about you fleeing; I'm talking about those guys mentioning that Orson."

"Don't worry about it. Take each day as it comes." Simon looked over to Dicko and could see him staring into space, lost in thought.

"You okay over there?" Simon asked and put his hands in his pockets.

Dicko smiled and nodded the once. "Just thinking about … old friends."

"Oh?" Simon was unsure whether to continue the conversation.

"Dead friends?" Yoler asked bluntly.

Simon opened his mouth, about to reprimand Yoler for such a harsh and unsympathetic question, but Dicko held up his hand to Simon and told him it was okay.

"I'm not sure. They were alive when I left them," Dicko said with a smile. "I hope not."

"What about you?" Dicko asked Simon. "I've only been told snippets about what you've been through…"

"That's rich coming from Mr Secretive over there," Simon nodded over to Dicko and laughed.

"I'm not much of a storyteller."

Simon puffed out a breath and looked at Dicko. He smiled thinly and decided to speak. "When we were awash with the Canavars," he began, "we stayed hidden and did everything the media told us. Then when the bombs fell we hid under the stairs, in a cupboard."

"Coming from a village, I never heard any bombs fall," Dicko announced.

"And then?" Yoler tried to hurry Simon's story along.

Simon told them that his family lived in their attic once the bombs had stopped falling, and a gang of people broke into their home and raided the place, took what they had left, which wasn't much. He told them that their car was still on the drive.

In the first days of Stage One he was convinced that thugs would arrive, so he siphoned his car and took the wheels off the vehicle. The car sat on a pile of bricks, a pile for each wheel. They eventually left in the vehicle, but didn't get far. He told them that he had turned a corner and crashed into a hedge, and then was surrounded by the dead. He gave them the shortened version and told them that he and Imelda escaped, but his wife and son didn't.

"I'm sorry this happened to you," Yoler said. "It must have been horrific."

"It was," Simon smiled thinly. "It is."

"At least you have somebody left," said Dicko. "She's a cracking girl, your Imelda."

"Thanks, mate. She's all I have left." Simon excused himself and told the pair of them that he was going to go upstairs and check on her.

He reached the landing and felt the room spin. His chest tightened and his breathing became shallower. He decided to go into the bathroom first and sat on the toilet with his head in his hands. "Not again," he moaned. "What's wrong with me?"

He lifted his head up and held out his hands in front of him. They were juddering, and Simon Washington was concerned this time that he was about to have a heart attack. "Please. Not now."

He sat up, placed his hands on his thighs and tried to take control of his breathing.

"Not today," he gasped. "Next year. If it has to happen ... then next year."

He stood to his feet and made slow steps to the bedroom where he and his daughter slept. He walked in and cracked a smile when he saw her sleeping. She had a hold of the cuddly toy that was found, Lambie, and almost slept with a smile on her face. Simon wasn't doing the night duty so decided that an early night wouldn't harm him.

He was going to inform Yoler and Dicko that he was turning in, but couldn't be bothered to go back downstairs. They'd eventually work it out for themselves, he thought.

He kicked his boots off and lay next to his daughter. He lifted his arm up and gave his armpits a quick sniff. Maybe tomorrow he'd go back to the pond and wash the clothes.

He felt his carotid artery and then put his hand over his heart. "Stay strong, you little bugger."

He closed his eyes and hoped for a long sleep. He also hoped that he wouldn't die in his sleep from heart failure.

*

Dicko looked to the ceiling of where he was standing, in the kitchen, and was certain that father and daughter were now settled. He took a swig of water from one of the jars and placed the palms of his hands flat on the sideboard. He was leaning with his head bowed and his arms straightened to keep him up as support. He took in a few deep breaths and tried to cool his face down. The face of his wife projected in his mind and he suddenly jumped when he could feel arms wrapping around his waist.

He didn't turn around. He didn't need to. He knew it was Yoler Sanders.

She groaned, "Are you up for it, or what?"

Dicko put on a brave face and cleared his throat. "Of course."

Yoler released her arms and Dicko turned around, now facing the gorgeous woman that he could never attract back in the old world.

The two of them stood kissing in the kitchen, with the window behind them, but Yoler could feel that Dicko's response was hardly full of passion.

She broke away gently, developed a small smile and asked him what was wrong.

"I'm not sure," was his vague answer.

"If this is about the first, and the last time, we did it, it's okay. I still enjoyed it."

"I just couldn't..." Dicko was struggling for words. "I couldn't finish."

"You went soft." Yoler tried to lighten the mood and added further with a snicker, "It happens to a lot of guys your age. Maybe, next time we go out on a run, we'll try and pick up some viagra from a chemist or something."

"I'm glad you think it's funny." Dicko didn't look impressed with Yoler's ribbing.

"Come on, Dicky Boy." She gave him a playful nudge. "I'm just pulling your pisser."

Dicko gazed at Yoler and then dropped his head. She could see he was embarrassed and asked him what was wrong.

He began, "What happened the other night, between us..."

"Yes?"

"That was my first time since..." He couldn't find the words and grunted, "I've only ever been with one woman before."

Yoler felt terrible right away and placed her hands on Dicko's shoulders and told him it was okay. She could see he was getting upset. He tried to shrug her away because the attention he was receiving was making him worse.

"It's okay." She leaned in, trying to hug the man, but he gently pushed her away.

"Leave me for a minute, will you?"

Yoler nodded and went back into the living room, and began to sing *Sexy Sadie*. Once Yoler was out of the room, Dicko put his right hand over his mouth and nose, and began to sob. He tried to be as quiet as he could, knowing that Yoler was in the next room and that Simon and Imelda were upstairs, but covering his mouth and nose, his way of suppressing the noise he was making, didn't work very well.

After a couple of minutes, Dicko began to calm down and wiped his beard that had been dampened by the tears that had fallen from his eyes, and blew a breath out. He could feel his temperature cooling down, and he could sense that Yoler was hanging around near the doorframe of the living room, wondering if he was okay.

He walked inside and was greeted with a smiling Yoler. She was sitting on the armchair and asked if he was okay now.

Dicko said yes and the pair of them sat down. Half an hour later the pair of them made love.

CHAPTER THIRTY-THREE

NEXT DAY

Simon opened his sticky eyes and turned his head to the side. Before lying on the bed, he had forgotten to draw the curtains. He could see from where he was lying that dawn was breaking. It was the start of a brand new day and Simon guessed that it was around four in the morning. He heard moaning to the side of him and could see that Imelda was beginning to wake up.

He sat up and rubbed his eyes with his fingers. A twinge of pain in his mouth made him wince. Toothache. There were many things that he missed and took for granted in the old world, like music, online shopping, television ... many things, but a dentist wasn't one of them. He thought about having to extract the tooth out himself. It could be worse, he thought. It could be appendicitis. Then he'd be fucked.

Simon rubbed his mouth, hoping the discomfort was going to pass, and stood to his feet. Fully dressed from the night before, he walked around the room. Maybe he should get up now, he thought. He could give Yoler or Dicko a chance to turn in early.

He stopped walking when he heard voices coming from downstairs, but it didn't sound like the voices of Simon and Yoler.

Simon put his boots back on and took the knife from the side table and placed it into his pocket. He left the bedroom and went onto the landing, where the voices could be heard clearer. He sat on the top step and listened to what was being said. A scuffle broke out, followed by more raised voices, and then silence.

"Right," a man's voice bellowed; a voice that Simon didn't recognise, "now that we've all calmed down, I'm gonna ask you two a few questions."

It sounded to Simon that these impostors were in control. He didn't know how they were in control. He couldn't see. Were there many of them? Or were Dicko and Yoler overpowered by them? Or did one of them have a gun? Surely if one of them had a gun then nobody would dare start a scuffle.

"Where's the other prick?" another man growled.

Simon screwed his eyes with confusion. *Other prick? How do they know someone else is here?*

"There is no one else here," Simon heard Dicko saying from the ground floor.

"The shitebag that ran off," the man yelled. "Where is he?"

As soon as Simon heard this, he knew it was the people from the visitor centre.

"Haven't seen him since he ran away," said Dicko.

"Bollocks! We saw that you were both in the car when you knocked our pal down."

"I'm telling you," protested Dicko, "he's gone."

"Then you don't mind if I take a look upstairs then, do you?"

Simon Washington felt his limbs shake with panic and was unsure what to do. Simon went into his bedroom, stopped moving and took a peep at his little girl who was fast asleep. He stepped over to her and gave Imelda a quick shake. "Babe," he said frantically. "Babe, wake up."

Imelda moaned, stretched and began to yawn. Simon grabbed her hand and urged her to get off the bed and stand next to her daddy, startling the girl.

"Is it morning?" she yawned.

"We might be in danger."

"What?"

"I know it sounds strange, but we could be in trouble."

"Daddy, what's going on?"

"Look, don't panic."

"Panic?"

"There're some people in the house. We need to hide."

"People? What kind of people?"

"Bad ones."

The sound of footsteps could be heard creeping up the stairs. Simon looked at Imelda and said, "You, in the cupboard. I'll get under the bed."

"But daddy..."

"Just do it."

Imelda stepped inside the clothes cupboard, and Simon shut her in before crawling underneath the bed. He could hear the individual, probably a man, walking across the landing and then trying the doors. Theirs was next.

Simon held his breath, heart racing, and waited for the door to be tried. He didn't have to wait long.

The door opened and the first thing, and pretty much the only thing, that Simon could see was the brown muddy boots of one of the intruders. He held his breath as the boots slowly went to the left side of the bed, Simon's eyes following. The boots then walked around the bed, going by the cupboard, and went to the right side of the bed. Simon released a long and quiet breath out and then sucked another one in. The boots stopped at the foot of the bed, inches away from Simon's head.

Simon had no idea how long the person had stood for or why. It felt like hours. The boots then moved, making Simon gasp, and headed towards the cupboard.

As soon as the person opened the cupboard, Simon crawled out from under the bed and said, "Okay, okay."

Imelda released a scream as Simon stood to his feet. He held both hands up and said, "Don't you touch her."

Simon then looked over to Imelda and beckoned her over. He recognised the man from the visitor centre and could see he was holding a knife. He gazed at Simon's pockets and pointed at his right one.

"I'll be taking that," the man said.

Simon slowly reached into his pocket and threw the knife by the man's feet.

The man with the grey hair and beard smiled, picked the knife up and opened the bedroom door wider. "The pair of you, downstairs."

Simon felt Imelda's warm silky hand grab *his*, and father and daughter went downstairs with the intruder behind them.

CHAPTER THIRTY-FOUR

Simon and Imelda entered the living room and could see Yoler and Dicko sitting on the couch with their hands on their lap. Simon stood next to them, with his little girl standing behind. The man with the grey hair went over and stood next to his two other companions, put his knife away and pulled out a machete from his belt that Simon had never noticed before when they were upstairs.

It was the same three people from the visitor centre. Simon and Dicko didn't know the names of the men, but they knew that the female was called Clare, because she had introduced herself when they first met.

The female told Simon to pass whatever weapon he had over. Simon looked at Dicko, and Dicko nodded at Simon. "Me and Yoler have handed ours over."

Simon huffed, "I've already given it to *him*." Simon pointed over at the man with the grey beard and patted his pockets, showing the intruders that he wasn't carrying, not anymore.

Simon did as he was told and remained standing by the couch with Imelda behind him.

"It took a while to find you folk," Grey Beard cackled. "And yet here you are, in a farmhouse and fully exposed. Not great thinking. Most people opt to find an abandoned house or stay in the woods, but you folk..."

"We have everything we need here," Dicko said. "Why live in the woods and live off berries? When winter comes..."

"Enough!" snapped the thin man that was clean shaven. "We're not here to hurt you. Despite what you did to our friend, we're just here to claim compensation."

"Compensation?" Yoler scoffed. "What the piss are you on about, compensation?"

A thin man with dark hair shaven stood holding a knife, and pointed over to Imelda who was cowering behind her father.

He said, "Right, cutie, you come over here and stand next to me."

"She's going nowhere," Simon snarled with his teeth clenched together. "You need to get through me first."

"Very touching," the man giggled and looked up at his two friends, Clare and the grey haired man with the thick beard.

"Tie these fuckers up," the man with the shaved head commanded to the other guy and the female.

"You can fuck off!" Yoler snapped and raised her fists.

"We're not going to harm you," Clare, the female, said. "We need to empty your supplies into your car that we're going to take. And that'll take a while with the three of us."

"We need you guys to be on your best behaviour when we do this," said Clean Shaven. "Tying you up is the only way. Now, where are the car keys for that Mazda?"

Yoler and Dicko remained tight-lipped.

"Come on." Grey Beard put his machete away, and tapped the machete handle and nodded over in Simon and Imelda's direction. "Do you really want me to harm the little girl to get a fucking answer?"

Dicko sighed in defeat and said, "They're in the kitchen. By the sink."

Clare went in to look for them and returned to the living room seconds later, shaking the keys. "Got them."

"Good." Grey Beard nodded.

"We could always lock them in one of the bedrooms," Clare suggested, looking at her two male companions.

"Nah, fuck that." Grey Beard shook his head. "They're staying here."

Grey Beard pulled out four black tie tags out of his pocket and began conversing with his other two colleagues.

Yoler turned to Dicko and Simon overheard her say, "We can't let them take everything, just like that."

Dicko nodded and whispered, "I know."

Once the three had finished talking, Grey Beard walked over with his hand on the machete handle and went over to Yoler first. He asked her to stand up. She did as she was told and held out her hands in front of her. Simon noticed that Yoler gave Dicko a glare, but had no idea what it was about. What were these two planning?

"Put your arms behind," Grey Beard snarled at Yoler.

She moved her arms behind her and Grey Beard moved to the side of her and bent over. Yoler was making it difficult for him to tie her up.

"Fuck's sake." Clean Shaven laughed. He had his arms folded and was standing next to Clare. "Let's hurry this up."

Grey Beard huffed, "Fuck off, Clare!"

"You're taking ages."

"I wouldn't mind a hand over here."

Grey Beard grabbed the standing Yoler's wrists and bent over, struggling with the tie tag. Dicko glared at the machete handle and shifted a few inches nearer to Grey Beard. Dicko could see that Grey Beard was still bent over, struggling with the tie tag, and was becoming exasperated, cussing under his breath.

Dicko and Yoler glared at each other one more time and Simon held his breath, knowing that something was going to happen.

Dicko reached for Grey Beard's machete handle and Yoler leaned to her left and took a bite out of the man's arm. Dicko punched the man in the throat and then pulled out the machete and stood up before Clare and Clean Shaven had a chance to pull out their own large blades.

Clare panicked and left the house, leaving a very confused Clean Shaven to ask where the fuck she was going. He never got an answer and decided to flee himself, running through the kitchen and out of the back door, the same way Clare had left.

Dicko ran after the pair of them, and Yoler turned to Simon and pointed at the bleeding Grey Beard who was lying on his front, injured and moaning on the floor.

Yoler screamed at Simon, "Kneel on his arm and whatever you do, don't let that bearded cunt get up!"

She then followed Dicko, picking up her knife on the way out. Simon told a confused and petrified Imelda to go upstairs, but she refused. She was quiet, stunned, and looked like she was in shock.

"I don't want to leave you, daddy," she groaned.

"Just go," Simon snapped, panting. "Get in the room and hide in the cupboard. I'll come up for you once we're ... done."

Imelda took the stairs and made progress to the room her and her dad had been staying in for days.

Simon was kneeling on the man's outstretched arm and could hear him gasping. He had been punched in the throat and Simon looked down and could see the blood pouring out of the man's right arm, in the triceps area. It was a hell of a bite from Yoler, a desperate bite. It was the similar kind of bite an individual would take out of an apple.

Simon twisted his neck, making it crack, and looked in the direction of the kitchen when he heard the sounds of a man screaming from outside. He had no idea what happened to the Clare character, but was convinced that Yoler and Dicko were attacking Clean Shaven.

Simon was praying under his breath. He was scared and was trying to block out the pleading from the man that was underneath him.

"Please, man," pleaded Grey Beard. "You're hurting me."

"Hurting?" Simon scoffed. "And what would you three scumbags have done to us after you'd emptied the house?"

"We would have let you go."

"Bullshit!"

"It's true. That was the plan. Orson told us not to kill you guys, unless it was absolutely necessary."

Orson! There was that name again.

Yoler and Dicko returned to the living room. Dicko's machete was stained with blood and so was Yoler's knife.

"We lost that Clare character," Dicko panted, "but the other one won't be giving us any bother."

Simon turned and asked, "Where did she go?"

"She was heading for the pond. She was too far away to chase. She must be going into the woods."

"This piece of shit mentioned that name again ... Orson. If that Clare character gets back to, wherever she came from, she'll tell that Orson guy where we stay."

"Well, let's hope she doesn't make it," Dicko sighed.

"Maybe she's heading towards Helen's camp," Simon wondered. "Maybe if..."

Simon never finished his sentence. He felt a dull ache in his stomach and fell backwards. Grey Beard had escaped and was now scrambling upstairs. Simon rolled around on the floor, winded, whilst Yoler and Dicko ran towards the door that led upstairs, after Grey Beard.

Simon quickly got to his feet, gasping for breath, and tried to warn his two friends that Imelda was in the usual bedroom upstairs.

Simon headed upstairs, for his room, and could see that Yoler and Dicko were already standing by the frame of the opened door. Simon stood behind them and looked in. Grey Beard had Imelda around the throat and was standing behind the little girl.

"I'm sorry daddy," she cried, once she clocked Simon's face. "I thought it was you coming in and I came out."

"Fucking shut up!" Grey Beard snarled at her.

"Don't you fucking touch her!" Simon screamed. He took a step forward, but he was being held back by his two other housemates.

Grey Beard revealed a devilish grin, "I swear, I'll snap her fucking neck."

"Don't you touch her!"

"Right." Dicko held his hand up to the assailant and added, "Let's not do anything stupid now. What do you want?"

"What?" Grey Beard looked perplexed.

"What do you want? You want to be allowed to leave?"

Grey Beard had lost all his confidence and swagger, and looked like a frightened and desperate man, which he was.

He nodded. "Yes, I want to leave."

"Then let the girl go."

"No." Grey Beard shook his head and looked to be close to tears.

"No?"

"As soon as I let her go, you'll kill me. I know where you live. You're not going to risk letting me go."

"Maybe that would be true if you were the last survivor of the three. But you're not. That woman knows where we live and she's gone, she's escaped. So what'd be the point of killing *you*? With that woman now on the run, we know we have to leave here now."

"I could talk to Clare, if she returns to our camp," Grey Beard said desperately. "I'll keep my mouth shut and I'll make sure she does the same. I'll make sure she doesn't tell Orson a thing. But I'll need to go now, try and get back before *she* does."

Yoler didn't believe him and was growing impatient with this standoff, and the frightened look on Imelda's face made her heart go numb.

Simon snarled. "Just ... let-her-go."

Grey Beard side stepped over to the bedroom window and opened it with his free hand.

"What the piss are you doing?" Yoler asked.

"I don't believe you guys. I'm gonna let this girl go and jump out of this window. Don't you fucking follow me."

"There's no need for that," Dicko tried to reassure the man. "We'll let you out downstairs. We'll keep our distance."

"Bollocks!" the man laughed. He opened the window wider and pushed Imelda towards Yoler and Dicko, and then jumped out.

Simon and Imelda immediately hugged and Yoler was about to move downstairs after the man, but Dicko held her back. A cry from outside from the man was heard, and Dicko just assumed that he had landed awkwardly before fleeing.

"Don't bother," Dicko said to her.

"But I can catch him," said Yoler. "I'm quick."

"You won't catch him. It's amazing how fast a person can run when they're scared to death."

A male moan was heard again and Yoler and Dicko went to the bedroom window and looked out.

Grey Beard was lying on the floor, trying to crawl away from the house, but his obvious broken left leg was preventing this.

"Ouch," Yoler said, and then winced.

"Looks like our friend isn't going anywhere for the time being," snickered Dicko. "Let's tie him up and put him in the spare bedroom. We might need him alive."

CHAPTER THIRTY-FIVE

Clare had been running for over five minutes. She was so out of breath that she had to stop once she passed the pond and was near the woods. She bent over and tried to catch her breath. She looked around and knew her only option was the woods.

She couldn't go back.

They'd be waiting for her. And to the side of her were just fields.

She straightened her back, placed her hands on her hips, and waited a minute. She placed her right hand on her side and felt for the handle of her knife. It was still there. At least she had some kind of protection.

She then pulled out the large blade and strolled into the woods, into the unknown. She had no idea how, but she wanted to find a road and try and get back to Orson and the rest of the crew. At the moment she was going the wrong way, but going back on herself and heading back where the farm was situated could be disastrous for the woman.

She made her way through the bracken and constantly scanned all around her with paranoid eyes. The woods were condensed, but she could still see about ten to fifteen yards in front of her.

She had been in the woodland for ... she didn't know how long, but to her left she could hear noises, people chatting. She couldn't see a fire, but she could see smoke billowing into the air from many yards away.

A camp, she thought. But was it a friendly camp?

She decided not to risk it, and crept around the camp. She made sure that she didn't get too close and was aware that guards could be around.

She held the knife with her shaking hands and relaxed a little when she was obviously moving away from the location. She looked behind her and could see the smoke in the distance and the chatter from people could not be heard anymore.

She put her knife back into her pocket and ran her fingers over her greasy hair and tightened her ponytail. She licked her dry lips and rubbed her throat. Jesus, she needed a drink.

The bracken seemed longer up ahead, and she hoped that there was some way out of the stifling woods real soon. She made a move, wiping her damp forehead with her sleeve, and sped up, hoping that she wasn't far away from a road. She wanted to be out in the open. She needed to feel the cool wind temporarily cover her frame.

Her feet continued to go through the bracken as her eyes looked around, and a sharp pain shot through her left leg. She released a scream and fell to the floor. She lay on the floor and cried out once more, feeling the white hot pain. She sat up and tried to lift her left leg, but it was no use. She searched through the bracken and could see that she had stood on an animal spring coil trap. She guessed that it had broken her ankle, and she tried to use her fingers to prise the metal jaws open, so she could release her foot, but she couldn't do it.

She cried out again and this time didn't care whether the camp from a few hundred yards back had good or bad people in it. She needed help. She needed to be heard.

She lay back down and put her hands on her head. The pain was intense and she cried out for help again.

She sat up and once more tried to prise open the jaws of the trap. Her head was lowered and she cussed as she struggled to get her leg free. The sound of disturbed plantation could be heard in front of her, which was followed by a growling. She gulped and looked up to see an Alsatian, only yards away from her. More noises could be heard, and this time a black slavering Pit Bull appeared to her right and another canine, a Red Setter, appeared to her left.

Clare never said a word. She didn't want to antagonise the situation. Were they just being inquisitive because of the noise she was making? Or were they going to...?

No. Surely not.

The Alsatian took a step forward and began to sniff her. She shook with fear and the black Pit Bull was the first of the three dogs to attack her. It ran and grabbed her by the throat and the other two dogs also attacked. Clare's screams never lasted long as the ravenous animals ripped her to bloody shreds. Once her head was torn from the rest of her body, the hungry canines bit into her torso and began to devour her insides, like pigs eating from a trough.

Their snouts became bloodier as they dipped further into Clare's cadaver. Not even the sound of a dozen moving bodies heading the dogs' way, bothered them. They were too busy enjoying their raw, bloody and delicious meal.

The twelve members of the dead, attracted by the screams of Clare, both whilst she had been trapped and whilst she was being devoured, headed in the direction of the culprit that started this mess: the spring coil animal trap.

The first one approached the Pit Bull.

The dogs were so engrossed in their feed that they were unaware of the dead that surrounded them. Until they were attacked.

Squeals of pain from all three dogs emerged once the dead, some of them dropping to their knees, began to rip the canines to pieces. There were twelve of the dead, four to every dog, and the only animal to fight back was the black Pit Bull. It turned and tried to gnaw away at the rotten face of one of them, but soon stopped when one of the creatures took a generous bite out of its neck. The dog was still conscious when they opened up its stomach.

The twelve ghouls made light work of the three dogs, and even one knelt and grabbed the decapitated head of Clare, forcing its arm in and scooping out her brains, then stuffing its face.

CHAPTER THIRTY-SIX

Helen had spent the last hour washing clothes. She and a male called Jason Martins had been at the pond and were now hanging the clothes on a line that had been tied to two trees. The wet clothes were washed in the pond with soap and then dumped in a bucket and taken back to the camp.

There was plenty of water filtered, but the food situation could have been healthier. Ten mouths to feed was a hard task to do on a daily basis, and the supplies were dwindling so much that Gavin and Donald had planned to go for a dangerous jaunt through the woods to see if there were any mushrooms, blackberries, chestnuts ... even an orchard.

Once the clothes were hung up on the lines, Helen walked over to the main hut to grab herself a bottle of water. She opened the door to the main hut to see a half-dressed Donald Brownstone. He had his back to her and was putting on a fresh T-shirt. She could see the tattoo on Donald's back. She had seen it before. It went from shoulder to shoulder and in old English the word "Charlie" was present. Helen had asked him about it weeks ago and he had told her that it was the name of a dog he had lost a while back. She didn't believe him, but never felt it necessary to dig any deeper. Everybody had secrets; even Helen Willis.

"Fuck's sake!" he snapped, realising somebody had walked into the cabin. "Doesn't anybody knock anymore?" He turned around and immediately apologised when he could see that it was Helen that had walked in on him.

"That's okay," she said with a smile. "Now, don't be hogging this place. Me and David have this place tonight."

Donald Brownstone snickered and said, "That's right. It's your turn tonight. It's better in here, isn't it?"

"What a difference, staying in this place," Helen laughed, and had a quick scan around in the cabin, making Donald reveal a rare smile. It was no secret amongst the others that he had a soft spot for Helen.

"Tell me about it."

Helen placed her tongue in her cheek and said with a cheeky smirk, "Shame me and David couldn't have it every night."

"You know the rules." Donald playfully wagged his finger. "We share the cabin. One night for every person, or couple."

"I know."

When they first arrived at this area, it was the abandoned cabin that made them set up camp. The other four huts were made by the people themselves from loose logs and branches that had been collected from the area.

Donald asked the woman, "What do you think of the new people, now that you've spent some time with them?"

Helen bit her bottom lip in thought, and then hunched her shoulders. "They seem okay. Just ... survivors like you and me."

"I don't know." Donald ran his fingers over his hairless head and added, "I don't trust them, you dig what I'm sayin'?"

Helen snickered, "You don't trust anyone, Donald."

"True."

"The trouble with you..."

A scream in the distance stopped Helen from speaking and made her gasp. "Did you hear that?" she asked Donald with wide eyes.

Donald seemed unsure. "I think so."

"You *think* so?"

Helen and Donald stepped out of the cabin and looked around and could see Gavin and Jamie Monk. She called them over and asked if they had just heard a scream, but both men shook their heads. "Maybe I'm going mad." Helen scratched her head.

"Are you sure it was a scream?" Gavin asked Helen. "It could have been an injured animal, or..."

"I'm telling you now," Helen panted. "I heard a scream. A woman. I also heard squealing ... like dogs in pain ... or something. I don't bloody know."

"From which direction?"

Helen pointed.

Gavin sighed and said, "Okay. I'll check it out."

Jamie Monk asked to join him and both men walked deeper into the woods, away from the camp, and headed in the direction where Helen had pointed.

Once the two men were swallowed up by the greenery, Helen and Donald waited anxiously.

*

"I have no idea where we're going," came the voice from Gavin Bertrand to his partner Jamie Monk.

The two young men stepped into an open part of the woods and could see bloody carnage in front of them. Twelve of the dead, all now standing, with bodies, bloody meat, and trails of intestines like thick spaghetti by their feet.

"Oh shit." Gavin placed his hand over his mouth once the smell hit him. It was a mixture of the rotting bodies of the dead that were on their feet and the dead human and the three dogs.

"What the fuck?" was all that Jamie Monk could manage.

Both young men stood in shock and gazed at the twelve standing cadavers.

Still chewing, every single one of the dead began to advance towards Gavin and his friend. They were slow, but very persistent, and Gavin screamed at his friend to run.

Gavin ran a few yards ahead but stopped when he realised his companion wasn't by his side. He turned around and could see that Jamie was still standing and staring at the advancing dead. He was in shock and his legs had frozen with fear.

Two of the dead grabbed Jamie and took him down, burying their heads in his neck. Gavin watched in horror as they ripped his friend's throat out, and could see the fresh blood spurting onto the faces of his killers. Jamie released an awful scream, but it was short-lived.

Gavin gagged when a third fell to its knees, bent over as if it was going to give Jamie the kiss of life, and began chewing his lips off.

Gavin was also in shock, but his legs thankfully worked. And when the other nine walked past his dead friend and headed for him, he turned around and ran like he had never run before.

*

A shriek filled the air, only yards away, and everyone that was inside their huts came out, wondering what the hell was going on.

Gavin darted out of the condensed part of the woods and back into the camp and screamed, "There's loads of the dead! They've got Jamie!"

"Wait, wait." Donald was the first to approach the young man and said, "Calm down. What happened?"

"They're coming!" Gavin shrieked. "The Canavars are coming!"

Donald gazed and could feel the blood draining from his face when he saw the dead emerging from out of the trees. He quickly found his voice. "Quick, everyone," said Donald. "Get inside your huts."

The dead all emerged from out of the woods and before anybody had a chance to move. There were twelve of them, and the camp was filled with screams once one grabbed a hold of a nineteen-year-old called John Duncan and bit into his neck.

Little David ran over to his mum and the three of them, Helen, David and Donald Brownstone, stood in shock and saw another resident being taken down. Gavin and three others fled to the left, leaving Helen, David and Donald standing alone.

David stood in shock and was unable to cry. Instead, he stood with his legs shaking and had dribbled a little in his underpants.

Not one of the dead pursued Gavin and the other three individuals; they had been distracted by something else. Every single one of the dead turned and gazed at Helen, her son and Donald, and moved in their direction. The dead headed towards them in almost an organised semi-circle and Donald grabbed Helen and said, "The pond! Both of you! Now!"

"What about the others?" Helen screamed.

"Fuck the others! They're gone." Donald grabbed Helen by the hair and forced her to look at her frightened boy that was by her side. "That's the only thing you should be worried about! Let's move!"

The three ran from the dead, leaving the camp behind, and headed into a more condensed part of the woods. Donald led the way, whilst Helen ran behind him, holding a petrified David's hand.

"Where are we going?" David cried, but he never got an answer. "Mum? Where're we going? Are we going to the farm?"

Helen had no idea where they were going to go, but Donald had an answer for David. "Yes," he panted. "We're going to the farm. I take it that it's this way."

"Yeah!" Helen yelled. "It's straight on."

"I hope these pricks let us in."

"They'll welcome us," Helen panted. "I know they will."

They came out of the woods and were at the pond, all three of them gasping. Donald told them to follow him around the pond, but Helen and David already knew where they were going.

David tripped over a thick tree root before they reached the cluster of trees and Helen helplessly saw Donald Brownstone running away from them, unaware of David's predicament. Helen tried to pick her son up and quickly managed to scramble to their feet. The sight of the twelve dead exiting the woods and following them around the pond had injected more adrenaline through their bodies.

Both mother and son ran through the group of trees faster than they had ever run before. The pair of them were still holding hands, and could now see Donald on the field and heading for the incline of the hill that led up to the farmhouse that was visible.

Donald Brownstone genuinely didn't know about David's fall and thought that Helen and David weren't far behind. He looked over his shoulder and stopped running when he saw how far away they were.

"Hurry!" he cried. "They're right behind you! Don't turn around! Just run to me!"

Helen ignored Donald's advice and looked over her shoulder. The dead were only ten yards behind her, and she knew that they would have been way ahead of them if it wasn't for David's fall. Their hideous faces made her gasp in fright, as it had been a while since she had seen any.

They were all the same. They were slow, thankfully, and stunk to the heavens. All of their eyes had a milky film over them, and their movement was awkward and clumsy.

Donald reached his hand in his pocket and pulled out a knife, but it was just a precaution. He couldn't take on twelve. That would be madness, and he was convinced that the incline would slow them down. But what about after that?

A high-pitched scream could be heard in front of them and all looked up.

"What the fuck's that?" Donald yelled, but Helen didn't answer him.

It was Imelda. She was standing at the back of the farm, staring at the three individuals.

She had seen the dead following the three of them, and she seemed hysterical.

CHAPTER THIRTY-SEVEN

Imelda Washington was drawing at the table with her pencil and paper. She came out of her little world briefly and looked up to see that nobody was with her. The living room was empty. Her dad couldn't have gone far, so she never panicked. She put her head down and carried on drawing.

She had so far drawn a picture of the farmhouse. She even drew a car by the side of the house, representing the Mazda Dicko had taken, and then underneath the house and to the side she put in the grass, albeit grey in colour, like everything else.

She then began to add clouds at the top of the paper and placed a circle in the right corner, representing the sun. She leaned back in the chair and had to think about how many people were staying in the house. She counted on her fingers. "One, two, three, four."

She began to draw herself and her father first. After all, they were the first to arrive at the house.

She made the drawing of herself wearing a dress and with a huge smile on the face. She didn't know why she drew this. She hadn't worn a dress or skirt since she last went to school, and smiling wasn't something she did on a regular basis, not these days. She had lost her regular smile when she saw her brother and her mummy being taken down by the Canavars.

The drawing of her was next to the front door of the house, and she even added her scar that was on the right side of her forehead, just below her hairline. Next to her, by her side and on the left, was her dad. In truth, it could have been anyone and wasn't a good representation of Simon Washington, not that that was something someone would say to an eight-year-old child. It was a simple drawing; she had given her father dark hair, and also a smile, but not as large as the one she had given herself.

She then looked up to the ceiling in thought, and tried to recall who was the next individual to join them. Her and her dad had found Yoler sleeping in their bed, but Dicko was already sitting in the living room when this incident had happened. So Dicko was the next person to join them, she thought. She spent a while on Dicko, even sketching a knife attached to his side, and then she immediately began to sketch Yoler.

The little girl tried to draw Yoler, but wasn't happy with the end result. She wanted to make Yoler just as pretty as she was in real life, but couldn't seem to pull it off. She knew if she kept on rubbing the drawing of Yoler, then she'd end up making a mess of the picture. She kept the third draft, but still wasn't happy with it. The only thing she was happy with was the hair she had given her.

Imelda placed the pencil at the side of the drawing and sat back, inspecting her work. She then felt a rush of emotion suffocating her. She felt like she was being slowly strangled, had a dull sensation in her chest and could feel her eyes becoming damp.

Then she had a mini breakdown.

The girl cried hard and her beautiful wet eyes continued to release water down her shuddering cheeks. She very seldom had breakdowns like this anymore, although for a month, after she had lost her mum and brother, it was all the time, but she knew how much her breakdowns affected her dad. Every time she showed she was hurting, Simon would become upset. As the days ticked by, the easier it had become. The pain was still there, but it wasn't as raw as it used to be.

Imelda dried her eyes and decided to go into the kitchen and use a small amount of water to splash her face. If her daddy saw her like this, she knew that it would upset him, and she didn't want that.

She sat back at the table and decided what to draw next. A minute later, she could hear footsteps and her dad entered the living room.

*

Simon entered the living room, stood by the front window and peered out onto the road. He was standing guard whilst Yoler and Dicko slept in one of the rooms upstairs, exhausted after burying the bodies of two men in the small wooded area: Clean Shaven and finally the attacker from the pond that Dicko had killed days ago.

He rubbed his jaw as his tooth began to ache again. It was going to have to come out one day, he thought. Just not today. The captive, Grey Beard, was in the other room, tied up, gagged and dosed by three solpadol tablets for his pain, and more importantly so Yoler and Dicko could get some shuteye.

They were still unsure what to do with the man. Yoler wanted him dead, Dicko was unsure, and Simon didn't want a man killed if it could be avoided. Imelda was at the table, drawing another picture with her pencil, and Simon felt at peace. It was quiet, but it wasn't eerily quiet. The fact that he had two people upstairs who were almost like warriors helped a great deal, and his confidence had never been so high since this shit had begun.

He took a deep breath and created a smile. His thoughts went to Diana and Tyler. He began to think about the time when they went to Lochgoilhead for a three-day break, but those thoughts were short-lived when he heard the sound of a chair scraping from behind him. Simon looked over his shoulder and could see Imelda getting to her feet.

"You okay, babe?" he asked.

She said, "I'm going to get a drink from the kitchen."

"Okay."

"I might pop out and get some air as well."

"Good idea." Simon faced the front window and glared out at the barren road. "I think I might join you." He then muttered under his breath, "There's a whole lot of fuck all happening here anyway."

Imelda went to the back of the place, went through the kitchen, took a drink and went outside to the back. Simon remained staring out the front window. He rested his hand on the handle of the machete that had been taken from Grey Beard and smiled when Yoler made a crack that they were now like the three Musketeers, as two of them now had machetes that were taken from Grey Beard and the now defunct Clean Shaven who was butchered out in the back.

A scream filled with fear alerted Simon, and he ran towards his daughter's screams, to the outside.

He exited the place and was now outside, standing next to her and could see three people running up the hill. He knew who they were and knew why they were running. A dozen of the dead were behind them.

Some of the dead were limping, some were dragging their legs as if they'd been shot, some shambled with their arms by their side, and others had their arms raised like something out of a black and white Frankenstein movie.

Simon shushed a hysterical Imelda and gave her a hug as Donald, Helen and David ran towards them. Yoler and Dicko had come from upstairs and exited the house bleary eyed. They stood next to Simon, both panting and confused.

"Jesus Christ on a cross," Yoler huffed once her eyes witnessed the figures coming towards her. "It's some of the guys from that camp. And where the piss did the dead come from?"

"What do we do?" Simon asked with panic. "What do we do?"

"We get rid of them," Dicko said calmly, and then turned to Simon and pointed at the bald menacing figure of Donald Brownstone who was getting nearer to them. "Can he handle himself?"

"Of course." Simon nodded. "I don't think Helen can."

"Okay." Dicko nodded. "Me, Yoler and baldy will sort the Canavars out. You, that woman, and the kids get in the house and hide upstairs."

"Bollocks to that, mate!" Simon snapped. "I'm doing this."

"Good." Dicko looked down at the machete that was tucked in Simon's belt and said, "You'll be using that in a few minutes."

163

Yoler pulled out her machete, and Dicko pulled his trench knife from the brown leather holster.

"Hopefully," Dicko began, "this'll be over quicker than you think."

"Well, if it's anything like your performance the other night," Yoler laughed.

Simon couldn't believe how relaxed the two were. He was shaking like a leaf in a hurricane, yet Dicko was up for the battle, and Yoler was cracking jokes.

"Well, let's hurry this up," Yoler snapped. "As soon as we're done, I desperately need to brush my teeth because my breath is like a tramp's cock."

Donald was the first to reach them; he nodded at the three of them, panting and unable to talk.

"Oh," Simon scratched his head, realising that Dicko hadn't met Donald. "Dicko, this is Donald. Donald ... Dicko."

Both men nodded at one another and Yoler asked, "Where did the dead come from?"

"They came into our camp and attacked us," cried Donald. "Helen said she had heard a scream from a woman, then the sound of squealing dogs. That's probably what attracted them to the area. I've hardly seen any for weeks and now this happens."

"A scream from a woman." Yoler scratched her head.

"Clare escaped in that direction," said Simon. "It must have been her. So, maybe Clare was taken by dogs first, and then the Canavars turned up and ate the dogs and what was left of Clare."

"Who's Clare?" asked Donald.

"She was part of a small gang that came here and..."

"What?" Donald looked confused.

"It doesn't matter now."

Donald pulled out his knife as Helen and David had arrived out of breath.

"Are we ready?" said Donald.

"Let them come a little closer," Dicko said. The dead were about twenty yards from the group, struggling with the incline.

A scream could be heard from behind and Simon, Yoler, Donald and Dicko turned and saw two more of the dead grabbing Helen and Imelda. The two ghouls had come from the front of the farmhouse and appeared from the side, taking everybody by surprise. Imelda fell with her female Canavar and Simon cried, "No!" on seeing this.

Dicko was the first to react, ran over to the girls and planted his trench knife into the back of the head of Imelda's attacker. Helen had managed to push the other creature away and Yoler drove her blade through the side of its head. It remained standing until Yoler quickly removed the blade, and then it fell in a heap. Simon released a cry and his panic stricken body ran over to his little girl.

"Are you okay?" Simon yelled, and his body flooded with panic. He went over to his shaken little girl. "Babe, talk to me."

"I'm fine," she cried and said with a quiver, tears in her eyes, "Daddy?"

"Yes, babe? What is it?"

Imelda's eyes filled with water and couldn't get the words out.

"We really don't have time for this, right now."

Imelda looked at her father with wet eyes and cried, "You told me that they were all gone."

"I'm sorry," said Simon. "We'll talk about that later."

Dicko said to Helen, "Let's not take any more chances. Get the kids upstairs. Go to Simon's room, the lot of you. Imelda will show you where to go. Just don't use the back bedroom."

"What's in there?" Helen asked.

"I'll explain later. Just don't go in."

"Daddy?" Imelda cried.

Simon, holding the machete with both hands, said, "It's okay, babe. Just go with Helen. I'll be up in a bit."

Helen took the kids into the house and shut the back door behind her.

"How do we do this?" Simon asked, his words drenched in panic.

"How many have you killed before?" Donald asked him, staring at the dead that were a matter of yards away.

"Just the two."

"Jesus wept," Donald moaned.

"Spread out!" Yoler yelled. "I don't want to be catching you men when me and Simon are swinging our machetes about."

"Are we all ready?" Dicko asked the other three. He could see that the dead gang had almost finished climbing the hill and were nearly on flat ground.

Simon, Yoler and Donald nodded in unison.

"I'm a bit out of practice," Dicko said with a smile, "but here goes."

Dicko took a couple of steps forward and rammed his blade into the forehead of the nearest one. Yoler also attacked them and, Simon could see Donald take out his first, a female, with a stab to the temple.

Simon could see the three individuals take the dead down with ease, and felt guilty for hesitating. He pulled his blade behind his head and embedded it into a creature that had its back to him. The machete blade went into the top of the skull by a few inches, and this made the creature fall to the ground with the machete still stuck, but it wasn't finished, and Donald had to step in and finish the creature off.

Simon pulled the blade out of the head and could see one of them coming over, a teenage girl in its former life with a bloody dress on. Its face was ashen, its eyes pale, and it looked like it had fresh blood on its chin.

Clare's blood, possibly?

He took in a deep breath and swiped at the female, but he missed. He swiped once more and this time the blade struck the side of its head, but it wasn't enough to kill the ghoul. With the blade still stuck in the side of the creature's head, the Canavar's arms were outstretched and grabbed Simon by the shoulders.

Simon tried to push the thing away, but it was freakishly strong.

He grabbed the female ghoul by the throat to stop himself from being bitten, took a step backwards, lost his footing, and the pair of them fell to the ground.

With the Canavar on top of Simon, he put his hands under its chin as it tried to bite, but it was a battle he was losing. His arms were weakening and the diseased mouth of the dead being was dropping closer to his face.

He winced as the smell from the female hit him. He retched as he could see a handful of maggots fall out of its rotten mouth as it opened to take a chunk out of him. He turned his head to the side to avoid the maggots from hitting him in the face, then turned to face the dead thing and focused on more important matters: not getting infected. He cried out as his arms quivered, and the female Canavar snarled and managed to free itself from Simon's weakening grip.

Its head dropped and Simon screamed out, knowing that he had lost the fight and could feel the teeth of the Canavar touch his neck.

He closed his eyes, winced, and waited for the inevitable bite.

CHAPTER THIRTY-EIGHT

Helen, David and Imelda hid in the room, listening to the commotion outside. Imelda was desperate to see if her daddy was okay. She attempted once to go over to the window and see how they were getting on, but Helen had pulled her back and they remained sitting in the corner of the bedroom, all shuddering like cats being cornered by a fox.

It had gone quiet all of a sudden.

Helen looked at her petrified son and then at the terrified face of Imelda Washington.

"What's happening?" Imelda asked Helen.

"I don't know," was Helen's response. "I really don't know."

"Go and have a look, mummy," David whined. "I want to know if the Canavars are all gone."

"Okay, son." Helen nodded and took a quick glance at Imelda. She asked Simon's daughter, "You okay, love? You look very pale."

Said Imelda, unconvincingly, "I'm alright."

"You sure? You're sweating as well."

"Yes," Imelda snapped.

Helen told the kids to stay where they were and slowly stood to her feet. She shuffled over to the window and reluctantly took a peep out, looking down. She could see dead bodies scattered across the back yard, and gasped when she saw Simon lying on the floor, on his back.

"What is it?" Imelda asked. She had heard Helen's gasp and could tell by her face that she had seen something upsetting.

"It's nothing," Helen lied.

"Is it daddy?" Imelda stood up and was about to walk over.

"Stay where you are." Helen pointed at Imelda and added, "I'm not gonna let you see this."

Imelda sat back down, next to David, and both children shook with fear, wondering what was and what *had* been going on outside.

Helen took another look outside and looked down where Simon lay.

A smile stretched across her face.

*

He opened his eyes and looked up to the grey skies. He raised his hand and felt his neck, then inspected his fingers.

There was no blood.

The faces of Yoler, Dicko and Donald Brownstone could now be seen in his vision, and the three of them were looking down on Simon Washington.

"You okay?" Dicko asked him.

Simon looked unsure. "I ... think so."

Dicko knelt down and gave Simon his hand and pulled him up until he was sitting. Simon scratched his head and looked to the side of him and could see his female attacker was lying defunct, stab wound to the back of the head.

"One more second and you would have been Canavar meat," Dicko laughed gently, wiping his blade on the tattered clothes of the deceased.

"Thanks," said Simon, still dazed.

"Don't mention it." He patted the holster where the trench knife was and said, "All thanks to Trevor once more."

Simon rubbed his head and decided that it was time to stand on his feet. He put his hands on his head and had a look around, staring at the dead bodies.

"The two that went for Helen and the kids..." Simon began. "They came from the front; from the main road."

Dicko nodded and said, "I'll check it out. See if there're more."

Once Dicko disappeared, Yoler asked Simon how he was feeling, whilst Donald stood near Simon, staring at the man with contempt.

"How's he feeling?" Donald scoffed. "You're asking how's he feeling? Embarrassed ... that's probably how he's feeling. I had to help him with the first one. Overall, he only killed one of them in the end, and that was from behind. I saw it with my own eyes." He then widened his eyes at Simon, and growled, "Your performance was fucking pish. You're about as much use as a stitched up cunt."

"Alright, alright," Yoler barged past Brownstone and stood next to Simon. "Leave him alone, you bald prick."

"No wonder. He was about as much use as a condom machine in a fucking nunnery."

"Simon was the first to come here," Yoler said, "so he has overall say who stays and who doesn't."

"So?"

"So, slap head, watch your mouth."

"You've got a big mouth for a little slag," Donald Brownstone took a menacing step forward, but Yoler wasn't for budging.

"I may not be able to take you on," she said, "but what I can do is cut your ball sack open while you sleep."

Donald opened his mouth to react to Yoler's threat, but the presence of Dicko returning stopped him.

"It's clear at the front," Dicko announced. "Must have been a couple of strays from the main road."

"The screaming didn't help," said Donald.

"That was my fault," Simon confessed. "I told her that the dead weren't around anymore, so she must have had quite a fright."

"Yeah, well, if that little bitch screams like that again..."

Donald never had chance to finish his sentence and staggered backwards, slowly realising that Simon had punched him in the jaw.

"You bastard." Donald rubbed his jaw and ran over to Simon, but Dicko went over and took out Donald with a left hook, making the burly man stagger and fall onto his backside.

"Another trick like that," said Dicko, "and it's curtains for you, Kojak."

"Are we gonna let this prick stay with us?" Yoler asked Simon. "Helen and little David are no bother, but this prick would make a priest kick his cunt in."

Simon looked down on Donald and watched as the large bald man rubbed his face where Dicko had struck him. He knew that he'd make a good warrior, be a great asset, but would living with someone with such a volatile temper be worth it?

Simon said, "We'll give him another chance. On one condition."

"And what's that?" Donald mumbled, getting ready to stand on his two feet again.

Simon went inside, and returned from the kitchen a few seconds later. He tossed a cigarette lighter over in Donald's direction. "Drag the bodies into a pile at the side of the house and burn them."

"But there's twelve of them, you dig what I'm sayin'?" moaned Donald.

"Then you should make a start now," said Dicko with a hard glare.

Simon turned on his heels, heading for the house again, and Yoler asked him where he was going. "I'm gonna see how my daughter is."

By the time Simon reached the living room, Helen and David came through the door that led to the upstairs.

"Where is she?" Simon began to panic.

"It's okay. Relax." Helen smiled and brushed her fingers through her dark bobbed hair. "She said she wanted to be left alone. Is it safe now?"

"Yes." Simon nodded. "The others are outside. No one got hurt ... not really." Simon squeezed past Helen and her son, but she grabbed his sleeve and said, "Your daughter said she wanted to be left alone."

"It's okay." Simon gave Helen a strange and confused look. "In case you've forgotten, I'm her dad."

He left the living room and trotted upstairs, approached the closed bedroom door where he and Imelda slept and gave it a gentle knock. "It's daddy," he announced, but opened the door before getting a reply.

Imelda was sitting up on the bed, and had her knees up. She had sheets of white paper; almost the same colour as her face, by her feet and was writing-or drawing with her pencil.

"You okay, babe?"

"Uh-huh." Imelda wasn't crying, but her eyes looked wet. It looked like she was close.

"Look," Simon gulped and paused, "the reasons why I told you that—"

"I know why you did it, daddy," she said. She never looked up at Simon and continued to scribble.

"You do?"

"You did it to protect me."

"I'm sorry you had to see that ... *them*." Simon took a step forward, but Imelda spoke and stopped him in his tracks.

"Don't come near me, daddy," she said.

"What?" Simon was mystified. "Are you angry with me?"

She shook her head, still scribbling. "I want to be left alone for a few minutes, then we'll talk. We'll all talk."

"What do you mean?"

"Daddy, please."

"Okay."

Simon never asked any more questions. He did as he was told and left the bedroom, closing the door behind him ever so slowly. He trudged his frame back down to the ground floor, his mind polluted by confusion.

CHAPTER THIRTY-NINE

Minutes had passed and Simon, Yoler, Dicko, Helen and young David watched from outside as the bodies burned. It didn't take long for Donald to drag the bodies in one spot, but trying to set the defunct creatures alight was far more difficult.

Donald asked if he could wash his hands with the water that was available and promised to take a trip to the pond himself to get more the next morning. Because of the large supplies of bottled water and sodas anyway, they all agreed and he went inside to the kitchen. The remaining individuals looked up when they heard a window opening and could see Imelda's face.

"Can you all come up?" she said. "I have something to tell you."

They all looked up at her, and Simon was the first to enter the house and make his way up.

Helen and David followed, and then Yoler and Dicko walked behind them.

"What's going on?" Donald asked Dicko.

"Stay down here," said Dicko, who was unable to answer Donald's query. "Keep guard."

Simon was on the landing and entered the room and went over to his daughter; he was quickly followed by the others. Imelda was sitting up; her blonde hair tied back, and had her hands resting on her lap. She looked pale and was sweating.

Dicko was the last to enter and shut the door behind him. Yoler, Dicko, Helen and David stood by the end of the bed, patiently waiting for what Imelda had to say, whilst Simon sat at the side and stroked his little girl's hair.

"So?" Yoler couldn't bite her tongue any longer. "What is it? What's happening?"

The little girl remained silent; her pale face quivered with nerves, and Simon continued to sit next to her on the bed, stroking her clammy head with his thumb.

"What is it, babe?" her father asked her. "What's wrong? Is there something on your mind? Is it because I told you that the Canavars were all gone, is that it?"

Again, there was no answer from the eight-year-old.

"Tell me."

Imelda cleared her throat, lifted her hands from her lap, and turned her hands around and showed them her palms. The left hand had a sock wrapped around it. With her right hand, Imelda removed the sock.

"It's just a small one," she said with sadness. "But it's enough. We *all* know that it's enough."

Helen gasped and Simon broke down when he saw the bite at the side of her left palm. It was small, and didn't look like a full bite, but Imelda was correct. It was enough. They all knew in the room, even young David, that it was enough to get her infected. And she was. She *was* infected.

Simon screwed his right hand into a fist and bit into it. He was sobbing quietly, but Imelda tried to remain calm.

"When they came from the side of the house, the first one tried to attack me, but I pushed it away, and then we both fell over. That's when it bit me, but I pulled my hand away as Dicko killed it."

"No, no, no." Simon grabbed his little girl and kissed her head. "Not my baby. Not my sweet little baby."

"Don't be sad, daddy," she spoke with calm and added, "It's okay."

"You can't go," Simon cried and hugged his little girl. "You can't."

Helen released tears of her own and gave an upset David a hug as they watched the sad episode unfold in front of their eyes.

"What do we do?" Yoler asked nobody in particular. "How do we handle this?"

The adults in the room all stared at one another, and Simon broke away from his pale daughter.

"I want to be buried in the back garden," Imelda said openly, stunning the people in the room. "I don't feel too well and I think I've got minutes left, if I'm lucky. I don't want to turn." She looked at Yoler. "Once I fall asleep, I want you to do it."

Simon flashed Yoler a look. Simon said, "Do it? What do you mean by *do it*?"

A silence fell on the room and all the adults knew what she wanted, but not Simon. What the hell was his daughter talking about? Do it? Do what?

Imelda spoke with a croak in her voice. "I want Yoler to kill me, daddy."

"Oh God." He placed his hands on his head and waggled his head from side to side. *Please tell me this isn't happening. Please tell me this is a dream.*

Imelda placed her cold hand on her daddy's thigh and said, "I would never ask you to do it, daddy. That wouldn't be fair."

"How?" Yoler asked the little girl. There was no emotion in Yoler's voice, but her eyes were moist, despite trying to be strong for father and daughter.

Imelda produced a thin smile and a tear fell from each eye. "A knife through the temple. Nothing too messy."

Simon fell to the side of the bed and now had his knees on the carpet, kneeling by the side of the bed and had his hands on his daughter's leg.

"Do you want a drink?" Dicko asked the little girl.

She shook her head and moved down the bed and lay down. She released a sigh and said to Simon, "I'm tired, daddy."

He touched her clammy head and released more tears. She was getting colder. It wasn't long now.

She closed her eyes and groaned, "Don't be sad, daddy."

"I can't help it," he sobbed. "You're my baby girl. The only thing I have left."

"I'm not sad, daddy. I'm going to see mummy and Tyler."

He watched her chest rising up and down as she breathed, and leaned over and kissed her on her cold, damp forehead.

He lowered his head and rested it on the bed, sobbing for the only thing he had left to love. He could hear whispering between Dicko and Yoler, but couldn't make out what they were saying. He didn't *want* to know what they were saying.

"Simon? Simon?"

Yoler's voice could be heard, but Simon never lifted his head.

She tried again. "Simon?"

Simon felt a hand on his shoulder, making him jump, and lifted his head and looked up to see whom the hand belonged to. It was Dicko.

"What is it?" Simon snapped, his cheeks stained with tears.

Dicko pointed at Imelda and could see that she had closed her eyes, but she was still breathing.

Simon turned and looked at his daughter. He leaned over and kissed her on her clammy head. "I'm so sorry I let you down, baby."

She didn't respond.

"It'll takes a few minutes for her to turn," said Yoler. "At least that's what they said on the news, when it first broke out. I think it's best if everyone leaves. Nobody needs to see this."

"I want to stay here," Simon said. "I want to be with her until she's actually gone."

Yoler walked over to her and felt her neck for a pulse. She gulped, and then gave Simon a sympathetic look by thinning her lips. "I'm sorry, Simes. She's already gone."

"Has she?" he cried, putting his shaking hands to his mouth. He looked at her chest and realised she wasn't breathing anymore.

"Leave the room." Yoler pulled out a knife from her pocket. "Everyone."

A tearful Helen walked around the bed and put her arm around a devastated Simon.

"Come on," Helen said to the broken man. "Let's go."

"I can't leave her," Simon sobbed.

"You don't want to see this."

"Everybody out," Yoler snapped. "And I mean everybody."

Dicko left with an upset David. Helen was the next to go, urging Simon to follow her, but he remained where he was.

"Remember what she said, Simes," Yoler said to Simon, gripping the handle of the knife tight. "She doesn't want to turn. So if you don't leave in the next thirty seconds, you're gonna have to watch me put this knife into the side of her head. Is that what you want?"

Simon wiped his tearstained face with his forearm and shook his head.

"Then go…" Yoler's voice quavered and a tear fell from her left eye. "Now."

CHAPTER FORTY

Simon reached the ground floor last and walked through the empty living room. He felt like he was floating, and gazed around with his wet blurry eyes. Where was everyone? Simon entered the kitchen and could hear voices from outside. He stepped outside and looked to his left where he could see the pile of smouldering bodies.

Would the fire attract more of the Canavars from afar? He wasn't sure. Maybe it was just noise that they followed. Maybe their vision was so impaired, like their movement, they couldn't see very well. Maybe some couldn't see at all.

He looked to his right and stared at the sympathetic faces that were gazing at him. The faces of Dicko, Helen, David and Donald Brownstone all looked away as Simon approached them slowly with dragging feet.

Dicko put his hand on Simon's shoulder. "I'm sorry, Simon. I really am."

Helen stepped forwards and hugged him, but there was no response from the shell-shocked man. She stepped away once she saw Yoler exiting the house.

Simon broke away from the embrace and could see the stare from Helen. He turned around and saw Yoler.

Yoler looked emotional and said, "I'll dig her grave myself."

Nobody spoke. Nobody responded. There was a deathly silence amongst the group.

"I'll take good care of her," said Yoler. "I'll wrap her up in a sheet, but I'll need a hand to bring her downstairs."

"I'll do it," Donald gulped.

"Me too," said Dicko.

Simon remained silent.

Yoler said, "I'll get a shovel."

*

It had taken half an hour for Yoler to dig a shallow grave for Imelda, and once she was done, she asked Donald and Dicko to go upstairs with her. Imelda was wrapped up in an orange sheet and her body was carried downstairs and outside.

Simon, Helen and David sat on the grass, with their backs to the house. They never conversed with each other. They just sat in silence. Yoler had dug a grave to the left of the house, a few yards away from the vegetable patch, near a few trees.

Simon turned to his left and saw the two men placing a wrapped up Imelda into the hole. Yoler walked over to Simon and crouched down next to him.

"Simes, I'm going to put her to rest," she said. "Do you want to say a few words?"

"I don't know." He hunched his shoulders. "No. What's the point?"

"Okay," she said, "If you change your mind."

He shook his head. "I won't."

Yoler stood to her feet and walked away, heading for the grave.

"Yoler," Simon called over.

She stopped walking and looked over her shoulder.

"Thanks ... for everything."

"It's the least I can do, Simes."

She walked over to the shovel and began to place the dug up soil that sat in a large pile over the body, whilst Donald and Dicko watched, ready to take their turn once Yoler became tired. But she never became tired. If she did, she never let on that she was. She did it all herself.

Yelling could be heard from inside the house. It was the sound of a male voice; it was the prisoner. It was Grey Beard. He was moaning about the pain he was in, and that he was thirsty. But it was mainly the pain that he was moaning about. Maybe the painkillers were wearing off. He *had* broken his leg after all.

After everything that had happened, Simon had forgotten about the intruder.

"I'll go and see to him," Simon heard Dicko say to Yoler.

"No, you won't." Simon stood up. "*I* will."

"But I was going to..." Dicko paused and decided not to finish his sentence. "Now that we know that Clare's dead, I was thinking that we might as well get rid of him. To keep the place protected."

Simon nodded. "You're right. He needs to be dealt with."

Simon strolled over to Yoler and held out his hand. Donald and Simon were now standing next to Yoler and were concerned about Simon's behaviour.

"What is it?" Yoler asked.

"Give me your knife," said Simon. "I'll do it."

"We need every room in the house, now that there's a few of us," Yoler said. "We can't have the room that he's in turning into a blood bath. If we need to do it, we can do it outside."

"We should go up and suffocate him," Dicko said. "No mess."

"I suppose that'll work." Yoler nodded.

"That's too easy," Simon snarled. "I want to kill him myself. If those bastards hadn't come to the farm, this wouldn't have happened. All of this shit started when they came here. Imelda's dead because of them."

"I'm not entirely sure about that," Donald said. "I mean..." He looked up and could see the vicious glare from Yoler, Dicko and Helen. He cleared his throat nervously and nodded his head in defeat.

"You want revenge." Dicko nodded. "I get it."

"I've never killed anyone before," said Simon with a shiver in his voice. "I may as well get my first out of the way and do it to someone who deserves it."

Yoler and Dicko peeped at one another, unsure what to do.

"Get him out the house," Simon said to the two of them. "Then everybody get inside and I'll do the rest."

Dicko nodded and went inside the house; Donald Brownstone went after him. A minute later, a screaming Grey Beard was dragged out of the place and dumped on the grass, a bone sickeningly protruding through his skin.

Yoler walked up to Simon and handed him her knife. Grey Beard was moaning and dragging himself across the grassy hill, desperately trying to get away. He wasn't going anywhere fast. His progression was very minimal, but he was trying, as he knew he was going to die. He had a strong feeling he was going to die.

Everyone, apart from Simon, went back into the house, but they all watched from the kitchen window. It was a precaution, just in case Simon struggled with the man or decided that he couldn't kill him. Yoler and Dicko didn't want another one of them escaping. If Grey Beard escaped and managed to get back to his group, telling Orson what had happened and about how Clare and the other man had died, it would be curtains for Simon and the rest. But how could a man, especially a man with a broken leg and couldn't walk, possibly get back to his camp in once piece, especially in this new and dangerous world? They weren't going to take the risk. He was going to have to die, and Simon wanted revenge anyway.

Simon sat back down on the ground and stared at the elderly man, who continued to desperately drag himself across the long grass. He didn't want to kill him straight away, he wanted to make him wait a while, make him suffer.

He stuck the large blade into the grass and pulled his knees up to his chest. He put his arms over his knees and rested his head on them, staring down at the grass.

He began to cry, and not only did he feel that he had let Imelda down, he felt that he had also let Diana down as well. "I'm sorry," he sobbed. "I'm so sorry."

He quickly lifted his head and angrily wiped his tears away. He pulled the knife out of the ground and stood to his feet. He glared at the injured man. He was almost thirty yards away and was making decent progress, still dragging himself away.

He must be exhausted, Simon thought. And with that broken leg, possibly catching it occasionally on the ground, it must have been sheer agony.

The injured individual was now on the flat part of the grass. Simon was certain that he didn't have the energy to reach the cluster of trees that needed to be passed to get to the pond, but Grey Beard was certainly giving it a damn good try.

Simon strolled down the hill, knife in his right hand, and slowly headed in the direction of Grey Beard. He reached the flat part and progressed another twelve yards before crouching down next to the injured man. He was still trying to get away, but he was tiring and panting hard.

"Stop struggling," Simon told him. "There's no point."

The injured man stopped crawling and looked at Simon with a look of defeat on his features. He sighed and went onto his back, panting hard, tears of pain in his eyes.

"You shouldn't have come to the farm." Simon stood over him and added, "My daughter's dead because of your arrival."

"If you hadn't have come to the visitor centre and killed our friend," Grey Beard spat, "then we wouldn't have come seeking for revenge, which is exactly why you're going to kill me ... for revenge, right?"

"Yes, that's true." Simon nodded. "I do want revenge, but you were going to die anyway. Clare's dead, which means that you're the only person from Orson's crew that know we live here."

"Go ahead," the man snickered, but it was clear in his face that he was frightened. Wasn't everybody frightened of death?

"Make it quick." The man slapped his chest. "Straight through the heart."

"What's the point of revenge if I'm gonna make your demise as quick as possible?"

"It's all I ask." He nodded down to his leg and added, "I think I've suffered enough, don't you?"

Simon knelt down next to the man and said, "You're not going to get your wish."

Grey Beard growled, "And why the fuck not?"

"Because you don't deserve it."

"I'm a survivor, just like yourself," Grey Beard continued to pant. "I had a family once, before meeting up with Orson's lot, had a job, worked in the prison service as a Human Resource Manager."

"Not anymore." Simon snapped. "What you used to be doesn't matter anymore, so stop your bellyaching. You're going to die the way *I* want you to die."

"And how's that?" He began to laugh, mocking Simon.

"Bloody and painful."

"Fucking cunt!" Grey Beard snarled and spat in Simon's direction, missing his face by inches. "I wish I killed that slag daughter of yours now. Blonde cunt. Yeah, if I could have my time over again I would have fucked that little bitch. I would have fucked her good—"

Simon rammed the blade into the man's side. "Sick bastard," Simon spat, and gave the knife a slow twist.

The man coughed and moaned. He yelped when Simon pulled the knife out. With the blood still running off the end of the blade, Simon stabbed Grey Beard in his midriff, again and again, and continued even when the elderly man had stopped moaning. Simon only stopped once he became tired and fell onto his backside with exhaustion.

The knife and his hands were covered in blood. He looked at the mutilated man and sneered at the corpse. He had been stabbed seventeen times.

Simon wiped his bloody hands on the grass, and then cleaned the blade. He stood up straight and glared at the corpse, gritting his teeth so hard that he thought they were going to shatter. Killing the man in such a brutal way didn't seem enough to satisfy his revenge. He took a step back and booted the side of the man's head and spat on his lifeless face.

He began to make the walk back to the farm. He looked over his shoulder, looking at the body, and decided to leave it for the crows, or whatever came first.

"Cunt," he snarled, and then placed the knife into his pocket, hitting the grassy hill and heading for the house.

CHAPTER FORTY-ONE

The evening was near; Simon decided to spend some time outside whilst some of the others were having a snack from the cupboard. He stepped out and closed his eyes as the wind tickled his face. He looked around the back of the farm and could see the Mazda to his right, sitting on the drive. He looked down across the field and could see the dead man had company. Six crows were sitting on his front, pecking away at the cadaver.

Simon had no idea why crows liked the meat from a human.

And where the fuck did they come from?

He once read that when an animal dies and begins to rot, a number of quite smelly chemicals are given off. Maybe the smell attracted the crows, like blood does to sharks.

He took a gander to his left and released a sad sigh. He looked over at the pile of charcoal bodies and walked by the vegetable patch that Yoler had made and then went over to Imelda's grave.

He looked at Yoler's work and realised there was no headstone or crucifix to state whom was resting in peace. He promised himself that he would make a crucifix for his little girl tomorrow. He wasn't a believer, but Imelda used to talk about God every now and then.

He crouched down by the grave and eventually sat down and crossed his legs. He closed his eyes and tilted his chin back, feeling the wind caress his features. He opened them to see the murky heavens above him. He brought his head back down, cleared his throat, and could feel his eyes fill.

"Hey, baby girl," he said with a tremble in his voice. He lowered his head and felt stupid for talking to a pile of dirt. He knew she was gone. Could she hear him? Of course not!

"I'm pretty sure you can't hear what I'm saying," he sighed. "In fact, I don't know why I'm doing this." Simon rubbed his face with both hands and felt silly for talking to himself. He looked at the grave, and then looked up to the side where the field was. His throat began to harden and he could feel his eyes filling.

He said, "I'm so sorry, Diana. I couldn't protect any of you. Keep our Imelda safe. *I* couldn't. Please forgive me."

Simon broke down and took a minute before he could compose himself. "All of you were my life. Now I have no one, apart from a few people I've met a couple of days ago. This hurts so much that I feel I can't breathe." Simon paused for a few seconds, wiped his nose, and then cleared his throat. "I've let you all down. And for that I'll never forgive myself. You have no idea how much I want to be with you guys. No idea."

Simon placed his hands on the dirt where Imelda lay only a couple of feet down. He was on all fours and dipped his head as he cried, the tears falling from his face like a dripping tap. He sobbed, "Sleep tight, baby girl. I will always love you. Always."

"Simon," a voice was heard from behind him. It was Helen. "You okay? You've been out here for ages."

Simon awkwardly stood to his feet, like a drunk after falling down, and wiped his dirty hands on his trousers. He turned around and walked over to Helen. She gasped and placed her hand over her mouth when she saw the state of the man. The pair of them embraced and Helen rubbed his back as he sobbed.

"Let it out, Simon," she whispered into his ear and pecked him on the cheek. "Don't keep it in. Let it all out."

They broke away and Helen placed her hand on Simon's wet cheek. "Let's go inside. You can't stay out here all evening. Donald said he'd do the night stint."

Simon nodded and announced, "I need a drink."

Helen put her arm around him and the pair of them walked inside. The first thing that Simon did was grab a plastic bottle of filtered water and took three gulps. He placed the bottle back and walked into the living room where he was greeted with glum faces.

Nobody spoke to him. Nobody knew what to say.

Simon smiled thinly at the sombre faces and headed straight upstairs.

He went into the bedroom where he and Imelda slept, and kicked his boots off before lying down on the bed. He turned on his side and could faintly smell his daughter. He wiped his eyes and sat up. He swung his legs to the side and sat facing the window. He had had enough. He was going to kill himself. With all his family gone there didn't seem to be any point carrying on.

He searched the bottom drawer of the side table to see if he could find a belt or a tie. There was nothing but underwear.

Still sitting, he opened the top drawer and saw two pieces of paper folded up.

He took out the two pieces of paper and opened up the first one. It was another picture. Imelda must have drawn it when she asked all of them for some privacy, after she had been bitten.

The picture was similar to one she had drawn a couple of days ago. The one she had drawn a few days ago was her and her dad on one side of the car, the dead on the other side, and her mummy and brother in heaven,

In this picture she had drawn a car, the family car, and surrounding the vehicle were a horde of Canavars. Simon was drawn at the far right of the picture, away from the horde. At the top of the picture were three figures: Diana, Tyler and Imelda.

Simon's heart went numb looking at the picture, and gently placed the A4 piece of paper on top of the side table. He opened up the second piece of paper and cried as soon as he saw Imelda's handwriting.

Daddy.

Don't cry for me, daddy. I know you will be sad, but please keep going for me. I'm going to see mummy and Tyler and I'll tell them what you did to keep me safe. You are my hero and I'll always love you.
Stay strong and keep living, no matter what it takes.

Imelda

It was such a brave and mature note from a girl so young that knew she was dying, and he read it once more before putting it on top of the drawing.

Simon jumped when he heard knocking on his door.

He gulped and asked, "Who is it?"

The door opened and Helen, Dicko and Yoler stepped inside.

"What's the matter?" he asked the three of them.

"Just making sure you haven't topped yourself," Yoler joked, but Simon could tell there was some seriousness in her comment.

Dicko flashed Yoler a hard look.

"What's up with you, Dicky Boy?" Yoler shrugged her shoulders. "You look like someone has shat on your new rug."

"A little tact would be nice," he said, shaking his head in disapproval.

"It's okay." Simon raised his hand up at Dicko.

"What's that?" Helen nodded over to the pieces of paper on the side table. Simon smiled and picked them up and passed them to Helen. Helen gasped when she opened up the drawing, and cried when she read the short letter. She passed the papers to the other two and went over to Simon and sat by his side.

"You'll get through this," Helen said to the distraught man. "We'll help you. Everybody's afraid of dying until you lose a child. Then you're afraid of living."

"I can't think straight." Simon took in a deep breath and continued, "I can't believe I'm never going to see her again. I can't believe I'll never see those lovely big blue eyes, blonde hair, her chunky cheeks and those gappy teeth. I'll never see my baby again."

"It's gonna be hard, Simes," Yoler said, handing back the pieces of paper. "But like Helen said … we'll help you through this. Like what Imelda said on the note: stay strong. She was your flesh and blood and it might seem like there's no option left—"

"She wasn't my flesh and blood," Simon said with his head lowered and his hands clasping.

"What do you mean?" Dicko said.

"My son was mine, biologically, but not Imelda."

"What are you talking about?" Helen spoke with a perplexed look. "You're not making sense."

Simon's head dropped an inch and the man began to chew his bottom lip, wondering if he should tell these folk about a period in his life that had always saddened him.

He said, "After Tyler was born, Diana and I began to argue. We just weren't getting along at all." Simon looked up at the confused faces, gulped, and then continued further, "Anyway, Diana had a fling with a consultant at work. She confessed a couple of months later and told me she was pregnant. It was *his*. I knew straight away that it was his."

Helen asked, "*How* did you know?"

"Because Diana and I hadn't had sex in months."

"Oh," Helen said in astonishment, "I had no idea."

"Why would you? Anyway, we decided to stick together and I raised Imelda like one of my own. I loved her like one of my own."

"You never told her the truth?" Yoler asked him.

Simon shook his head. "No. Even the consultant that Diana had an affair with never knew. I think after a few months he moved to a different hospital anyway."

"Raising her as your own chid was a very noble, yet very difficult decision to make," Dicko said with a succession of nods.

"I suppose I would have been a hypocrite if I left her for the affair."

"What do you mean?" Helen questioned the heartbroken man.

Simon shook his head and sighed, "I was hardly a saint myself."

"You strayed?" Yoler asked.

"When Diana was pregnant with Tyler." Simon nodded and shamefully lowered his head, unable to look his new friends in the eye. "And a couple of others before that. She never knew."

"That was a different world. A different life." Yoler walked over to him and kissed him on the head. "I'm going downstairs, Simes. Get some rest, and stop beating yourself up about past misdemeanours that don't matter now."

Yoler left with Dicko, leaving Helen alone with Simon.

"I'll be downstairs as well," she said. "If you need me..."

"Thanks, Helen."

"Do you need anything before I go?"

"No." Simon shook his head.

He lay down on the bed and turned on his side. He heard the door shut and Helen's steps heading to the ground floor. He curled up and closed his eyes. He knew he wasn't going to get any sleep tonight, but he closed his eyes anyway.

He released a melancholic breath out and his thoughts took him to a time when the family went to a caravan holiday in Wales. It had rained the whole time, and the holiday had been made worse when Imelda, who was only a toddler at the time, fell off the guest room's bed and had banged her head, causing a one-inch mark on the right side of her forehead, just below her hairline.

It was then he knew that he loved her just as much as Tyler. He freaked out when she fell and was riddled with panic as they drove to the nearest hospital. It turned out to be a minor cut and mild concussion.

His eyes filled and when they opened, water fell out. Then he remembered the words on Imelda's note.

His little girl had only been dead hours, but he told himself that he needed to see some light despite the darkness.

He closed his eyes once more and took in deep breaths. He felt exhausted, but even a full bottle of bourbon wouldn't have been able to put Simon Washington to sleep. He then began to think about the poem that his son would say to Imelda to frighten her.

Tyler was always reprimanded for teasing his sister, but he had said it so many times, and had been caught so many times, that even Simon knew his son's poem off by heart.

The Canavars are coming, so you better hide and pray. If you don't believe me then you're going to die today. They'll eat your flesh, they'll eat your brains, and they'll eat your heart and more. The Canavars are everywhere; you better lock your door.

Simon kept his eyes closed, but his psyche was plagued with Imelda's goodbye letter, especially the last line. It was easier said than done, but he was going to try if that was what she wanted.

Maybe that last line had saved his life, because minutes before reading it he was thinking about ending his existence. The words from the last line of the letter swirled around in his head like cigar smoke, and Simon released a sad sigh.

Stay strong and keep living, no matter what.

THE END

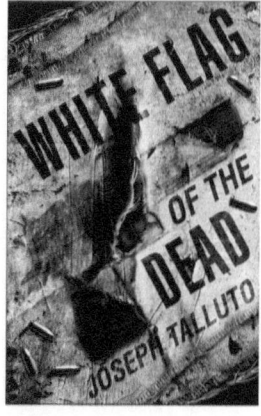

CHECK OUT OTHER GREAT ZOMBIE NOVELS

Z BURBIA
by Jake Bible

Whispering Pines is a classic, quiet, private American subdivision on the edge of Asheville, NC, set in the pristine Blue Ridge Mountains. Which is good since the zombie apocalypse has come to Western North Carolina and really put suburban living to the test!

Surrounded by a sea of the undead, the residents of Whispering Pines have adapted their bucolic life of block parties to scavenging parties, common area groundskeeping to immediate area warfare, neighborhood beautification to neighborhood fortification.

But, even in the best of times, suburban living has its ups and downs what with nosy neighbors, a strict Home Owners' Association, and a property management company that believes the words "strict interpretation" are holy words when applied to the HOA covenants. Now with the zombie apocalypse upon them even those innocuous, daily irritations quickly become dramatic struggles for personal identity, family security, and straight up survival.

ZOMBIE RULES
by David Achord

Zach Gunderson's life sucked and then the zombie apocalypse began.

Rick, an aging Vietnam veteran, alcoholic, and prepper, convinces Zach that the apocalypse is on the horizon. The two of them take refuge at a remote farm. As the zombie plague rages, they face a terrifying fight for survival.

They soon learn however that the walking dead are not the only monsters.